The House Always Wins

B Baskerville

Hyem Books

- Chapter 1 -

Her long, pale legs glowed in the moonlight as she staggered across the road in high heels. It was late, almost midnight, and the streets of Roker were deserted. He didn't know who she was or where she'd been drinking. But he knew three things: she was intoxicated, she was alone, and she was easy pickings.

The Sunderland sky was clear, the stars lighting the sky like strings of lanterns. He followed, listening to the build-up to the big fight through Bluetooth earbuds. Ahead, her heels click-clacked on paving slabs, but his trainers made no sound. He hung back, keeping his distance and lurking round corners to observe her from a distance.

Yes, Jim. I think Ahmed will be feeling the pressure tonight. He's a seven-to-one favourite. Many argue that this fight isn't for Jones to win; it's for Ahmed to lose. The entire northeast will be rooting for Abdul Ahmed –

The Tyneside Terror. In fact, I'd go so far as to say all of Britain will be rooting for the Benton boy made good.

A street light flickered as she passed it on Side Cliff Road, casting an elongated shadow of narrow waist and delicious hips. It was a broad residential street lined with terrace homes on one side and plush semi-detached houses on the other. A purple beech tree at the edge of a garden rustled in the icy wind, its deep red leaves almost black in the moonlight. An onshore breeze whipped her long curls into a dishevelled mess, bringing with it a scent of salt and seaweed. And like a thin reed on a windswept beach, she swayed in the gusts, fragile and vulnerable to both the elements and those with sinful intentions.

You're right, Hamish. I can't say Jones has many fans on this side of the Pond, not after his antics at the press conference. I'm pleased to see so many Union Flags being flown here at Madison Square Garden. I dare say they outnumber the Stars and Stripes.

She continued straight at the crossroads, where the southern side of the street transitioned from homes to parkland. This park, with its model railway and children's play area, was familiar territory for him. He recalled fond memories of visiting with his grandmother – may she rest in peace. They would sit, savouring 99s topped with a flake and monkey's blood while watching elderly men dressed in white playing bowls. Those were days of innocent pleasure, now replaced by his yearning for a more thrilling form of entertainment.

Sorry to interrupt, Hamish, but I hear the penultimate event of the evening is about to begin. A women's flyweight bout between America's Taylor and Mexico's Gutierez. Gutierez has been looking sharp in training.

The commentary faded in his mind as he crept closer. The woman looked to be in her mid-twenties. She paused to remove her shoes, almost toppling over as she undid the metal clasps. The heels swung like pendulums from her left hand as she walked on, turning right onto Roker Terrace. All the while, she used her right hand to push her hair from her eyes with each puff of wind.

He almost couldn't believe it when she left the main road, choosing to walk through a grassy esplanade above the beach. The land sloped downwards, concealing her from the occasional passing car.

Some might say she had every right to walk there and enjoy the sobering sea air. But bare feet on stony ground reduced her ability to run away. Long, loose hair obscured her vision, preventing her from spotting threats.

Yes, some might say she had every right to be there; others would say she was asking for it.

His heart quickened, adrenaline coursing through him. He paused by a bus shelter, its recent paint job already flaking from constant exposure to the North Sea's wind and rain. Moonbeams played on the water, illuminating the choppy sea state outside the piers. He flexed his fingers in soft leather gloves and checked his weapon.

He lowered the mask over his face.

It was time.

- Chapter 2 -

She couldn't see the danger, but he could. The threat was almost upon her now. He was a soft-bodied man in his forties with faded jeans and a zip-up hoodie. He watched him trot to catch up with her, his unkempt hair flopping around his fleshy face. He called her *pet* and slung an arm over her shoulder. She pulled away, her intoxicated eyes scanning his face to see if she recognised him. She didn't.

The man in the mask stayed low, using the balustrades to his advantage. He moved like an animal on all fours; he called it *beast mode.*

"Come on, darlin'. I'll walk you home. Help tuck you in."

He wrapped his other arm around her waist, pulling her into his chest. He ran his hands over her back, telling her how good she felt.

The woman's face was one of confused fear. To her credit, she tried to knee him, tried to slap her palms into his chest. But it only seemed to turn Hoodie on more.

"Feisty," he cackled. "Relax, pet. I'll get you home soon."

The man in the mask could feel the cold concrete through his knee pads as he edged forward. Repulsion flooded through him, and he clamped a hand over his mouth, watching Hoodie push her to the ground, his revolting hands fighting the tight material of her dress.

In one swift motion, he vaulted over the wall and into the grass. The slimy bank was wet with dew, but he kept control of the skid as he descended. Through the eye holes in his mask, he honed in on his target like a lion on a lame gazelle. With practised ease, he reached over his shoulder and pulled the weapon from the long canvas bag strapped to his back.

He was standing over them now, only two steps away.

"Get off her," he growled at the piece of shit. "NOW."

Hoodie snapped around, annoyance rather than fear curling his lip – until their eyes locked and he took in the mask.

"Who the fuck do you think you are? Jog on, Batman. I'm having some alone time with my lady."

His words were confident; the tone of his voice told a different story. All front.

"She's not your lady."

Holding the weapon, he twisted, filling his body with torque before unleashing the baseball bat into his temple with all his might.

The woman's scream echoed with the dull thud of wood on bone. Hot blood, like black oil in the dark, painted her face and dress.

"Run," he told her. "You don't want to see what happens next."

She didn't need to be told twice. Wiggling herself free from Hoodie's weight, she legged it barefoot through the slick grass. For thirty seconds, she ran on before falling. Coated in mud, she looked back, defying his orders.

Hoodie was down but not out. Despite his head injury, he grappled the masked man, resisting the inevitable. It was a struggle to drag him up the bank, but a battle he relished. No great victory ever came easy.

At the top, he gulped cold air and quickly scanned the road. The coast was clear as he grabbed Hoodie by the back of his hair, jerking his face towards his would-be victim. "Apologise," he demanded.

Hoodie tried to pull away. He got one step before another swing of the bat hit him cleanly in the obliques. He doubled over, clutching broken ribs.

"Sorry." The word was breathless, barely audible.

"Louder. So she can hear you."

Hoodie winced in pain, trying to beg for his life as blood filled his villainous lungs.

The masked man swung the bat once more. Then, like a marionette with severed strings, Hoodie tumbled down the bank, limbs waving in a grotesque dance of surrender until, with a sickening thud of death, his body came to rest outside an amusement arcade.

He stared at the body, the heat of satisfaction warming him up.

Hoodie deserved it.

Some would say he was asking for it.

Looking south, he saw the woman standing transfixed, her eyes red, her mouth open.

He saluted her – happy to be of service – then increased the volume on his earbuds and walked away.

Taylor's laying it on Hernandez, Jim. Two, three, four heavy shots unanswered. I can't see this going much longer. There! There we have it. The ref has put an end to her misery. It's a technical knockout for Boston's Leanne Taylor.

- Chapter 3 -

DC Saffron Boyd looked out the passenger window into the inky night, covering her mouth as she yawned. At the wheel, newly promoted DS Elliot Whyte tried to stifle a yawn of his own. He gave up and opened his mouth like a roaring lion.

Boyd chuckled. "I'm the alpha."

"What?" Whyte frowned, heavy brows peaking above his dark eyes.

His wavy black hair and aquiline nose, combined with the slightly golden hue of his skin, gave the man a Mediterranean appearance. Still, he was Wearside through and through.

"In the animal kingdom, when the alpha yawns, the other members of the pack copy. If a lesser pack member yawns, the alpha doesn't do a thing."

Whyte shot Boyd some side-eye. "You've been watching too much Discovery Channel. And it's a good job we're humans and not animals."

Boyd lowered the window an inch, flooding the pool car with frigid air.

She was an attractive young DC with blonde hair and a spread of freckles over her nose that darkened whenever she blushed – which was often. She was seeing Whyte's flatmate, Oliver Martin, and stayed over most nights, making her practically his flatmate too. So when he got the call shortly before one a.m. to drive to Roker and investigate a death, he only had to bang on the wall dividing their rooms to summon her.

"Humans *are* animals. We might wear clothes and have a technology addiction, but we're still just hairless apes."

Whyte parked the car on Roker Terrace. This was his old stomping ground, and though he always enjoyed returning to Wearside for pleasure – to see his father or meet up with old school friends – it was business that brought him here more often than not.

"You can be a hairless ape all you like, Saff." He unbuckled his seatbelt and got out of the car. "But I'm going to be a detective."

He approached the cordon, recognising a stout PC with a round face shaved to perfection. "Alreet, Dex?"

Dex nodded at Whyte and tipped his hat at Boyd.

"Anonymous caller?" Whyte asked.

"Aye." Dex motioned down towards the beach. "Some lass slurring her words told us to go to the amusements. Said a man had fallen down the bank."

Whyte leant over a stoney barrier and peered towards Marine Walk. It was a steep bank but not overly high. Twenty feet, he estimated. "Fallen, you say?"

"Nope. *I* didn't say he fell. Our anonymous witness said he fell. I'm reserving judgment. Go on down. See for yourself."

Dex held out a cardboard box for Whyte and Boyd to take plastic gloves and booties from.

Whyte checked his watch as he pulled on the gloves. One-thirty. "You know if the fight's started yet?"

Dex shrugged. "Nee idea."

"The walkouts should be starting now," Boyd said, and both men turned to look at her. "What? Can't a lady take an interest in a bit of mindless violence now and again?"

"Yes," Whyte said. "But not you."

As far as Whyte knew, Boyd's interests were as far from mindless violence as one could get.

"You're right," she said with a teasing smile. "Keaton's been going on about it all week." She counted the facts on her fingers as she spoke. "Walkouts at one-thirty. Starts at one forty-five. Ten three-minute rounds."

"Let's crack on then. With any luck, we'll catch the end of it."

They took a paved route down to Marine Walk where the stench of death was mercifully diluted by briny air and a lingering scent of fried fish. Roker was a popular tourist area north of the River Wear. A vast expanse of blond sand lined with coffee shops and chippies. A striped lighthouse marked the end of a great curved pier protecting the harbour from the worst of the North Sea swell. They reached a roundabout surrounded by heavy boulders. The DB was resting facedown between two jagged rocks. Half on the road, half on the pavement, his limbs were sprawled in unnatural angles.

Whyte looked up at the amusement arcade to his right. It seemed oddly forlorn at night, robbed of its usual dancing lights, music and beep-beep of various machines. The expected happy shouts of children and the tinkling of copper from coin pusher machines were replaced with the sombre footsteps of scene of crime officers and the murmurs of police officers.

"Annie Fitzgerald," Whyte murmured as much to himself as anyone. "Year ten. Took her on a date here. I won enough tokens to buy her a stuffed toy. She chose a purple teddy bear, and I got a kiss on the cheek for my efforts. Stunning lass. Wonder what she's doing now."

"Isn't that what social media's for?" Boyd approached the body and knelt down next to a local doctor who had arrived to confirm the death. "Male, late forties to early fifties."

She felt the man's pockets and pulled out a phone. She pressed the power button and, finding it locked, held the sensor against the pad of his index finger.

"Worth a shot," she muttered when it didn't unlock. Feeling further into his pockets, she found a debit card and handed it to Whyte.

"Mr Lee R Edwards."

Boyd turned her head and looked at the bank, taking in the areas of grass flattened by his body as he rolled down the hill. She was quiet for a while, then cast her torch over the rocks on either side of him. "I can't see any blood on the rocks. Can you?"

Moving closer, Whyte examined the area with his torch. "No. Not a drop." He angled the white beam of light over the victim and grimaced. "Riddle me this, Saff. If Mr Edwards tumbled down this grassy verge, didn't hit the rocks and landed face down, why the hell is the back of his skull completely caved in?"

"I don't know," Boyd answered. "But something's telling me you're not going to catch the end of the fight." She walked back up the bank, scanning her torchlight back and forth in front of her. "Get up here, Whyte."

He caught up, seeing what she saw. Across the road from the Roker Hotel, the pavement branched from Roker Terrace down to the seafront. He examined a railing directly above where the body lay. At first, it looked like specks of red rust. He dabbed it with a gloved finger. Not rust. It was damp with blood.

"He didn't fall," he said.

Boyd stood beside him and gazed out at the choppy sea. "He didn't fall," she echoed.

- Chapter 4 -

While Madison Square Garden was just a five-minute drive from Times Square, New York, it was a hell of a long way from Times Square, Newcastle, where the bars were alive with local pride as sports fans, young and old, gathered to watch the Tyneside Terror defend his belt.

Hope East sipped a Midori and lemonade and adjusted the hem of her floral dress. The Pink Elephant didn't usually show sports, but tonight was an exception. The whole city would be tuning in. Not screening the fight was bad for business, and in these troubled times with rising rent and utilities, pubs and bars did what they needed to survive. Still, the Pink Elephant wasn't just surviving; it was thriving, and seats were at a premium. Hope didn't mind. She shared a chair with her wife, perching on her knee. Catalina bit her lip, eyes glued to the screen. She placed her pint of Carling on an art-deco table beside her and wrapped her arms around Hope. A buxom woman, Catalina cut a stylish figure in a waistcoat and matching trousers, while Hope was softer, preferring feminine prints and muted tones. She wasn't usually one for late nights in bars and nightclubs, but Hope couldn't resist. This was a special occasion.

The atmosphere in the 1920s-styled bar was electric, with the buzz of excited conversation and modern jazz music filling the air. Rose gold accented a predominantly black interior. Vintage movie posters adorned the walls; staff wore crisp white shirts and bowties. The bar was heaving, but while the dancefloor was crammed with warm bodies, no one moved in time to the music; they were too engrossed in the action on the screen.

Jones threw a powerful right. Ahmed ducked, firing back into his opponent's solar plexus.

"Go on, son," shouted a bald man from the back of the room. "Get in there."

Feeling Catalina's legs tremble with nerves, Hope nestled in closer, her hand resting on her wife's arm, offering silent support.

The crowd gasped collectively as Jones landed a heavy blow. Ahmed stumbled backwards, first hitting the ropes, then careening to the canvas with a thud.

"No!" Catalina's face was etched with worry as she pushed strands of golden blonde hair behind her ear.

"He'll get back up," Hope assured her. "He always gets back up."

Catalina took an anxious sip of lager while the referee began his count. "I'm not so sure."

But with eyes filled with fierce determination, the boxer pushed himself off the mat, rising to his feet before the count ran out.

Hope clapped her hands as the bar erupted with applause. This was great for the city, she thought. Abdul's rise to stardom shone a light on Newcastle and united the toon in only the way sport could. She beamed at her wife, who still looked like she was suffering palpitations from the knockdown, and kissed her lips. "He's unstoppable."

AN HOUR LATER, A baby cried in the predawn darkness of North Tyneside. Detective Chief Inspector Erica Cooper scooped Danny into her arms and tickled his tummy. She was one of the few people who hadn't stayed up late to watch the fight, choosing to go to bed at seven p.m. instead – but for good reason. She had an early flight to catch.

"Passport. Currency. Driver's license," she muttered, meticulously inspecting her carry-on.

Despite the difficulties of Danny's birth and the pressures of her job, Cooper was slim and healthy, her body nourished with good food cooked by a good man. And while she was short in stature, her buzzcut hair and hard stare meant she could sit before any hardened criminal and meet their eye.

She tried to push thoughts of work to the back of her mind. Northumbria CID had come under close scrutiny after serial killers and missing persons cases had plagued their recent years. A new DI had finally been assigned to the unit, and Cooper looked forward to working with him. Unfortunately, his start coincided with her long-overdue holiday. Still, she knew the team would look after him.

Cooper double-checked her tickets. Newcastle to Cancun. Two weeks of tequilas and tacos in Tulum.

"Are you sure we have everything Danny needs?" she asked quietly to avoid waking her teenage daughter, who slept in the next room and had chosen to stay home rather than miss the start of the school year. "Did you pack a bottle brush? What if it's cold on the plane? Do you have baby shampoo?"

A calming hand rested on her shoulder. "Yes, I packed a bottle brush. We have his hat and mittens if it gets cold, and the baby shampoo is in our hold luggage. Relax, Erica. We have everything."

"I am relaxed. Look."

Cooper handed Danny to her good man, Justin Atkinson, and gestured at her casual outfit. "I'm an eight-hour flight and a couple of Dos Equis away from perfect Zen."

While Cooper was short, Atkinson was tall. While she liked metal music, he preferred classical. And yet, they worked. When Danny arrived, Atkinson took paternity leave for six weeks, allowing Cooper to continue the work she loved. When he returned to the lab, Atkinson reduced his hours, sharing Danny's care with Cooper's mother. Still, fatherhood suited Atkinson, Cooper thought as she smiled at him. He was a fair few years older than she was, and his hair had greyed considerably more since becoming a dad again, yet his face seemed more youthful, more fulfilled.

"Do you want me to carry the cases downstairs?" Atkinson asked, checking his watch. "The taxi will be here any second."

"No, it's okay," she said, taking a suitcase in each hand. "You have our precious cargo."

She followed him downstairs, where her mother waited in the kitchen. She sat at the kitchen table listening to the Abdul-Jones fight on BBC Sounds.

"How's he doing?" Cooper asked.

"It's all over. Ahmed won, good lad. Jones almost had him, though. He knocked Ahmed down in the fifth, but he got back up during the count and managed to finish him in the seventh." Julie Cooper paused the boxing post-mortem and got to her feet. "Just brilliant for the northeast. Now, have the best time, you two." Her eyes glazed over as she pictured Mexico. "A fortnight of sunshine and sunbathing? I'm not jealous in the slightest."

Cooper laughed. "We don't really do sunbathing, Mum. Besides, you know you still have a villa and bar in the Canaries, right?"

"It's your father's bar, dear," Julie replied with a hint of sadness in her voice. "And though I bet it's going crazy right now with the ex-pats watching the boxing, it wouldn't feel right being there without him. The sooner I can sell it, the better. Now, I have Tina's schedule and her list of clubs." She waved a printout that Cooper had typed for her. "We'll be just fine. You two have—"

Cooper cut her off. "You won't try and force feed her—"

"Well, in my day, you ate what you were given," Julie said. "But it's been made abundantly clear that we don't live in *my day* anymore, so no, I won't insist that Tina eats anything too horrible like, you know, fruits and vegetables."

"She actually..." Cooper was about to go over her daughter's needs for the millionth time when the taxi rolled silently into the street. Tina was more than capable of going toe-to-toe with her grandmother and was stubborn enough and intelligent enough to win any argument that came up.

The taxi stopped outside Cooper's door, and the driver opened the boot. Cooper kissed her mother on the cheek and dragged the cases down the dimly lit path, but as Atkison slid into the backseat with baby Danny in his arms, his phone began to ring.

Cooper was halfway through saying, "Ignore it," when her phone started to chirp as well.

Great.

Atkinson squinted at his iPhone. "It's HQ," he sighed.

Cooper pulled her phone from her carry-on bag. She didn't need to look at the screen to know who it was, and yet her heart sank all the same. "It's

Nixon," she said as images of Mayan pyramids and pina coladas faded in her mind.

The driver glanced at them in the rearview mirror, started the engine and pulled away from the curb.

"Shit," Cooper sighed, tilting her head back and squeezing her eyes shut in frustration. "Stop the car."

If something had the superintendent out of bed at this hour, it had to be big.

- Chapter 5 -

It was close to three forty-five when Cooper and Atkinson arrived at a renowned gay club in the city centre. The taxi driver had been kind enough not to run the metre while they handed Danny over to Julie and changed in record time. Cooper swapped her linen trousers and lacy vest for a sleek suit and smart shoes, putting her dreams of a holiday back on the shelf beside her sunglasses and beaded necklace.

The streets were deserted save for a few walk-of-shamers and stragglers who had partied till last orders, their giggles and hushed conversations fading into the morning fog. As Cooper approached the crime scene, the neon-lit entrance glowed a soft aura through the misty air and a sense of unfairness settled over her. Unfairness at being denied the break she so badly needed, but much more so, unfairness that two lives had been cut short.

Dampness shimmered on the pavement, reflecting the pink lights above. There was an eerie, unsettling quiet to the scene. Just an hour or so ago, the place would have pulsated with uptempo beats, hormone-filled seduction and adrenaline-fuelled morale.

Cooper adjusted the collar of her raincoat as Atkinson left her side to join the team of SOCOs donning their bunny suits and booties. She fastened the top button to keep the cold air off her neck, gave herself a pep talk and approached a nervous-looking PC standing by the cordon.

His slim frame shivered as he spoke, his voice quivering. "I was the first one here, ma'am. I..."

His voice faded. He covered his mouth with the back of his hand.

"I've never..."

"Your first DB?" Cooper asked.

He nodded.

"Spewed yet?"

He shook his head. "No, ma'am."

"Then you're doing better than I did. Got vomit all over my new Kurt Geigers and almost contaminated the entire scene. Had to be escorted from the building."

His face brightened somewhat.

"What can you tell me?"

He pointed behind him to an alleyway opposite the club that curved around between an upmarket chain hotel and office buildings. A large screen covered each end of the alley, protecting the dignity of the deceased.

"A bloke called it in. He and a friend went into the alley to, well, get better acquainted. That's when they found them. His friend ran off while he was on the phone to 999. I was only around the corner. Can't have taken me more than two minutes to get here after the call was placed, but the caller had scarpered as well by the time I got here. Can't blame them. It's fucking horrific." He remembered who he was talking to and gulped an apology. "Sorry, ma'am."

"Call me Cooper. And swear as much as you like as long as the public can't hear you."

Atkinson and the others used gloved hands to lift the yellow tape and disappear behind the screens. A smell of cigarette smoke and alcohol wavered over the damp tarmac.

"Two women," the PC said. "They've been badly beaten, and their throats are slit wide open." He looked away. As if he could look away from the image now burnt into his young retinas.

A familiar shadow fell over a reflection of a neon pink elephant in a puddle. Pink faded to black, and Cooper turned to see the round face of DS Paula Keaton. A powerhouse of muscle and self-assurance, she not only felt like stone, but she was the rock many of the team depended on. Accompanying Keaton was DC Oliver Martin. A baby-faced pretty boy with gelled hair and a gullible demeanour.

"Hate crime?" Keaton asked.

"Two women murdered opposite a gay club? Looks that way," Cooper replied. "You okay?"

"I'm fine," Keaton said.

Martin scrunched his face. "In Newcastle? Doesn't feel right. Geordies are famously tolerant."

Keaton gave him a sceptical stare. "Think I'll be the judge of that."

Admonished, he raised and lowered his shoulders. "Aye. Fair enough."

"Erica," Atkinson called for Cooper and beckoned her over. She followed, ducking under the tape and behind the screen.

Jesus. She saw why the first responder was on the verge of tears. The first woman, well-built and fair-haired, had not only had her throat cut, but her head was practically severed. The cervical bones of her neck and tissue of the oesophagus clearly visible. The second woman, slender with wavy dark locks, lay face up in a puddle. She'd been badly beaten, her nose and cheekbones crushed into what had once been a pretty face. Her mouth was slightly agape, revealing a jaw with several teeth missing.

Around them, the forensics team set up lighting. As it illuminated the alley, it shimmered off fragments of shattered glass, creating a mosaic of twinkling lights. In the corner, startled by the sudden illumination, a rat scurried from its hiding place behind a drainpipe, seeking refuge in the shadows.

Atkinson let Cooper observe the scene for a moment before saying, "I'm no detective, but—"

"But this isn't your average mugging gone wrong," finished Cooper, spotting two teeth on the ground, at least five feet from their owner. She turned her head and blinked several times before she could continue. The first-responder had summed it up perfectly; it was fucking horrific. "This is nasty. This was done by someone with pure hate in their heart."

Picturing a long night ahead of her, Cooper asked optimistically, "Any ID?"

"Actually, yes."

That was a turn-up for the books. At least she wouldn't have to wait around for a worried relative to report a loved one missing or chase DNA results only to find the victim wasn't in their database.

He extended an arm toward the larger woman with lighter hair.

"In the first victim's pockets, we found a roll of twenty-pound notes and two sticks of chewing gum." He handed a clear plastic evidence bag to Cooper, which she glanced quickly at.

"And?"

Atkinson sucked his lips into his mouth. "And there was a driver's license in the second victim's shoulder bag." He hesitated before handing it to her. "I guess we know why they called Nixon at this ungodly hour. And why, he, in turn, called us."

Holding the bag up to the light, Cooper squinted at the ID. Though slightly blurred by the plastic wallet, a name was clearly visible.

"Hope East?" Cooper staggered back a few steps. "You're shitting me?"

Looking back at the petite woman with the wavy, blood-stained hair, Cooper suddenly recognised her.

She now knew why her leave had been denied at the last second. There were hate crimes, and then there were hate crimes that threatened to tear a city apart.

"Hope East," she repeated. "Someone's murdered the goddamn Mayor of Newcastle."

- Chapter 6 -

Hope for Change. Vote Hope for Newcastle.

Hope East had been in power for over a year. She'd been in the public eye for much longer, campaigning on social media and in the local press for causes popular with young, liberal members of the electorate, both Geordies and those who came to the northeast for university or a more affordable cost of living.

Cooper had met her twice before. Once, at a Northumbria Police recruitment event where she'd spoken about the importance of a diverse police force, one that represented the rich fabric of local society. More women, more representatives of different races and religions, and more members of the LGBTQ+ community. The second event was a fundraiser for a charity supporting disadvantaged children by providing work experience in the music industry. From classical to rap, Hope approached stars and execs alike to find opportunities in a world often dictated by nepotism. Cooper wouldn't claim to know her or be friends with her, but from their short conversations, she found her charming, eloquent and charismatic.

And now she was dead. Murdered in a grotesque and senseless act of violence. Cooper felt sick to her stomach as she walked out of the alley, searching for Keaton and Martin. They needed witnesses, CCTV, and evidence. They needed to inform the families.

"Coffee?" Keaton brandished a paper cup in Cooper's direction, which she took gratefully. Goodness knows where she'd got it from at this hour, but she wasn't about to ask questions.

"You're a star."

Keaton ran a hand over her short, brown ponytail, which she kept tight and smooth. "Martin's talking to a homeless man who was sleeping in a doorway further up the street. He says he didn't see anything."

"Believe him?"

Keaton shrugged. "Maybe he's too scared to say owt. I'll give Martin more time to chat with him. He's got that sweet, puppy-dog thing going. People open up to him more than they do me."

"That's because you put the fear of God into them."

"Don't I just?" Keaton folded her thick arms and scanned the street for CCTV cameras, her eyes resting on a Greek takeaway promising the best gyros in the city. To its left was a store selling school uniforms, and to its right was an adult toy store.

This area of town was ever-evolving. The impressive Life Science Centre, part museum – part laboratory, was at the cutting edge of genetic disease research and pioneering fertility treatments. Towering, modern apartment blocks rubbed shoulders with famous hotel chains and swanky, glass-fronted office spaces, dwarfing the many rainbow-clad bars and clubs. But amongst the shiny glamour of modernity and hip nightlife, there were still pockets of neglect. Places where people slept rough, addicts shuffled aimlessly and the most vulnerable members of society were forgotten.

Cooper sipped her coffee. It was weak and lukewarm, as disappointing as not being in an airport lounge about now. She thought of the two women lying just metres away with their throats cut open. Who could do such a thing? And why? Was Hope targeted at random, a sick attack based on sexuality? Or was this politically motivated because of her position and power?

"Listen," Cooper said, breaking the silence and trying to shake the image of Hope East's lifeless eyes staring at nothing, her body mutilated and defiled, "Martin might be right. This might not be a hate crime. Well, not exactly."

Keaton turned to her. "What do you mean? And let's not tell him that. You use the words *Martin, I think you're right* and he'll never shut up about it."

"One of the women in the alley is Hope East."

There was a pause while Keaton inhaled deeply, looking troubled.

Oliver Martin jogged over to join them. He rubbed his upper arms for warmth and blew out a billow of condensing air. "Poor bugger. That's no life," he said, shaking his head. "If he did see something, he's not talking."

Keaton's head fell forward, and she put a hand to her forehead, pain written all over her usual tough exterior.

Martin looked concerned. "What's up?"

"One of the victims is Hope East," Keaton said.

"The other is likely her wife. Catalina, if I remember correctly," Cooper added.

"Hope East? Hope East? Why do I know that name?"

Keaton rolled her eyes at the young man. "Because she's the effing mayor of effing Newcastle, that's why."

His mouth fell open. "Ahh."

"Ahh indeed," Keaton said, mocking him. "Find out who owns that gyros place and access their camera. They might have caught something. And speak to the manager of every bar on this block. We need to talk to their staff. Let's find out where they were before this happened. Switch? Digital? The Pink Elephant? Who were they here with, and what time did they leave?"

Martin nodded, dipped his head against the wind and set off.

Cooper rubbed her temples, feeling the weight of the investigation already. A city buoyed into the early hours by sporting victory only to awake to the sinking news of a brutal double murder. Because if Newcastle had a face, it was Hope East's. And now her image would dominate the news. News that their corner of the northeast wasn't the diverse, accepting place they thought it was.

Keaton's jaw worked overtime, chewing something invisible. "We need to get a handle on this quickly. Once word gets out, it'll be a media circus."

"And don't I know it."

Cooper swallowed the last of the mediocre coffee, crumpled the cup and walked to the north end of the road, towards the Life Science Centre. The sun was beginning to melt the foggy darkness of the night sky, painting it a paler shade of blue. She found a bin outside a bar called The Yard and deposited the cup into it.

"But, Coop," Keaton called, her long strides easily keeping pace with the smaller DCI. "An openly gay public figure and her wife murdered here." She gestured to a string of pride flag bunting. "If this isn't a hate crime, what is it?"

Cooper pinched her nose and shuffled her feet before meeting Keaton's eye.

"A political assassination."

- Chapter 7 -

Whitney Chambers stood outside her daughter's new-build in the La Sagesse estate of Jesmond. Sunlight gradually dried the morning dew on neatly trimmed hedges and pristine lawns. Colourful flowers adorned the new neighbourhood built on the grounds of an old Catholic school. It was a place where tranquillity intertwined with status. Whitney tutted and knocked again, louder this time.

"Just phone them," shouted her husband, Nick, from the car's passenger window. Behind him, an infant with a bad case of the terrible twos squirmed in his car seat, banging his tiny fists against the glass.

"I *have* phoned them. You literally just watched me phone them."

"Try their mobiles. No one answers their landlines anymore."

"I just—" she cut her reply short and returned to the front door. "Oh, why do I bother?"

Whitney had tried their mobiles. Repeatedly. She'd arrived early, hoping for a warm embrace, a cup of tea, and a chat. It wasn't like her daughter to change plans and not tell her. She wasn't flighty or impulsive; she was sensible and rigid with her timekeeping.

Whitney knocked on the door again, her knuckles meeting the wood with rhythmic desperation. As no response came, a growing feeling of unease gnawed at her. She moved from window to window, trying to find a gap in the curtains, but alas, there was no way of seeing into the home.

"Their cars are still here," she sighed.

"Whose cars?" Nick asked.

Whitney bit her tongue. *Whose do you think?* "Your daughter's. And Catalina's."

"Right," said Nick, his eyes darting like they always did when he was confused. "They're probably hungover," he assured her. "Let's get a coffee and go and see Jim."

Whitney empathised with baby Brandon having his tantrum in the car seat. She wanted to join him. To scream and rage. Jim had been dead for six months, and she couldn't face telling Nick that. Again.

Could Hope be hungover? Having a lie-in? Oblivious to Whitney's banging on the door and constant calls? She didn't think so. Hope never drank much, and although Catalina did, she could certainly handle her booze. They both adored

Brandon; he was their world, and they were never late to collect him when he had a sleepover at his Nan Nan's.

Something was wrong; she could tell. Mothers could always tell.

With shaking fingers, Whitney searched for the number of the nearest police station.

"Are you calling Jim?"

"Shh."

She hit the green call button. The woman she spoke to was sympathetic but not forthcoming with any real help. At least she didn't spin the old *we can't do anything for twenty-four hours* nonsense. Whitney didn't like having to use her daughter's name to gain favours and Hope herself would give her daggers and chastise her for using her title in that way, but needs must, and she knew Hope and Catlina were ill or injured. Or worse.

The call handler relented and agreed to prioritise the call, but still, it might be hours before someone arrived. Feeling unable to do anymore, Whitney decided to drive Nick and Brandon the short distance to the Osborne Coffee Co. on St. George's Terrace. But she had barely sat down and fastened her seat belt when a police car appeared in the rearview.

"That was quick," she said, briefly lifted by the police's efficiency.

Her next thought came with more foreboding.

Too quick.

The police car pulled up next to hers, followed by an unmarked car. Two women and a man, all in suits, got out. Detectives, Whitney thought, her chest tightening. This was no welfare check.

BEFORE COOPER COULD REACH the house, a frail woman in her early sixties came running over.

"What's happened? Where's Hope?"

She stumbled on the curb, landing on her knees and palms. Cooper went to help her up. Her thin trousers were torn, and blood seeped into the material. Shaken, she opened her hands and dusted small stones from open wounds.

"Get the first aid kit," she called to Martin. He was already a step ahead, opening the car boot. "I'm DCI Erica Cooper. You know Hope?"

She knew the answer before it left the woman's trembling lips. "I'm her mother. I have Brandon with me."

"Brandon?"

"Her son. Her and Catalina's son."

Cooper glanced at the car and noticed the youngster staring back at her with curious eyes. He looked to be about two, just a baby with no idea how his world had changed in the blink of an eye. One moment, he had two mums; the next, he was an orphan. His big blue eyes and sandy hair reminded her of another toddler who lost his father without ever knowing him, and the comparison broke Cooper's heart.

"We'll get you cleaned up," Cooper said, taking the woman's hands. "What's your name?"

"Whitney."

"Do you have a key for the house, Whitney?"

She shook her head. "Yes, but it's at my house. Why won't you tell me what's happened?"

Martin had donned gloves and was holding antibacterial wipes. "Whitney, please come and take a seat." He motioned to the open door of the car. "I've got this," he mouthed to Cooper, leading Whitney away. "I can break the news."

Cooper mouthed her thanks, trying to hide the emotion that had stirred inside her at the thought of that young boy losing both his parents. She shook her arms, trying to flick the dark thoughts out the very ends of her fingers before joining Keaton at the front door. A uniformed officer was working on the lock, but it was stubbornly refusing to budge.

"I can do this the tidy way, but it'll take a while," he said.

"The quick way is fine," Cooper told him.

Keaton grinned. "If you're getting the big red key, I call dibs."

"Soz," said the uniform. "Just a plain old crowbar today."

Within thirty seconds, he'd pried the front door open. Cooper listened for an alarm system but couldn't hear any beeping, only the faint tick-tock of a grandfather clock. The parquet floorboards pointed forward, guiding them into the entrance hall. It was styled in a sleek, modern design with glossy grey walls, a brilliant white ceiling and a crystal chandelier. A large, abstract painting hung on the wall to Cooper's right, its bright colours contrasting with the monochrome space.

Their feet echoed on the wooden floor as they stepped inside. The house felt oddly cold and morose, as if the building itself – the very bricks and mortar – could sense it had been deserted, like an abandoned dog that knew his owners would never return home.

A flash of movement caught Cooper's eye, followed by the sound of shattering glass.

"Stop," Cooper yelled. "Police!"

They raced forward in time to see a person crashing out the back window into a garden walled with old trees and stone walls.

"Stay where you are."

He was a big bloke with dark skin and garish orange trainers. Keaton reached the back door first, opening it with a ferocious shoulder charge and a grunt of pain.

"He's got something," Keaton yelled over her shoulder, sprinting down the lawn and around a pine tree.

The man pushed something into a backpack as he ran, slinging it over his shoulder in time to leap the wall. Keaton grabbed the top edge with both hands and hauled herself over. Cooper was less graceful, pulling on vines and using a neighbouring tree to help her up. Sitting astride the stone wall, she sighed, seeing the man disappear down Jesmond Dene Road into the expansive stretch of woodland trails.

- Chapter 8 -

"Get a car down there," Cooper shouted, pointing down Jesmond Dene Road.

"Can't, ma'am," said a uniform from the other end of the Easts' garden. He shook his head apologetically. "It's closed to vehicles. Bollards both ends."

Over the past decade, Jesmond had edged towards becoming a low-traffic neighbourhood, and each year, it seemed more and more roads were closed to vehicles. It was a divisive scheme, and those who loved it cited cleaner air and safer streets for pedestrians and cyclists. Still, all that traffic had to go somewhere and for every closed road, another saw constant gridlock and exhaust fumes. Journey times increased, and emergency vehicles struggled to get to some areas.

"Oh, for crying out loud." Cooper slipped over the other side of the wall, grazing the right side of her face against the stone but landing otherwise unharmed.

The man in the orange trainers had been in the home of two murder victims. He fled from the police and was carrying an unknown object, presumably from the victims' home. As far as Cooper was concerned, that made him a suspect. Or, at the very least, a person of interest. Who was he, and why was he in Hope and Catalina's home the morning after their deaths?

"Then block off the exits," she said through gritted teeth.

His face popped over the wall, and he peered down at Cooper. "What? All of them?"

"I'm sorry, do you have other plans today? Yes, all of them. Get on the radio and get a car or officer at every path leading into the dene." And though she knew she had no chance, she added, "I'm going after them."

THE TREES WHIPPED PAST as Keaton sprinted down the winding trail, her breath burning in her lungs. Her ankle rolled on a loose stone, and she stumbled, catching herself on the trunk of an old horse chestnut.

Not good. She was already losing ground.

He was fast, even by Keaton's standards, and she had the sprint speed of a professional rugby player. Because that's precisely what she was. Or used to be.

The man she pursued veered off the path, sliding down the steep bank in a shower of dirt and leaves, his longer legs giving him an advantage on the slopes.

"Stop! Police!" Her shout echoed through the trees unanswered.

Gritting her teeth, Keaton descended after him as he swerved left and took the stepping stones across the Ouse Burn two at a time. The unstable ground threatened to give way with every step, but she pushed on. Couldn't lose him now. Her foot caught on the first stepping stone, and she crashed into the shallow water, pain exploding through her wrist as it took the brunt of her fall. With no time or desire to assess the damage, she scrambled up, scanning the dense undergrowth for any sign of movement. There. A snapped branch. The faint rustle of footsteps heading east.

Keaton broke into a run once more, heedless of the throbbing in her wrist. He turned back towards the river, pausing for a second on the stone bridge by the falls, contemplating a jump. It was only a second, but it was enough for Keaton to make up ground. She almost had him, a feint feeling of recognition falling over her.

He darted south, covering the picnic field like a man running for his life. Or freedom. Keaton's breath came fast and shallow as she followed him down Red Walk, a paved footpath running parallel to the water. This was a battle of wills. Whose body could tolerate the most lactic acid? Whose lungs could burn the most without giving up?

The pathway widened. Families queued for the ice cream van, enjoyed a morning walk and visited the walled garden. There was far less manoeuvrability, and the contest changed from sprint speed to agility test.

He darted into the petting zoo, ripping a section of fencing away and letting a pair of angry goats free into the park. Chaos ensued. Parents scooped their children up, fleeing from the horned beasts. The goats attacked each other, butting heads and kicking their hooves. Roosters crowed, ducks quacked, pigs oinked, and humans screamed.

Keaton took the opposite approach, hopping the fence into the now empty enclosure, using it as a shortcut towards the exit. But as she stumbled out of the small zoo and turned up the hill towards Armstrong Bridge, she found herself fighting through a sea of joggers from a local running club. There must have been fifty of them.

She stopped, gasping, mouth open, head turning right and left in desperation, trying to find the man amongst the crowd. Bodies jostled into her. Some breathlessly apologising, others muttering annoyance at her getting in their way.

They had PBs to beat; she had a suspect to apprehend.

As the last of the joggers passed, leaving her alone on the trail, Keaton's chest heaved with disappointment. She felt the sting of failure like a punch in the gut. She'd had him, and she'd lost him. He could be on the bridge or the underpass, back on a trail or hiding in the trees. She interlaced her fingers and put her hands behind her head, swearing at the sky.

- Chapter 9 -

Cooper burst onto Red Walk, her face stinging from the graze she'd sustained dropping down the stone wall at the back of the La Sagesse estate. Searching for Keaton, she found her on the north bank of the Ouse Burn, crouched on her haunches, elbows resting on her knees, face resting on closed fists. The sun filtered through the canopy, illuminating the defeated DS.

Keaton looked up, squinting against the glare. "Lost him. Sorry, guv."

If there was anything Keaton loved, it was the thrill of a good chase. And if there was anything she abhorred, it was losing.

A swan floated in their direction, padded onto the bank, spread his expansive wings and hissed angrily at Keaton.

Keaton hissed back.

"What happened to your face?" she asked, turning back to Cooper.

"Trying to keep up with you, that's what. Should've known better." She crouched next to the DS. Across the stream, a boy in baggy shorts and wellies fished for sticklebacks with a nylon fishing net on a stick. "We've got cars posted on the main exits to the dene looking for him. I suspect we're too late."

"He'll be long gone," grumbled Keaton, and she was likely right. The dene sprawled into other parks, hundreds of trails spiderwebbing out into several different suburbs.

They stood and climbed the hill in silence until reaching Matthew Bank, turning into Jesmond, Tower Avenue and back into La Sagesse.

The Easts' home was a three-story new-build with a drive leading to a two-car garage. Above it, a balcony overlooked a manicured lawn filled with aromatic herbs and bushes trimmed into spirals or spheres. The front door was still ajar, guarded by a different officer than earlier.

Cooper took a left into a lounge area. "Let's see if anything obvious is missing. I refuse to believe that man's presence here was a coincidence, that he just happened to burgle a home the morning after its occupiers were killed."

"He didn't look like your average meth-head looking for something to pawn for a quick fix," Keaton said. "And he didn't run like one either."

The living room was exquisite and chic. Long dusky-pink sofas and lush palms in marble planters surrounded a sheepskin rug. An open plan layout led to a creamy, modern kitchen so immaculate Cooper wondered if either of the Easts actually cooked or ate anything at all.

"They must have a cleaner," she said, trying to justify the lived-in appearance of her own kitchen despite having her mother popping by most days to help out.

"How much do you think a place like this costs?" Keaton asked, opening a drawer in an antique desk in the study.

"A million? Maybe two?" guessed Cooper, admiring the luxurious surroundings. "I didn't know being mayor was so lucrative."

Keaton closed the drawer. "It's not. Not really. I think it's her wife's money. She mentioned it in her campaign. The last bloke was a bit of a dodge-pot, allegations of corruption and backroom dealings. Hope said she had everything in life she ever needed and therefore couldn't be bought."

In Cooper's experience, everyone could be bought with the right offer or influence. She'd sent one of her own DIs down for his part in people trafficking. He hadn't needed the money but took it anyway when his daughter was threatened.

"Do we know where Catalina worked?" Keaton asked.

"She was some kind of agent. Estate agent, maybe."

Keaton nodded her head as if the affluent surroundings made more sense now. "Must get a staff discount."

"You thinking what I'm thinking?" Cooper asked, running a gloved hand along the silky smooth surface of the kitchen top.

"That this place is a little too tidy for a burglar trying their luck? That bloke knew what he was looking for and where to find it."

"Exactly."

"You spotted any laptops or tablets yet? Because I haven't." Keaton nodded back towards the desk. "Nowt in the drawers."

They moved from room to room, checking every drawer, shelf, cupboard and storage unit. No tablets. No laptops.

"Son of a bitch," Cooper said, looking out a bedroom window into the back garden. "Something on their laptops holds the key to why there was a political assassination on the streets of Newcastle last night. And either the killer or someone who works for them was right here." She felt frustration bubbling up inside her. "Right here, and we bloody lost them."

Keaton's face betrayed her hurt. An almost imperceptible twitch of her cheek and a lowering of her eyes.

"Oh, not you, Paula. You did a damn site better than I did."

"I'll get him next time."

"I don't doubt it."

And when Keaton got hold of him, Cooper would give him hell. If the Easts' emails, files or data held clues to the killer and their motive, Cooper needed access to it. She removed her gloves, unlocked her phone and scrolled her contacts until she found the name she was looking for. Rebecca Hogg: Becky the Techie.

The call connected, and Cooper heard a long yawn before Becky spoke.

"Shouldn't you be in Mexico?"

"Don't remind me."

Cooper filled Becky in on all they knew so far. She could picture the cyber whizz with her colourful beanie and round glasses. She had dark hair and a darker sense of humour.

"I've got a crime scene with missing electronics. Is there any way you can access them remotely?"

Becky slurped on some sort of drink. "You got their phones?"

"SOCOs have them."

"Good. That makes things easier. I might be able to retrieve passwords from one device for the other. I'll head over to the evidence lock up and get started."

"One of the vic's had an office at the Civic Centre. I'll arrange the necessary paperwork for you to take her work computer too. Hopefully, you'll have it by later today."

More slurping, followed by, "You think the mayor ruffled the wrong bird's feathers?"

"I think someone had it in for her. She was a beautiful young woman in the public eye. That's enough in itself to annoy some. Now add to it her left-leaning, pro-environment, anti-corruption stance..."

"If she's got enemies and they've been silly enough to leave a digital trail, I'll find it. Just give me time."

Cooper thanked Becky and hung up, tapping her phone into the palm of her hand and staring at a framed photo on a bedside table. A happy couple, frozen in time with their young son, pride bursting out his mothers' eyes.

"Poor kid," said Keaton, reading her mind.

Cooper couldn't help but wonder if their son would remember his loving parents or if his memories would be replaced with the media circus and political scandal that would inevitably follow their murder. She shook her head, pushing those thoughts aside for the moment. She had work to do.

- Chapter 10 -

Martin sat on the front lawn with baby Brandon on his lap. The infant smiled and laughed while his grandmother sobbed next to them. When Martin saw Cooper and Keaton approaching, he apologised to the grieving mother, got to his feet and went to meet them.

"You'd better not let Saff see you playing with that baby," whispered Keaton. "Her ovaries might burst."

Martin gave her a look but didn't dare tell her to shut up. "I've treated her wounds from the fall. There's not much I can do for the other pain she's feeling, though. She's distraught and doesn't know who to choose."

"Who to choose?" echoed Cooper. "What do you mean?"

"Her husband or the kid." He glanced back at Whitney, who twirled a buttercup in her fingers, trying to entertain the toddler. "Her husband suffered a severe head injury a few years back and hasn't been the same since. Changed his entire personality and even changed what foods he likes and dislikes. He needs help with any tasks requiring fine motor skills, tying his shoelaces, things like that, and he has memory issues. Can't remember his own daughter's name some days."

Little Brandon started to whimper. Cooper recognised the beginnings of a meltdown. He'd be screaming the place down within a minute.

"Where is the husband?" she asked, eyes sweeping over the empty car.

"I called Whitney's neighbour. He came to take Nick for a walk and a tea. I don't think he understands what's got his wife so upset," Martin said. "What a horrible situation. Whitney says she takes Brandon once a week so Hope and Catalina can have a night out, go for a meal or go to the cinema. But she can't take him full-time. She can't look after Brandon and Nick."

His face clouded, and Cooper couldn't blame him. Whitney faced an impossible decision. Put her grandson into care, or her husband?

"Right, Mary Poppins," she addressed Martin. "Go work your magic with the toddler. He needs distracting in the next twenty seconds. Keaton, call the SOCOs and get someone to check the house for prints. Maybe we can identify Mr Orange Shoes."

Cooper adopted a sympathetic expression and went to sit with Whitney. The frail woman looked even smaller than when she'd come running towards Cooper earlier. Her thin legs shook, and there was a pained emptiness in her eyes.

"I just don't know what to do," she said, looking up at Cooper.

"We'll make sure Brandon is taken care of. You don't need to make any decisions today. He'll be looked after. I promise."

"I just can't believe she's gone." She drew her knees up to her chest and worried with the torn fabric on her knee.

"I'm so sorry. I met Hope a couple of times. She was a lovely woman."

"And a lovely daughter."

They sat in silence until Cooper added. "Your daughter made a real positive impact in this city. She won't be forgotten, and I swear I will do whatever it takes to bring the person who did this to justice."

Whitney picked up the buttercup and twisted it in her fingers until the stem disintegrated, staining her skin green.

"Did Hope ever mention anyone having a grudge against her?" Cooper asked. "Or Catalina?"

Whitney lifted her chin, thinking. "Other than the bigots?"

Cooper nodded.

"Not Catalina. She was the life and soul of the party. Everyone loved her. And she had a real way with Nick, always managed to get a smile out of him." She sighed. "She was like another daughter to me."

The tears returned as it dawned on her she'd lost not one daughter but two. Fat, silent tears rolled into hollow cheeks.

"And Hope?" Cooper asked.

"She was the LGBTQ+ face of the city. I'm sure plenty of people hated her just for existing. But..." Her brows lowered.

"What is it?" Cooper asked, watching Whitney try to remember something.

"Nick and I had come over for dinner one night. Must have been a month ago now. Hope was just about to serve a delicious shepherd's pie when there was a knock on the door. Hope answered, and I could hear shouting. A man was having a real go at her. He told her to keep her nose out of his business, or she'd regret it. Then Catalina stormed down the hallway and shut the door in his face."

Interesting.

"Any idea who he was or what he looked like?"

"Hope didn't want to talk about it, didn't want to spoil family time, but I got the feeling he worked with her. I got a good look at him from the kitchen window, so the next day, I went on the council's website and found his photo. Frank McKenna's his name."

Cooper wrote all this down. She was keen to chat to this McKenna as soon as possible.

"Sorry to interrupt." Keaton stood a few metres away. "Atkinson wants you to give him a ring," she told Cooper before addressing Whitney. "Can I get you anything, Mrs Chalmers?"

While Keaton chatted to Hope's mother, Cooper found her phone and saw three missed calls.

"You must be psychic," she said when he answered. "I was just about to call you. Rebecca Hogg's on her way over. She needs both Hope and Catalina's phones."

"That's why I was calling," he said. "Catalina's phone wasn't locked. I took the liberty of taking a quick look."

"And?"

"And this might be much simpler than we first thought."

Cooper itched the graze on her face and turned her back to the sun, her shadow stretching across the driveway. "Go on."

"There was a text exchange on Catalina's phone between her and a man named Patrice. Patrice appeared to have a bit of a crush on Catalina. Begged her to let him take her out on a date. He didn't take her rejection well."

She asked Atkinson to send her screenshots of the conversation and Patrice's number. If this really was a case of unrequited love rather than a hate crime or a political assassination, then Atkinson would be correct: It would make the case a hell of a lot simpler.

Still, the revelation didn't make her feel any better. Too many women lost their lives this way. At the hands of possessive men with the attitude, *if I can't have her, no one can.*

"I'll order from Lobo Rojo tonight," Atkinson said, breaking her thoughts of Frank McKenna, Patrice and the man in orange trainers.

"Huh?"

"I'll get a range of tacos and a batch of *carnitas* fries for half six. I might not be able to take you to Mexico, but I can bring Mexico to you."

For the first time that day, Cooper smiled.

- CHAPTER 11 -

THE TACOS WORKED WONDERS, and Cooper awoke on Monday feeling better about her aborted holiday. She and Atkinson desperately needed some time away, but it would wait. She might not be gazing out into the Caribbean Sea, but her children, mother and boyfriend were healthy and safe. No one had done to the Cooper/Atkinson family what had been done to the Easts. And for that, she was grateful.

Tina tucked into a croissant while she gazed at her phone at the kitchen table. Cooper kissed her on the top of the head and took in the smell of hair dye. Tina was sporting a more gothic appearance these days after breaking up with her long-term boyfriend, Josh. Cooper liked Josh; he was a sweet kid, but they'd been through a lot. Cooper didn't know the exact reason for their break up, but Tina seemed to be handling it well if you didn't count her black hair and plum lipstick.

If this new image was an act of rebellion, an attempt at riling her mother, it hadn't worked. Cooper thought Tina looked incredible and was hoping for the day she started listening to Metallica. She might still be Cooper's shy but brilliant little girl, but she had an edge about her now.

"First day of sixth form. You ready?"

Tina rolled her heavily lined eyes as if Cooper had asked the silliest question ever. "Ready for what? All we'll do today is stupid team-building stuff. Then we'll meet our subject tutors and be told to forget everything we learned at GCSE. At uni, I'm guessing they'll tell us to forget everything we did at A-level. Why don't they just teach it the right way in the first place and save us all the bother?"

She finished the last of the pastry and checked her lipstick for crumbs.

"Beats me," said Cooper, hoping Tina's new teachers knew what they'd let themselves in for.

A NEW FACE GREETED Cooper at the glass doors of HQ in Wallsend.

"You must be DCI Cooper?"

He was a tall man who towered over Cooper, broad too. His thick, black beard was neat, shiny and healthy. His eyes crinkled at the corners as he gave the sort of smile that could light up a room. He wore a charcoal suit and matching turban.

He extended a hand. "Detective Inspector Daljit Singh."

Cooper gripped his hand and shook it enthusiastically. "Very, very pleased to meet you, Daljit. You have no idea how much we need a new DI around here. Come on. I'll give you the tour and get you a coffee."

"Actually, I arrived early to get myself orientated and arranged for a Starbucks delivery. It's on your desk."

Impressive. The new DI would fit in just fine with an attitude like that.

Once settled upstairs in the incident room and sipping a delicious Americano, Cooper concluded a brief get-to-know-you by giving Singh a list of names he needed to know.

"You met Nixon yet?"

He shook his head.

"Lucky you. Well, our other DI is Neil Fuller. You'll know his name from the Summer Holt disappearance. He has a couple of DSs working with him on a fraud case at the moment. We have DS Paula Keaton – the fastest woman in the north. If you ever have a suspect who's scared of strong women, send her in. Then there's DS Elliot Whyte. He's the quiet type, and so is DC Saffron Boyd, who he usually works with. He's more quiet and brooding, and she's more quiet and shy. They're both highly intelligent, especially Boyd, and they work well together. They'll be helping us with the East case but also have a suspicious death in Sunderland they're dealing with. Last but not least is DC Oliver Martin. He's young and image-conscious. Keaton teases him mercilessly for it, but he's a gentle soul, and people take to him."

Singh clapped his hands and rubbed his palms together. "I look forward to meeting them all."

"You won't have to wait long. They can smell free coffee from a thousand paces."

Right on cue, Martin walked through the door sniffing the air. Singh handed him a drink and introduced himself.

Martin shook Singh's hand, then revealed, "We have a witness."

Cooper opened her mouth, ready to thank a higher being, when he added, "Don't get excited. It's not a great one."

Dejected, her shoulders slumped. "Better than nothing. Go ahead."

"Remember the guy I was speaking to? The homeless man? I took him breakfast this morning, and he finally admitted to hearing screaming and seeing someone running away from the direction of the alley."

Cooper shared a look with Singh. This had some promise.

"He didn't get a good look; it was dark, middle of the night, but he described a heavy-set male, probably five-ten to six feet. He was wearing dark clothing and a woollen beanie hat. He said he looked like he was carrying a baseball bat."

"Good work, Martin," Cooper said, thanking him. A baseball bat would explain the severity of some of Hope and Catalina's injuries. She turned to Singh. "Did Keaton send you everything we have so far?"

"Yes." He tapped his temple. "Committed to memory. I checked the text exchange between Catalina and Patrice. There's nothing there to help identify him, and the number he used is a burner phone that's either turned off or destroyed. We can ask the Easts' family and friends if they know of him, but for now, I agree with your assessment, DCI Cooper. Frank McKenna should be at the top of our list."

He stood, and Cooper did the same.

"Care to join me for a little trip to the Civic Centre, Daljit?"

"I wouldn't miss it."

- Chapter 12 -

The Civic Centre was as synonymous with the Newcastle skyline as the Tyne Bridge or St. James' Park. A towering white column topped with the heads of seahorses reminded residents of the city's connection to the water and its seafaring heritage. A bronze sculpture of the River God Tyne, oxidised green, crouched high on the wall, staring down at mortals as they passed beneath. Two such mortals, Cooper and Singh, strode purposefully towards the entrance, not even stopping to notice tens of bunny rabbits nibbling the grass lawn. Beyond the bunnies, a television crew broadcast live from Mayor East's former place of work, and a group of students with rainbow flags draped over their shoulders sat in a circle, holding a silent vigil.

The Civic Centre was the political focus of the city, but its banquetting hall was also a favourite wedding venue and played host to many an awards event or corporate do. Though

Mayor Hope East's job was primarily diplomatic, welcoming dignitaries, championing good causes and conferring freedoms of the city, she also chaired all city council meetings. What decisions had been made in this grand building? What secrets weren't recorded in the minutes?

Inside, Cooper felt the familiar eerie silence of a workforce rocked by the loss of a colleague. Two men in suits gossiped in a doorway, casting uneasy glances as anyone walked by. A cleaner engaged in a hushed conversation with a temp, both clutching their chests as they spoke. Seeing Cooper and Singh approach, a receptionist hastily put down the mobile she was texting on. She broke into an automatic smile, then wiped it from her face, sucking her lips in and looking down.

"How may I help you?"

The news was out. Hopefully, between the scandal, slander and back-fence talk, witnesses would come forward and new theories would be born.

Cooper showed her ID. "Frank McKenna, please."

The receptionist tucked a strand of chestnut bob behind an ear bejewelled with pearls and straightened her posture. "He's in the Council Chamber. They're hosting an emergency meeting because of... You know."

"I do know," said Cooper. "As part of the investigation, we'll need to speak to as many of Mayor East's friends, family and colleagues as possible. When is the meeting due to end?"

"There's no scheduled end time. I'm sorry. It's just that this is rather unprecedented."

Singh leant on the counter and read the ID hanging from her neck by a lanyard. "Sarah Sweetland? What a lovely name. May I call you Sarah?"

She looked away, "Sure."

"We need to speak to Mayor East's colleagues. We'd like to start with Frank McKenna, and we're not prepared to wait an unknown amount of time. The least intrusive, most subtle way to do that is for you to go and whisper in his ear that two detectives from Northumbria Police are here to see him."

Sarah Sweetland got the unspoken hint that a more intrusive, less subtle option was available. She closed her computer screen, seemed to brace herself, and left the lobby for the chambers. She returned in under three minutes with McKenna.

Having seen McKenna's image on the council website, Cooper now suspected it was taken a few years ago or that he'd used an app to enhance his appearance. He walked with a slight hunch to his shoulders and his skin was dry and creased. Still, he wasn't unattractive in his expensive suit and short beard. He met them with a curt nod and a face etched with annoyance.

"You've got five minutes. Make it quick."

If McKenna felt no need to waste time with pleasantries, then neither did Cooper. She cut to the chase. "What was your problem with Mayor East?"

McKenna's eyes narrowed. "Excuse me? I don't know what you mean. Hope and I were very amicable."

"We have a witness," said Cooper. "Who can place you outside her home, shouting and acting aggressively. Threatening even."

The receptionist averted her eyes and made a beeline for her desk, where she picked up her mobile again.

"Perhaps we should talk in your office?" suggested Singh.

They followed him through a maze of corridors until they reached a door with a small brass plaque denoting McKenna's name. Inside, he fixed his puffy, bloodshot eyes on the detectives.

Someone clearly hadn't been sleeping well. Guilty conscience?

"Interesting choice of haircut, detective," said McKenna, sitting. "I prefer a more feminine look on a lady."

Was he for real? They'd just implied his status as a suspect in a double murder, and his first move was to criticise Cooper's appearance. That was a first.

"Funnily enough, I don't base my appearance on the approval of men I've never met," she replied deadpan.

"And as far as I'm aware," Singh said, "there is no correlation between hair length and feminity. But maybe I'm more your type? My hair comes past my waist." He flashed McKenna a winning smile, which made him recoil. "Now, why were you threatening Mayor East?"

"I didn't threaten her," he replied. A veil of defensiveness descended upon him. He crossed his arms and adopted a bitter tone. "But she was a meddler. When I went to her house, it was to tell her to keep her nose out of my marriage."

He took his left hand in his right and subconsciously rubbed at an invisible wedding band.

"Divorced?" Cooper asked.

"Separated. Thanks to that bitch."

Cooper bristled. "Mayor East and her wife were murdered in an absolutely sickening attack. I suggest you keep your misogyny in check and tell me why you blame Hope East for your failed marriage. Did Hope and your wife have an affair?"

"God, no. Ciara's not... one of those." He stopped worrying his missing wedding band and clenched his jaw. "And that's all I have to say on the matter."

Singh picked up a copy of The Sun that was open on page three. He closed the paper, folded it and placed it on McKenna's desk. "Where were you?"

"What?"

"Where were you in the early hours of Sunday morning?"

McKenna's expression shifted, a flicker of discomfort crossing his face. "Are you serious?"

Neither Cooper nor Singh answered him.

"If you're looking for an alibi, I don't have one. I live alone. But I can tell you this for nowt, you can't place me in Times Square because I wasn't there. I have no desire to hang out at those clubs. They're really not my scene." His voice faded as he checked his watch. A none-too-subtle hint that their five minutes were up. "Though I hear a lot of straight women go to the bars around there."

"Yeah, they go to avoid being hit on by creepy divorced dudes," Cooper said bluntly. "Just one more question. Do you own a baseball bat?"

"If you're asking me if I play baseball, detective, the answer is no. No one in Newcastle plays baseball. I prefer more sophisticated sports, like squash or golf. Much more refined. But that wasn't what you were really asking me, was it?"

"No," said Cooper. "It was not."

A flicker of amusement danced in McKenna's eyes. "I need to return to chambers," he said. "We're having a minute's silence, and I don't want to miss it."

He stood and gestured at the door, but as Cooper and Singh showed themselves out of the Civic Centre, Cooper's scepticism lingered. Frank McKenna had avoided answering two of her questions. He clearly didn't like Hope East, and his words hinted at misogyny and homophobia. Whatever truth lurked beneath the councillor's polished facade, she would find it, no matter how sophisticated his sports preferences might be.

- Chapter 13 -

The incident room at Northumbria Police HQ buzzed with anticipation as detectives poured over evidence and discussed their next moves in hushed tones. It was a cavernous, sterile space with the sort of lighting that triggered migraines. Windows lined one wall; the other three were covered in scribbled notes and maps of Northumberland and Newcastle.

Cooper sat on a desk at the front of the room before an interactive whiteboard displaying images of Hope and Catalina East. She'd brought everyone together for an evening briefing to introduce DI Daljit Singh to the team and to review their findings so far.

Singh had some big shoes to fill, and Cooper hoped the team would judge him on his performance rather than compare him to the man who should have taken the DI position had he still been here. It pained her just to think about it. Her eyes wandered across the room until they settled on Paula Keaton. Their eyes met briefly, sharing a silent understanding.

"Welcome to the madhouse, DI Singh," said Keaton as she sipped from a can of Coke Zero, her desk littered with files and cereal bars. She clicked the top of her pen, as she often did when she was bored or agitated, then said, "I say, if you can swing a golf club, you can swing a baseball bat. Besides, that McKenna sounds like a right prick."

Singh smirked. "He is. But alas, neither of those facts are grounds for arrest. We can lean on him again tomorrow," he suggested. "Or we can speak to his wife. See if she can shed some light on her ex-husband's dislike of the mayor."

"I want some solid evidence that links McKenna to the murders," Cooper told the room. "Something more than *he said, she said.* Which is where Martin comes in. Care to share your glimmer of hope?"

Martin cleared his throat and got to his feet. Beside him, Saffron Boyd gave him a reassuring smile.

"Ethan Williams of no fixed abode was sleeping rough in Times Square on Saturday night. He reported hearing screams before seeing a tall man, approximately five-ten to six-nothing, running north on Marlborough Crescent carrying a baseball bat. He is described as wearing dark clothing and a woollen hat."

The room fell silent as they contemplated the horror of being beaten with a baseball bat before having their throats cut.

"On its own, it's not much," he said, his voice carrying a note of excitement. "But early this afternoon, I managed to find this." Martin pressed a button on the interactive screen and brought up a blurry image from a traffic camera. He zoomed in. "This is the man Ethan Williams saw. This backs his account."

The image was grey-scale and low-resolution but showed a man in dark clothing and a beanie hat carrying what looked like a baseball bat.

Cooper craned her head around and squinted at the board. Could it be McKenna, the man seen yelling at Hope East on her doorstep? It could be. His build was undoubtedly similar, but she wasn't convinced. Not yet.

"Well done, Martin," Cooper said as he returned to his seat. She pointed at the screen, and when she spoke again, it was to the entire room. "This is likely our perp. Find a clearer image of him. One with his face visible. Check every camera in the city if you have to."

But as everyone stood, ready to start their shift or go home for the evening, the double doors to the incident room opened. Rebecca Hogg – Becky the Techie – entered carrying a shoulder bag.

Becky was out of breath. She wore a TopGun hoodie over baggy jeans and a pair of Converse low tops. Her presence injected a burst of energy into the room as she opened the bag and handed Cooper a can of Michelada.

"What's this?" she asked.

"Mexican cocktail made of beer, lime juice and spices. Personally, I think it tastes like

Worcestershire Sauce mixed with regret, but I think you might need it when I show you this."

With a triumphant smile, Becky pulled a manilla folder from her bag and extracted a sheet of paper. "I managed to access Mayor East's emails."

Everyone who had stood ready to go home at the end of their shift sat back down, eyes on the cyber genius.

"I found a threatening email from an account linked to Chen Long."

The name didn't mean anything to Cooper.

Singh pursed his lips and exhaled. "The Dragon."

"The one and only," Becky said.

Cooper gestured for Singh to stand. "Elaborate, please."

DI Daljit Singh's voice was heavy with knowledge. "Long was born in London to Beijing parents. He was raised in Manchester, turning his back on medical school when he got caught up in gang culture. Wicked smart but with an equally wicked temper, he wanted to establish his own gang, so he moved to Newcastle, setting up a construction firm as a front."

Cooper felt a flash of recognition. "Wait. Long as in Longevity Building Solutions?"

"The very same."

"Shit," said Cooper. "They did my roof."

Becky chuckled. "I'd keep an eye on it the next time it pisses it down. Longevity applied to build thirty luxury homes on the Town Moor. Hope was extremely vocal in opposing it. It's all there in the minutes of the planning committee. The Dragon didn't take too kindly to that."

Cooper read the email. "Subject: Your actions have consequences." She raised her brows. "Mayor East, your opposition to my plans is noted. Refusing progress will have repercussions not only for the city but for you personally. Reconsider. The Dragon is watching."

Keaton leant back in her chair, balancing it on two legs, laughing to herself. "The Dragon is watching? Seriously? Talking about yourself in the third person is bad enough. Using your sad, little, self-appointed nickname is another."

"Says Pitbull Paula," Martin said with a cheeky grin.

"Listen, L'Oréal. I didn't give myself that name, and I certainly never signed any emails that way. And while we're at it, what sort of narcissist would even think about applying to build a bunch of homes on the Town Moor? As if the people of Newcastle would ever let that fly."

Cooper scanned the email again, her eyes lingering on the word *repercussions.* "Does this man have a history of violence?" she asked Singh.

"You could say that." Singh rubbed the back of his neck. "He served three years for hitting his former girlfriend."

"Three years?" asked Cooper. "How hard did he hit her?"

"Well, that's just it, DCI Cooper. He hit her with a baseball bat."

- Chapter 14 -

Cooper picked Tina up from Tynemouth Academy. The place held bad memories for both of them, and Cooper couldn't help remembering one snowy night when Tina was still fourteen every time she drove past.

Tina jumped in the passenger side of the BMW and smoothed her newly dyed hair in the vanity mirror.

"Well?" probed Cooper. "How was your first day?"

"I've been going here since year seven."

"You know what I mean. First day of sixth form."

Tina shrugged. "Fine."

Fine could mean anything from it being the best day ever to the building caving in.

"At least tell me if they made you do *stupid team-building stuff*?"

Tina caught sight of something in the vanity mirror and slumped down her chair. "Drive."

"What? This isn't an action film." Cooper checked her rearview and saw why Tina had suddenly turned into a fugitive.

Kenny, Tina's father, was standing on the corner looking straight at them.

The same man whom Cooper had an injunction against.

"Drive!" Tina repeated.

She hit the accelerator and turned down a maze of side streets and back lanes until finally pulling up outside the Dolphin Pub on King Edward Road. Tina wiped a tear away, smudging the eyeliner she'd taken so much care in applying.

Whatever Kenny's flaws – and there were many of them – she never thought he would hurt his daughter. Embarrass her, yes, but hurt her? No, Cooper didn't think so. Still, his presence near the school boiled her blood for what effect it was having on Tina.

"Oh, T," Cooper said, reaching across and holding her hand. "You know your father would never hurt you."

"That's not the point," she said, almost yelling. "He's not supposed to be anywhere near where you might be. I think outside my school at four-thirty would come under that category. Don't you?"

"I do." Cooper squeezed her fingers. "He probably just wanted to see how you were doing. He hasn't seen you since—"

"Since he completely violated your privacy and trust?"

"Yeah. Since then." She worked to keep her emotions in check, but the physical feelings of pounding heart, hot skin and a sensation that she was being choked still took hold of her.

"He's not supposed to come near you," she repeated, softer this time. Sadder.

"You don't need to worry about me, sweety." She gripped Tina's hand harder.

"Don't I? First, you get sick and nearly die, then you're kidnapped. And I know what happened in the woods that day with Jack. It could have been you. And Danny's birth..." Her speech came in fits, panic evident in every breath between her short sentences. "If something happens to you..."

"Nothing is going to happen to me." But even as she said it, she knew it was an empty promise. She couldn't guarantee that, not in her line of work and with her medical history. Still, at least now, Tina had a support network. Her grandmother had moved home to Tynemouth, and should the worst happen, she knew Atkinson would care for Tina as much as he did his three sons.

Tina worked to calm herself, taking deep breaths and focusing on a cat sitting on a bin outside the pub. "I just don't want him to hurt you again."

"He can't. I won't be that stupid again."

"You're not stupid," Tina sniffed. "You're badass." She forced a smile and rubbed Cooper's buzzcut.

"Speak for yourself. You look like a Geordie Morticia Addams."

"Who?"

Cooper started the ignition. "I'm going to pretend you didn't just ask that, young lady. We are going straight home to watch the Addams Family. The black and white sitcom, not the films."

But as soon as she turned onto the A193 to take them back to Latimer Terrace, her phone rang.

"Cooper here."

"It's me, Daljit."

"What's up, Daljit?" She took Percy Park Road.

"Are you hungry?"

"Why?"

"The Dragon. He's at Bamboo Grove on Stowell Street. Care to join me for dinner?"

Cooper pulled up outside her home and looked over at her daughter.

"I'm fine," she mouthed. "Seriously. I just had a moment. Go and be badass." She unbuckled and got out, but just as she was about to close the door, she added, "And bring back dim sum."

- CHAPTER 15 -

CHINATOWN WAS CAUGHT BETWEEN two worlds. On one side stood Newcastle's past – the old medieval walls. Thick stones from the thirteenth century that defended the city until it fell to the Scots during the English Civil War. On the other, Newcastle's present – multistory car parks, a Premier Inn and The Gate, an entertainment complex housing a Wetherspoons, casino, cinema and steakhouse.

Stowell Street, one of only five Chinatowns in England, originally started as a single Chinese supermarket in the seventies. Now, Eastern culture had burst out of Stowell Street, and Japanese, Korean and Vietnamese restaurants had popped up in the neighbouring area.

Cooper found Singh, Keaton and Martin at the corner of St. Andrew's Street, where a towering red gate adorned with golden dragons marked the entrance to Chinatown.

"Long arrived around forty minutes ago," Singh told her. "He's here with his wife, Chardonnay."

Cooper couldn't help pulling a face. "Chardonnay? Really?"

"Really. Uniform are here and ready to assist," Singh told her, pointing down Stowell Street to where several officers were hugging one side of the street, staying out of view of anyone looking out of the restaurant's upstairs windows. "He's a violent man. I didn't want to take any chances."

"Back entrance?" Cooper asked.

"The back lane next to the city walls. It's covered."

Cooper nodded. "What are we waiting for then. Let's go."

As the four of them walked further into Chinatown, Cooper noticed elements of the district she'd never picked up on before. The lack of traditional street lamps, for one. They'd been replaced with dainty lanterns of red and gold lattice, and the street sign was coloured jade green and featured Chinese jiǎntǐzì. The various smells emanating from the different restaurants were overpowering. Cooper's stomach grumbled in response, and her mouth began to water. When they reached Bamboo Grove, she asked, "Anyone eaten here before?"

Martin nodded. "I came here with Saff over the summer. Excellent duck."

"And how did we get this intel?"

"I saw one of their posts on Instagram. Thought it looked tasty—"

"Not the duck," laughed Cooper. "How do we know Long is here?"

Singh brought both hands to his chest. "Good fortune. As soon as I knew we'd need to speak to Long, I put a bulletin out to my brothers in the Northumbria Police Sikh Society. My friend, Paramveer from Forth Banks station, was dining here with his wife and two children when he spotted Long arriving."

"About time we had some good fortune," Cooper said. "Now let's go and see what this so-called Dragon has to say about that aggressive email he sent the mayor."

They took the stairs up an entranceway lined on both sides with bamboo. Low lighting and small lanterns cast unusual shadows until they reached the first floor, where the hall opened up into a bright, airy restaurant. Pale green walls and soft instrumental music gave the room a tranquil aura. Bamboo had been used to create fences that divided the tables, forming booths to give patrons privacy. But between the bamboo stalks, slithers of light allowed a peak into others' lives. A large family gathered for a special occasion, their laughter and chatter floating above the bamboo like their helium-filled balloons. An attractive couple on a date shared quiet conversations, stealing kisses and flirtatious glances between bites of flavourful food. Professionals, straight from the office, engaged in animated discussions, striking deals over delectable dumplings.

To their right, Cooper looked into the open kitchen where masterful chefs in clean whites combined flavours and techniques to create dishes that smelled too good to be true. No wonder the place was this busy on a Monday.

"Welcome to Bamboo Grove. Table for four?"

Cooper spoke quietly, explaining to the graceful waitress who she was and why they were there.

"Mr Long?" she repeated, checking her tablet for the name each table booking had been reserved under. "Ah, yes. Table seventeen."

She was mid-turn, about to point out the table in question when a crashing noise caused uproar.

"That's Long!" shouted Singh.

Long sprinted through the restaurant, toppling tables and sending crockery and food flying. Angry voices and children's squeals followed him as he did his best to stop anyone from following him. Instead of heading for the fire exit, he leapt over the counter into the open kitchen, swiping a chef's knife from a chopping block.

"He's armed, be careful," Cooper called out as she ran.

He wore tight, black jeans and a fitted t-shirt that revealed a muscular physique. Despite the restrictive clothing, he moved quickly, darting through the kitchen and bursting through a door and out of sight.

Chefs and wait staff pressed themselves against fridges and store cupboards, avoiding the melee. Singh grunted as he tripped on a mop and bucket, spilling soapy water over a laminated floor. There was a yelp as Keaton slipped on the slick surface, hitting the deck with some force. Martin stopped to help her; Cooper and Singh pressed on.

The door led to an unlit stairwell. They could hear Long's footsteps descending in the darkness.

"Long," Cooper called after him. "We just want to talk."

He didn't slow, passing the ground floor and continuing to a basement, where he charged through a closed door, slamming it behind himself, almost hitting Singh in the face.

Cooper almost choked as she fell into the room, which was so thick with smoke it was like fog. White, carcinogenic plumes obscured most of the furniture and objects, but Cooper could make out enough green felt and coloured chips to know they were in a casino.

A literal underground casino.

"Police!" shouted Singh. "Move." Then, over his shoulder to Cooper. "This way."

Long darted into a bathroom and through a hidden door into the basement of the neighbouring restaurant. He turned, brandishing the knife in Cooper's direction. It was brief but enough to halt her in her tracks. She'd made a promise to Tina and had no intention of dying today. She stalled, extending an arm to hold Singh back as Long jumped onto a sink and rolled out a high window into the back alley.

Cooper caught her breath, the image of the knife in front of her nose not leaving her. After a second, she climbed onto the sink and looked through the window in time to see Long, with cat-like agility, jump onto a commercial waste bin and over the city walls. She could hear the footsteps and shouts of uniform as they sprinted to either end of the alley.

Swearing, she dialled Keaton's number. "You okay?"

"Got a bruised butt and a newfound respect for gravity. Tell me you got him."

Cooper remained silent until Keaton swore.

"Bollocks. That's two–nil. Well, never mind. Martin and I have got something you might be interested in."

Cooper started to make her way back through the basement and out of the haze of smoke. "Dim sum?" she asked.

"How about a nice cool glass of Chardonnay?"

- Chapter 16 -

While Oliver Martin calmed diners and helped the restaurant staff right tables and chairs, Paula Keaton used her frame to keep Chardonnay Long from the exit.

Chardonnay's red nail varnish sparkled as she pointed a finger in Keaton's face and told her to stop harassing her husband. Her tan was as fake as her icy white hair, but the labels she wore were all genuine. A Michael Kor's bag, some LK Bennett heels and London Road jewellery adorned a form-fitting Dior dress that came to her knees. Even in her heels, she was only five-four, but despite her height, she carried herself with confidence and attitude.

"You in charge?" she asked Cooper when she joined them by the exit. "I demand to know why you're persecuting my husband. Is this how we treat people in this country? Demonise those who come to these shores to build a life for themselves?"

"Take a seat, Mrs Long," Cooper said, gesturing to an empty table. "And don't give me the poor immigrant line. Your husband was born in London, raised in Manchester and could have been a doctor earning six figures by now. And while we're at it, I haven't persecuted anyone. All I did was walk in the door. Your husband armed himself and legged it of his own accord. Any idea why a legitimate businessman would do that?"

Chardonnay sat down with a humph. She folded her arms, but her posture remained resolute. "He must've known you were here to accuse him of something."

Cooper sat opposite as Keaton poured both women some water from a glass jug.

"Your husband sent a threatening email to Mayor East shortly before she was murdered. What can you tell me about that?"

Chardonnay took a slow breath and a slower sip of water. "If Chen emailed Mayor East, I'm sure it was to respectfully ask her to reconsider her position. My husband is a good man and a business owner. He just wanted to provide homes for the people of Newcastle."

Singh joined them at the table and helped himself to a prawn cracker. "Newcastle needs affordable housing. They don't need their beloved green belt sacrificed for over-priced five-bedrooms made of MDF and Sellotape."

"How dare you." Chardonnay placed her glass on the table with a thud. "That's slanderous. Longevity Building Solutions are—"

"Are a financial front for your husband's criminal activities," finished Singh.

"What do you want?" Chardonnay fixed Cooper with a stare, her dark eyes accentuated with smokey eyeshadow and winged liner.

"I want you to tell me everything you know about Chen. His associates, his drug distribution network, his money laundering operations, everything."

Chardonnay scoffed. "You watch too many films, detective. Chen has nothing to do with drugs or money laundering."

"Then tell me about the Mayor. How he felt about her, how he acted after his application was turned down, and most importantly, where he was on Saturday night."

The petite woman fished a prawn cracker from the bowl, examined it between her manicured fingers, and then put it back.

"What makes you think I'd do a thing like that?"

Around them, the restaurant was returning to normality. While some diners had left, others sat back at their tables to enjoy their meals. Dishes began to flow from the kitchen, delivered by graceful staff with fake smiles. Conversations picked back up, and wine began to flow once more.

Cooper propped her elbows on the table and leant forward. "Because he's a violent man who put his ex-girlfriend in hospital. And one day, he might go at you with a baseball bat the same way he did to

Megan, only instead of putting you in the hospital, he puts you in a grave."

Chardonnay lowered her eyes, her mask of self-assuredness slipping. "He's a loving husband, faithful and kind. He'd never hurt me."

"That's what Megan thought."

Singh ate another prawn cracker, then said, "How about I make this a little easier for you?" He placed his palms together and looked to the ceiling while recounting a memory. "You two have been together three years?"

"I see you've done your research."

"So you were with Chen when we almost nailed him after the drug bust at the coke factory in Dinnington?" asked Singh. "We based our case on the presence of his DNA in several locations throughout the building, including the cutting room and the toilets. What didn't come out in court was that we also found a bra in the toilets. The bra contained the DNA of an unknown female, and – how shall I put this? – your husband's bodily fluids. Now I know that wasn't your bra, Chardonnay, because you're a stylish lady, and I don't think leopard print is your thing. Also, you're a slender lady, and the label on this bra read 38E."

Chardonnay's face flushed a similar shade to her nails. She tried to compose herself by taking a sip of water, but her husband's infidelity – confirmed in such explicit detail – had clearly hit her hard. She clenched her jaw and gripped the edge of the table. Cooper could see the struggle within the woman, torn between loyalty to her husband and the knowledge that he had betrayed her in such a classless manner. Cooper handed Chardonnay a paper serviette, and she used it to delicately dab the inner corners of her eyes.

When she met Cooper and Singh's gaze again, Chardonnay's face was hardened with rage. Four words came to Cooper's mind.

Hell hath no fury.

"I'll tell you everything you want to know."

- Chapter 17 -

Cooper tried to contain her excitement as she sat in a corner of the bustling restaurant. The aroma of sweet chilli passed by as a dish was delivered to a neighbouring table.

Opposite her, Chardonnay Long toyed with a pair of metal chopsticks, but this was no nervous fidgeting. She held one like a dagger, pressing and twisting it into a serviette until the paper disintegrated into a million rice-sized pieces. She'd made the risky decision to become an informant against her husband, entrusting her safety to Cooper and the team. Cooper couldn't promise her protection, but she'd do what she could, and the weight of that responsibility sat heavily on her shoulders.

"Where should I start?"

"At the beginning," Cooper told her.

As Chardonnay recounted meeting Long in the sauna at the Ramside Hall Hotel, where she'd been enjoying a spa weekend for her twenty-first birthday, Cooper's phone vibrated. Discretely, she glanced at the screen and saw a text from DC Saffron Boyd.

A surge of anticipation coursed through Cooper's veins. Whyte and Boyd had uncovered dashcam footage from Roker. *Sorry to interrupt*, it read. Boyd was nothing if not polite. *But we think you should see this.*

"I need to nip back to HQ," she told Singh.

Excusing herself from the table, Cooper offered Chardonnay a reassuring smile. "DI Singh and DS Keaton will take care of you."

With measured steps, Cooper navigated through the maze of tables and down the steps, emerging on Stowell Street in the heart of Chinatown. She checked in with the uniformed team, but Long had got away. They'd find him soon enough, she told herself. Especially now they had his wife on their side.

BUOYED BY THE THRILL of marital betrayal, Cooper hurried through the corridors of HQ, her footsteps echoing against the cold, sterile walls. She found Whyte and Boyd in a meeting room, staring intently at a monitor, the atmosphere charged with excitement.

"What you got?" she asked, pulling up a chair beside Whyte.

He reached across to grab the computer mouse, his arm brushing against hers.

In another universe, Cooper and Whyte might have ended up together. As young adults, they worked side by side when they first joined the force. They got on well, great, actually, until the day he ruined their friendship. It was all water under the bridge now, and Cooper had as fine a working relationship with him as she did with Keaton.

"As you know, we suspected foul play in the Roker death," Whyte said. "The victim's injuries weren't consistent with an accidental fall. Saff put out an appeal for information, and this just came in. Makes for interesting viewing."

He clicked play. "It's dark, but we enhanced the footage as much as possible."

The three detectives leant in, their eyes fixed on the screen as the grainy footage played. They watched in silence as a woman, alone and possibly inebriated, walked along the dimly lit street. It was a creepy scene, shadows enveloping her as she strayed from the road, taking a trail towards the beach.

Cooper's eyes narrowed as a figure emerged from the darkness, tailing the woman with an unsettling determination. A sense of unease settled in the room. Whyte swallowed, Cooper pulled at her collar, Boyd looked away.

"Pause it," Cooper commanded, her voice steady but tinged with disgust. "You think this is your DB?"

The image froze, capturing the moment the man turned to follow the woman down the embankment, disappearing from view. Whyte nodded. "Lee Edwards. I know the camera's a decent distance away, but it looks like him, and it's the right time frame. Here's where it gets interesting."

As the footage began to play again and the car moved closer to the scene, Cooper's eyes darted to a sudden movement on the left. A third figure, concealed by a bus stop, jumped over the stone railings and disappeared from view.

"He moved like an animal," Cooper said.

Whyte rewound a second and paused the footage. Cooper pointed a finger at the screen. "What's that on his back?"

"You'll see in a second," Whyte said, skipping forward.

Just as the car was about to pass by, the dashcam captured one man dragging the other back up to Roker Terrace. Though the footage was silent, Cooper swore she heard the crack of the baseball bat hitting the man's body.

"The driver witnessed this and waited until now to come forward?" Cooper asked, hitting rewind to watch it again.

"He was a bit cagey," Whyte said. "Saff's got a theory."

Boyd shrugged her shoulders. "It's just that, a theory. I can't prove it. But it was fight night. I think the driver might have been drunk and was too busy concentrating on driving in a straight line to notice what happened over here. She pointed at the corner of the screen where the action had occurred. "If you watch it again, you'll notice him swerve a few times. Not massively, but enough to make me think he wasn't sober. I think he waited until every ounce of alcohol left his system before handing this to us."

Cooper watched again, then sat back and rubbed her eyes. "Do you think this is the woman who called it in?"

"Probably," Whyte said. "Three murders on the same night, all involving baseball bats. You don't think they're connected, do you?"

Cooper wasn't sure. "I don't know. It's possible. I mean, there is enough time between this incident and the Easts'. Theoretically, someone could drive from Roker to Times Square in that time."

"Especially with the roads being so quiet that night," Whyte said.

Boyd pursed her lips. "But this seems to be some sort of vigilante killing. I know we don't know that for sure, but it certainly looks like this unknown male killed Lee Edwards because he was assaulting the unknown female."

"And we're looking at Chen Long for the Times Square murders." Cooper zoomed in on the image of the unknown male jumping over the wall. Could it be the man who called himself The Dragon? She thought of how fast Long had moved through the restaurant, down the stairs, through the casino, out the bathroom window into the alley and over the old town walls. She zoomed in further but couldn't tell either way.

Cooper stood and stretched her back. "Two crime scenes involving baseball bats in one night. I'll admit, it's a bit too much of a coincidence for my liking," she said, "but for now, we assume they're not linked."

- Chapter 18 -

The familiar streets of North Tyneside bathed in a gentle glow as the street lamps flickered to life. Cooper was almost home, and a hefty bag of dim sum slid precariously back and forth on the passenger seat every time she rounded a corner. Her thoughts had shifted from the double murder investigation back to her family; she ached to see Danny, to have him grip her finger in his soft, tiny hands and gaze into his blue eyes. There was something therapeutic about babies' eyes, how everything was new and wondrous.

She stopped at Tesco Express at Billy Mill to top up her fuel and grab some bread and milk. Keaton called. Cooper answered in the queue for the checkout, her voice coated in both weariness and curiosity. "This is the second time I've almost made it home this evening when someone's called me."

"Sorry, boss. You don't need to come in. Just wanted to give you an update."

Cooper paid and walked across the forecourt to her BMW. "Go on."

"Singh and Martin had a good chat with Chardonnay Long. After Singh's revelation, she didn't have a nice word to say about her husband."

"Understandable," Cooper chuckled. She started the engine and joined Beach Road. "As long as her hatred for him doesn't cloud her honesty."

"It's always a risk. Chardonnay doesn't know – or claims not to know –much about Long's business dealings, legal or otherwise. She says Long didn't have much respect for women, that he thought her little girlie brain didn't need troubling with his complex affairs."

"Complex affairs?" Cooper laughed. "He has kids dealing drugs and launders his money through a construction firm. It's not rocket science."

"Apparently, he completely lost it when Hope East blocked his plans to build a development on the moor. Called her every slur under the sun and started smashing his own kitchen up, throwing plates and glasses around."

"We already knew he had a violent streak, Paula. Did Chardonnay give us anything else?"

"She's willing to stay with him and pretend we never spoke. If he returns home, she'll let us know."

"She understands the risks?" Cooper asked. It was great news that Chardonnay Long was on their side, but she didn't want anything to happen to her.

"She understands. She also talked us through what we might find at their house. He has quite a stash of weapons. Loads of knives and, get this, a baseball bat."

Cooper's grip on the wheel tightened. The pieces of the puzzle were starting to fall into place. They had two suspects to focus on, both with grudges against the liberal mayor. She didn't know what McKenna's problem was, but she'd find out one way or the other. And as for Long, she hated that he'd evaded capture and was out there somewhere, but at least they'd turned Chardonnay.

Cooper pulled into her street, the welcoming warmth of home beckoning her. She stepped out of the car and made her way to the front door.

"Thanks, Paula. Let's get that bat to the lab. Do it subtly, though. If Long's watching his house, we don't want to endanger his wife. See if someone can pose as a delivery driver or something."

"Got it, boss. Have a good night."

Inside, the sounds of laughter and chatter reached her ears as she entered the bustling kitchen. Tina looked up from her homework and greeted her with a smile. Atkinson cradled Danny in his arms. Either he'd changed into his pyjamas early or he hadn't bothered to get dressed that day.

Cooper held up the bag of food and swapped it for her baby. As she fussed over her young son, delighting in his innocence after a day of murder investigations, Atkinson reheated dinner. The smell quickly filled the room, triggering a colossal belly rumble from both Cooper and Tina.

"Glass of white?" offered Atkinson, handing her a drink. "Thought you could use one."

"You thought right." Cooper kicked off her shoes. "But tell me it's not chardonnay."

He frowned. "It's not. Why?"

Cooper chuckled as she took a seat at the dining table and played with Danny's toes. "No reason."

WHILE COOPER SLEPT SOUNDLY in the dead of night, two people lurked outside a warehouse in Team Valley Trading Estate. The building was shared by multiple businesses, each with its own parking spaces and roller-blind entrance. It was the unlabeled lot at the end of the building that interested the pair. Officially, the lot was unoccupied. There was a reinforced side door with no windows, only a small sliding hatch allowing someone on the inside to vet who was on the outside before granting them access.

"Someone's coming, GA."

"Are you in position?" he asked.

Justice's reply was quick. "Affirmative."

GA watched the two men approach on foot; they weren't foolish enough to have their cars seen in the area. Dressed in smart suits, they walked with a certain confidence brought about by the entitlement of power. The taller one nudged the shorter as if they were on their way to a funfair. GA supposed they were, in a way. He tried to get a look at their faces, but they wore peaked caps, keeping their images hidden from any nearby security cameras.

GA observed silently as the men knocked on the side door. He knew from his research that two guards would be monitoring the door that night. They'd be big, beefy blokes with no neck and little between the ears. Still, while it was unlikely they had firearms, they could be armed, in which case, darkness would be his friend.

"Okay, Justice. Any second now," GA told his crew. "On my word. Make it quick."

"Don't rush me. I hate heights."

"You could have done it remotely. You said the servers were woefully protected."

He heard Justice sigh. "Doing it manually gives us more time. They could get the servers back online in minutes."

Atop a utility pole, with unsteady hands, Justice pulled a pair of insulated wire cutters from a shoulder bag and carefully readied them on the power lines that supplied electricity to the nearby streets.

"Once I make the cut, you have twenty seconds before the door's backup battery kicks in. Unless they have a generator, everything else will stay off."

The hatch in the heavy door slid open for a second while one guard asked for a password. The men pushed an envelope each through the hatch, then stood back as the door opened and they disappeared into the building.

"Now."

The faint hum of electricity ceased, replaced by an eerie silence as the area plunged into darkness.

Task accomplished, Justice took a deep breath, whispered a prayer, and then jumped, descending using a simple rappelling system.

The guard opened and closed the door several times, wondering why the magnet-controlled security feature wasn't automatically locking. GA wasted no time. The guards would be dead before Justice could unclip and run the length of the street.

- Chapter 19 -

A tip-off came during the early hours from a woman speaking broken English between bursts of hysterical crying.

Daljit Singh's usual bright and cheerful face was dour, and his amenable attitude more formal and stiff that morning when he greeted Cooper and Atkinson. "Prepare yourselves," he said. "I've seen some heinous things in my time. Nothing like this."

The area was in darkness save for the blue strobes of emergency vehicles.

"When can they get the power back on?" Cooper asked.

"They're working on it now," Singh said, pointing to a row of orange barriers erected around a utility pole. "Until then, you'll need this." He handed them high-powered torches from the back of his car. "There's a DB right inside the door. You'll need to step over it."

Cooper and Atkinson donned PPE and headed for the side door of the warehouse, where they found the first body. It was that of a large male, white, late thirties. Singh was right. There was no moving around him, so she carefully stepped over, mindful not to touch the victim, both out of respect and to preserve evidence.

She cast her torch around and found the vast room divided into sections. It looked like a showroom with catalogue furniture styling different areas as a lounge and several bedrooms. Unlike Ikea, the beds here were unmade, and the lounge was a mess with upturned tables and a bowl of what looked like cocaine spilt on the floor. The body of a half-naked man was slumped in an armchair, an empty beer bottle on its side by his feet. She looked round a corner and found another victim, this one fully undressed, skinny and pale.

"What the hell is this place?" Cooper asked.

"A funfair for fucking paedos, that's what."

She turned around to see Keaton, stony-faced and fists clenched.

"Some sort of pop-up brothel by the looks of it," she told Cooper. "Only the girls weren't getting paid, and it wasn't a career choice they made willingly."

Cooper's initial respect for the victim by the door dissipated.

DC Saffron Boyd appeared with tears in her eyes. She threw a clear, plastic evidence bag down on an empty sofa. Inside was a small pink t-shirt covered in glittery hearts.

"The label says age twelve to thirteen. I'm going outside to get some fresh air."

Martin followed her, catching up to take her hand.

Cooper tasted bile rising in her throat. She couldn't imagine the horrors that the owner of the pink t-shirt had endured. She scanned the room, her torch illuminating the sickening details: Pornography and paraphernalia catering to various fetishes. Her jaw tightened as she made her way to the next section of the warehouse, where she found another body, this one belonging to a man in his twenties. He was lying on a bed, face down, his arms outstretched as if he was trying to crawl away before he was killed. The bedsheets were stained with bodily fluids, and Cooper had to fight to keep herself from retching.

Atkinson went to check the other side of the warehouse, but Cooper had a feeling it was more of the same. She wondered just how many more bodies they would find in this nightmare.

"Fourteen," Keaton told her as if reading her mind.

"And the girls?"

"Nowhere to be seen. The woman – I mean girl – who called said the lights went out and there was a lot of commotion as people fell over each other or crashed into furniture. She said she hid under the bed while the place steadily got quieter and quieter. Then someone shouted that they were safe, that they'd killed all the bad guys. They told them to count to one hundred before leaving. When we arrived, the doors were wide open."

"Ma'am."

Cooper turned to see DS Elliot Whyte holding a stuffed toy in an evidence bag. His face was stained with tears, which he made no attempt to hide. Cooper had never seen him so emotional. He was usually stoic and reticent. She let the use of *ma'am* go. The situation called for formality.

"Dr Swanson would like a word," Whyte said. "She's back there." He illuminated the way with his torch.

Pathologist Margot Swanson had an ex-boyfriend in common with Cooper. Though it was water under the bridge, Cooper still found the woman's flirty nature annoying. She had an hourglass figure, which she knew exactly how to flaunt, and looked pristine even at this hour. Cooper's old DS – Jack "Tennessee" Daniel – had been terrified of the woman.

"Margot."

"Erica." Margot stood up. She'd been kneeling next to the body of a man in his fifties with dark skin and nicotine-stained fingernails. "This is..." She shook her head. "Well, words fail me."

The lights flickered and came back to life. Cooper gave the victim a once over but couldn't see any obvious cause of death.

"Any chance you have a COD for me?" she asked the pathologist.

"That's just it," said Margot, hands on hips. "No gunshot wounds. No stab wounds. In fact, no open wounds of any kind. I've got several dislocations. A dislocated shoulder in the lounge area, a dislocated knee and ankle in the pink room and a dislocated elbow in the room with the green sheets. Though none of those things would kill a person. There's some bruising, and one of them has a broken jaw, but nothing to imply severe blunt-force trauma. This leaves me with possible strangulation, though they can't have used anything harsh like a garrotte. Or some form of poisoning, which I won't know until we run toxicology."

Margot crouched down to her haunches and tucked a stray lock of brown curls behind her ear. "You ask me... Whatever the COD, it wasn't painful enough."

It was a shock to hear Margot speak this way. Despite her vixenish tendencies, she was a professional and always treated the dead courteously, no matter who they were.

But everyone had their limits.

And whoever killed these men may have reached a limit of their own. A former victim, perhaps.

All Cooper knew was that the killer or killers – the girl on the phone had said *they*, after all – knew what they were doing. They severed the power, blocked the exits, killed all these men without them putting up much of a fight, and then left the doors open for the workers.

Not workers, Erica. Victims.

She was roused from her thoughts by shouting.

"Boss!"

It was Keaton.

"Quick. Whyte heard crying. A poor lad's hiding in a wardrobe."

- Chapter 20 -

Cooper gathered the team at HQ. She arranged comfort food in the form of burgers and fries from a local restaurant, but no one was in the mood to eat much. Most picked at the fries or opened the burger buns to play with the salad.

"First things first," she said. "None of us woke up today expecting to be faced with fourteen murders. Not to mention the circumstances of their deaths. If anyone needs to speak to a professional, make sure you do. Failing that, speak to your colleagues. We'll get through this together, but it's going to be tough."

"Any news on the little boy?" Boyd asked. She pushed her untouched cardboard box of fries towards Martin.

The little boy Whyte found cowering in the wardrobe was actually fourteen, but he looked much younger with his malnourished frame and fearful eyes.

Whyte nodded. "Moroccan national, trafficked here by someone pretending to be his dad. Promised him a shiny new life in the UK, but when they got to England, he sold him."

"Effing awful," said Keaton. She turned to DI Singh. "You never met Jack, did you?"

Singh shook his head. "No. But I've heard only good things."

Keaton forced a smile. "We called him Tennessee. Those blokes who were killed last night, he'd have said men like that should be locked in a room with men like him. He was a gentleman, but heaven help anyone who tried to harm his wife or son."

Singh bowed his head in respect. "I think I would have liked him."

"Everyone liked him," said Cooper, her stomach filling with the familiar ache of survivors' guilt. "And I think whoever is responsible for last night's massacre—"

There was an audible gasp from those assembled.

"Yes, I said massacre. Fourteen dead. That's what we're dealing with. A massacre on Tyneside. And whoever executed those vile excuses for human beings was of the same opinion as Tennessee. Someone locked those men in and took them out one by one without the use of a gun, knife or piano string, and our only witness is a terrified boy who doesn't speak a word of English."

Cooper propped her elbow on the table and rested her forehead in her palm.

"What do we tell the press?" Singh asked.

Cooper thought about it. "We tell them there was an incident involving the deaths of numerous males between the approximate ages of twenty-five and sixty-five and that we have yet to identify any of the bodies. If anyone's son, husband, or father didn't return home, they should contact us."

Singh stood and put on a smart double-breasted coat. "I'll see to it."

"In the meantime," Cooper said, following Singh's lead and pulling on her jacket. "I'm headed to the morgue. Paula?"

Keaton stretched her arms above her head and rolled her shoulders numerous times. "Right behind you, boss."

PATHOLOGIST MARGOT SWANSON MET Cooper and Keaton at the main entrance to the Royal Victoria Infirmary in Newcastle's city centre. The RVI had a larger morgue than the Freeman Hospital, where Margot usually worked, and was more suited to large-scale events such as the one they were facing.

After initial greetings, the three women walked silently, following a labyrinth of corridors to the basement. With pale grey walls and arctic air, the basement housed neat rows of steel tables, each topped with a corpse and a white sheet.

Cooper dabbed Tiger Balm under her nostrils, but it didn't quite mask the stench of formaldehyde and disinfectant. The atmosphere was as ghostly as its inhabitants. Only the squeak of a gurney or the muted shuffling of feet on cold tiles punctuated the silence. It was a quiet not of respect but of disgust. It brought bile to Cooper's throat and numbed her fingers. She gazed upon the rows of bodies, wondering where the other victims – the real victims – were. Where was the owner of the pink t-shirt with glittery hearts?

"We found no ID on any of them," said Margot eventually. She tied her curls into a loose bun and folded her arms. "But I've made an initial list of identifiable features from tattoos and gold teeth to scars and birthmarks."

Cooper nodded, her mind racing with questions. "Any further forward with the COD?"

Margot tilted her head and pursed her filler-filled lips. "Some form of asphyxiation or strangulation." She beckoned Cooper towards the body of a grey-haired man with lined features. "Petechiae," she said, pointing at tiny-burst blood vessels around his eyes and neck. "Pinpoint haemorrhages. I found them on almost all the victims."

Margot moved to another body, pulled the sheet back to reveal his torso and asked a lab assistant to bring her a coffee.

"Would you like one, detectives?"

Both Cooper and Keaton shook their heads. Nothing about the morgue made Cooper crave food or drink.

When the assistant left, Margot added, "We've X-rayed everyone on this row. The other row will be done this evening. So far, three have fractures to the hyoid bone, a small U-shaped bone in the neck. This supports the strangulation hypothesis. However, I'm yet to find any ligature marks, so I doubt a rope or wire was used. There's some bruising on a couple of the victims' necks, but none are shaped like fingerprints."

"Anything else?" asked Keaton.

"We're running all the usual tests," Margot said with a shrug, "But for now, I'm sticking with asphyxiation. Someone took their time and choked the last breath out of these men, holding it until their brains were so starved of oxygen that there was no way back. We found some black fibres under a couple of fingernails. I've already sent them over to that handsome fella of yours," she said to Cooper. "It's possible they came from the killer's clothing."

Cooper's thoughts were interrupted when the first of the victims' relatives came forward after hearing the news report. A short, brittle lady with thinning hair tied in a tight bun was shown into the morgue. After a tense few moments, she identified a muscular man as her son. It was one of the men Cooper had stepped over as she entered the crime scene.

"He worked the doors in town. A nice gin bar just off the Bigg Market."

The woman's lower lip trembled as a white sheet was pulled back over her son's torso and head. She told Cooper his name was Isaac; he was thirty years old and still lived at home. He'd gone to work as usual but hadn't returned home.

"Did Isaac ever mention working for anyone else? A second job?" Keaton asked.

She shook her head. "No. Never." She worried a paper tissue between her fingers.

"What is it?" Keaton pressed.

She hesitated before answering. "I was worried he'd started dealing drugs. He knew a few lads who took steroids and dealt them on the side. Isaac wasn't into that. He called them roid monkeys. But, I wondered if he'd started selling them or other substances to supplement his income. He had more disposable income lately, nice new clothes, leased a white BMW."

Keaton raised a brow at Cooper while Isaac's mother fumbled her tissue.

"It's drugs, isn't it? They tried to recruit him off the estate when he was a bairn. He always resisted. Can't believe he turned that corner at his age."

Keaton patted the woman's arm and offered her a fresh tissue. "I don't think your son was dealing drugs, Mrs— Mrs?"

"Hamble."

"Mrs Hamble. I think your son was earning extra money by working security for an illegal gathering."

She looked confused. "Like a rave? I saw on the news there was something like that on farmland down in Cleveland."

"No, Mrs Hamble. Not a rave."

Cooper cut Keaton off. "Your son was working security for some terrible people. In fact, I'd go so far as to say, evil people. He was protecting men who paid to have access to children."

"Access? What do you— Oh." Her face crumpled like the tissue in her hands. "But Isaac wasn't? He didn't actually...?"

Cooper bit her tongue. *Mothers and their sons.*

Her little boy was still an angel as long as he wasn't directly involved. She could justify his actions as just another job, but as far as Cooper was concerned, he was an enabler. Wasn't there a quote about those who commit evil deeds and those who do nothing to prevent them? Atkinson would know. Still, it wasn't Cooper's place to make Mrs Hamble's day any worse. She'd already lost her son. Others would have plenty to say on the matter in the coming days and weeks, so Cooper simply replied, "I'm sorry for your loss."

- Chapter 21 -

Cooper brought her car to a stop at the traffic lights by the Cradlewell. A bus pulled up alongside her, its sides adorned with a *Hope for Newcastle* campaign poster defaced with homophobic slurs.

And so it begins.

As the light changed to green, she wiped her forehead, feeling the day's grime clinging to her like the metaphorical dirt she'd left at the morgue. Her thoughts muddled between the Easts' murders in Times Square and the hellscape they'd uncovered in Team Valley. Eight members of the public came to the morgue to identify their relatives. The pain of their loss was etched on their faces until the horrifying discovery that they were mourning men they never really knew. Men capable of heinous acts.

The Coast Road opened up ahead, and Cooper accelerated to fifty, then to seventy. She planned on organising some financial forensics. If she followed the money like Hansel and Gretel followed breadcrumbs, it could possibly lead her to the very top, to the gangs and organisations that arranged such sick events.

Chances were they only dealt in cash.

The road stretched before her, but her thoughts were far from the asphalt beneath her wheels. Cooper hit the brakes suddenly as someone merged from the slip road without checking their mirrors. A near miss. She took a few deep breaths and continued home, her mind now firmly on the road.

Parking on the street, the dull hum of her engine ceased, replaced by the tranquillity of her coastal home. She exited her vehicle, breathed a lungful of salty air and unlocked her front door. The clacking of her heeled boots on a tiled entranceway mingled with the sounds of family life. Her mother's commentary accompanied the familiar sound of a soap opera playing on the television.

"Don't take him back," Julie said, eyes rolling. "He got your sister pregnant." She turned to the door as Cooper entered. "Hello, dear."

"Hi, Mum."

Cooper went straight to the sofa to kiss Tina on the forehead. Her daughter was multitasking. Reading a chemistry textbook, cradling her baby brother, and texting furiously, her thumb dancing across the screen. It was a group chat entitled *Senior Team*.

"One week to go," said Cooper. The first netball match of the season was approaching, and Tina had moved up to join the senior squad. As always, Cooper worried about how her daughter would fit in, but training over the summer had gone well.

Tina put her phone down and handed Danny to Cooper. She pulled a piece of white fluff from her black leggings and flicked it away. Her nails were chipped and painted a deep shade of aubergine. "I'm not playing goal defence," she said.

"What? Why?" Cooper sat next to her, her protective instincts kicking in. "I saw you at tryouts. You were way better than that lanky girl with the giant feet."

Tina snorted. "Relax, Mum. I'm not being benched. They want me to play goal attack."

Cooper frowned. "But you play defence."

She lifted her shoulders in a what-can-you-do shrug. "Apparently, my shooting accuracy rate is wasted in defence."

An ACL tear had kept Tina off the court at the end of last season. Her rehab had gone well, but despite Tina insisting she was stronger than ever, Cooper couldn't help but worry. She didn't want to see her daughter on crutches again.

Julie made pained noises as she got to her feet. "Silly woman, getting back together with that loser."

Cooper frowned until she realised Julie was still talking about the soap opera.

"Dinner will be ready soon. When should we expect Justin?"

Cooper thought of Atkinson sifting through the warehouse in Team Valley, of the illegal drugs and magazines. She'd been present for a few precious moments, her mind on family instead of work.

"He's in Team Valley," she said. "He'll be late. Would you put a portion aside for him?"

"Of course." Julie shuffled to the kitchen. "We're having chicken Kyiv." She used the Ukrainian pronunciation. "I'll give him double helpings. He'll need it. What on Earth happened in Team Valley anyway? They're being oddly vague on the news. Was it carbon monoxide?"

Cooper shook her head. "You don't want to know." Her voice was low and full of sadness.

She hardly registered Tina as she said something about signing up for an additional A-level. Chemistry, biology and physics weren't challenging enough, so she'd signed up for maths as well. *Just for fun.*

Amid her reflection, Cooper glanced out the window, watching as the sun began to dip below the horizon. The soft lustre of the gloaming blanketed Tynemouth in warm hues, and she tried to tell herself that even the darkest cases could be illuminated with family, friendship and love.

Right on cue, Danny cried.

- Chapter 22 -

In the face of the gruesome September Fourth massacre, Hope and Catalina East's murders were put on the back burner. But, later that week, as Elliot Whyte alighted at Monument Metro and took the stairs from the underground station to the surface, he saw that the city was refusing to let the memory of Hope East fade.

It was early evening, and he had a date with Annie Fitzgerald. He hadn't seen her since sixth form, but following Boyd and Martin's badgering, he had sent her a friend request. She accepted. He liked her photo. She sent him a DM.

Whyte heard the protest before he saw it. He emerged on Grey Street and turned a one-eighty to face Grey's Monument, the towering monolith where Grey, Grainger and Blackett Streets collided. Public outrage seemed to burn brighter with each day that passed since the mayor's murder, and now Newcastle, once known for its cheeky charm and welcoming spirit, found itself the epicentre of a cultural storm threatening to tear it apart.

Rainbow flags fluttered defiantly in the autumnal drizzle, and banners demanding answers were waved high. Whyte couldn't help but feel a pang of sadness as he thought about the couple who had been brutally taken from the city, leaving a void that seemed impossible to fill. Young liberals mingled with eco-warriors and trans-rights activists, all united in their loss.

Whyte was a straight caucasian male raised in a conservative household. He wanted the same traditional things his father had once had: a church wedding, a happy wife, and healthy children. His idea of a good time was sinking a few pints while watching the footie. Still, Whyte leant left on most issues. He wanted higher taxes for the wealthy and better funding for the NHS. He thought gay marriage, a woman's right to choose, and green energy initiatives were all good for society. He wanted greater social safety nets and affordable housing. He had no problem using the singular they, but Xe or Ze was pushing it.

As he made his way through the crowd, he couldn't help but notice the heightened police presence. Officers in riot gear stood guard, their expressions grim and watchful. The mayor's supporters, driven by grief and anger, gathered to mourn their fallen leader and call for swift justice. They saw the couple as promoters of progress and champions of love. They refused to let their legacy wane.

Whyte spotted Annie waiting for him outside Waterstones, her coppery hair tied in a ponytail. She wore a cropped jumper and jeans, her brown eyes sparkling as she caught sight of him. He felt his heart rate pick up as he approached.

"Hey," she said, standing on tiptoes to give him a peck on the cheek.

Time had been kinder to Annie than to Whyte. She'd aged since sixth form, of course, but her skin was bright, healthy and smooth. Over ten years of policing had carved the first faint wrinkles around Whyte's eyes.

"Long time no see," he said, then casting his eyes around, added, "This is all a bit intense."

"It's about to get more intense." Annie gestured down Blackett Street, where a markedly different crowd had assembled around Old Eldon Square. This one, predominantly conservative and driven by a deep-rooted fear of change.

Someone unfurled a long banner: *Traditional Values Matter*. A group chanted, "Protect our city. Protect our city." Whyte shook his head at one sign that read *It's Adam and Eve, not Adam and Steve.* Yes, he wanted an old-school family one day, but there was a difference between being old-school and being a bloody bigoted dinosaur.

"Should we get out of here?" he asked, sensing the tension mounting. Getting caught in the middle of the action when things turned violent wasn't the ideal first date. Though technically, it was their second date, he thought, reminiscing about the amusements by Roker Beach.

They walked west, trying to block out the sounds of whispered victim-blaming. The hushed and not-so-hushed insinuations that the Easts had been too out, too proud. That they had brought their fate upon themselves.

"I know I'm a Sunderland girl," started Annie, "but I hate seeing Newcastle like this."

"Same." Whyte steered Annie away from an old man with dyed hair who was in a screaming match with a young skinhead woman. "My dad might disown me, but I'm basically an adopted Geordie at this point. Been here since I was twenty-two."

"I've only been here a year," Annie told him. "It's nice." She paused. "Usually."

Someone had sprayed *Love wins* on the side of a bus stop. The O of *Love was* shaped like a heart and coloured like a rainbow from red to indigo. Over the top, someone had replaced the W with an S. *Love Sins.*

Whyte gulped. The divide was palpable, the city's very identity at stake.

"Let's get out of here," Whyte said as the two groups edged closer to each other.

"Where are we eating?"

"A place called My Delhi," he told her as they walked on, heads down but eyes ahead. "They have loads of meat-free options if you're still vegetarian."

She was, and the look she gave him told him he'd just earned a few Brownie points for remembering. Still, as much as he wanted to concentrate on Annie when he sat opposite her in the colourful restaurant, he couldn't help but tune into the sirens of police cars and fire engines. The sickening sounds of a mass brawl carried far enough to reach them, piercing the ambience of the friendly eatery.

Whyte ordered beetroot tiki and Grandma's aloo matar. The dishes were delicious but couldn't entirely rid him of the bitter apprehension lingering at the back of his throat. Newcastle needed to unite and heal the strains and splinters before they tore completely. As elusive as it seemed, the solution was buried somewhere in the fractured city. All Whyte knew was that it started with finding Hope's killer.

- Chapter 23 -

The air in the incident room on Friday was thick with solemnity. Ever since Cooper uttered the word *massacre*, she'd felt the shift in attitude. The room was veiled beneath its usual stench of coffee and smoker's breath, but there was something else, something more grave and troublesome.

In a rare change, Keaton wore her hair down with one side tucked behind her ear, causing half the attendees of that morning's meeting to do a double take. Martin and Boyd sat beside each other, mouths straight, faces drained of colour. Whyte lurked at the back of the room, posture hunched, brows lower than usual. Singh paced.

Cooper paused for a moment to take it all in. In the past few days, they'd faced an apparent vigilante killing in Roker, a political assassination in the heart of the gay community and the mass murder of a paedophile gang.

"Right," Cooper said, removing the lid from a dry-erase marker. She spoke quietly, but it was enough to get everyone's attention; the incident room wasn't exactly buzzing with chitchat and gossip.

Images of the fourteen deceased men were attached to the board. Some were accompanied by pictures of them while they were alive.

"Isaac Hamble," she said as she wrote the man's name under his photograph. "A door supervisor from Newcastle. He had a similar role at Team Valley. As did Hamza Faizan. Both identified by their mothers." She wrote Hamza's name under his image.

Cooper pointed her pen at a third picture. "This is the gentleman we found in the armchair with his trousers round his ankles. Anyone recognise him?" She raised her brows. "Because you should."

"Jesus H Christ." Whyte unfolded his arms. "That's not Marcus Lightfoot, is it?"

Boyd craned her neck to look at him. "The news reader?"

"The very same," said Cooper. "Gives his extensive coverage of the Summer Holt case a sickening undertone, don't you think?"

The room nodded as one, noses wrinkled.

She continued down the list, revealing the names of those killed. Business owners, community leaders, and even a bloody school teacher.

"Whyte, did you speak with the witness this morning?"

He nodded, and she motioned for him to come to the front of the room.

"Tarik, the fourteen-year-old Moroccan boy, has been incredibly brave. He's told us about the house where he's been living on Teesside. He was kept there with three other boys. Another North African and two Middle Eastern. He doesn't know the exact address, but the translator is working with him to narrow it down. Tarik said all four of them were at the warehouse that night, along with three IC1 girls. He doesn't know their names but has given detailed descriptions."

"Is that information with child services?" asked Cooper.

"Yes. And *mispers*." Whyte took a breath before continuing. Tarik also helped us identify two of the deceased. Jamal Al-Mansoori and Viktor Petrovich."

Whyte added their names to the board. Jamal was the man in his fifties with dark skin and nicotine-stained fingernails who Margot had been examining when Cooper walked through the warehouse.

As Whyte returned to the back of the room, Cooper stared at the wall. "That still leaves us with three vic— three deceased to identify."

Keaton leant forward in her chair. "Excuse the segue, but we need to address the tension in the city. The division between the progressive and conservative groups is only growing, and it's not going to end well if we don't do something."

"Agreed," said Whyte. "I was in the toon last night as it was all kicking off. Not pretty."

Cooper had been thinking the same thing. On the morning news, a lecturer at Newcastle University had his car set on fire after a group of students found an almost two-decade-old social media post where he'd shared concern about the same-sex marriage act.

"Dr Swanson released Hope's body," Keaton said. "Her family have scheduled her funeral for a week today."

"We should arrange a police presence," said Whyte. "Both as a show of respect and in case..."

"In case the far right and fundamentalists hi-jack it," Cooper finished for him. She sat on the edge of a desk and added, "Let's reach out to the council and community leaders, see if we can come up with a plan to bridge the gap and bring some peace back to the streets."

"I'll speak to Nixon," Keaton offered.

At the mention of his name, the man himself entered the room.

"Wow," whispered Keaton in Martin's ear. "Speak his name, and he appears. He's like Beetlejuice."

"Only paler," whispered Martin.

The fluorescent lighting in the incident room did Nixon's pallid skin tone no favours. He shuffled towards Cooper. Back straight, chin dipped, and his hands buried deep in his trouser pockets.

Cooper jumped to her feet, sensing something in the superintendent's demeanour. "Sir?"

"It happened again." He spoke quietly, directly to Cooper, as if the others weren't even there.

"Excuse me?" asked Cooper, eyes narrowed.

"Another load of DBs in a warehouse. Another one of those..." His mouth chewed for the right word before spitting it out. "Parties. If you could call it that. Six men. One woman."

Cooper's heart pounded. "Where?" she asked.

"North of the border. Not that I'd wish this case on anyone, but I'm glad it hasn't fallen on us again. We're stretched thin enough."

"And don't I know it," said Cooper, somewhat relieved she didn't have another seven homicides to deal with. "When was this?"

"Wednesday night. The bodies weren't discovered until early this morning, but rigor suggests they died around forty-eight hours ago. Police Scotland confirmed there was a power outage at the time."

"They cut the power? Any other similarities to Team Valley?"

Nixon nodded. "Same modus operandi. Cut the power, choked them out in the dark, left no trace."

"We should consult with Police Scotland," Cooper said, lowering her eyes to the floor. Thinking not of the dead but of the poor youngsters. She wondered where they were, where they ran to in search of safety. "We can share our findings and evidence. Set up a joint task force."

"That won't be necessary," Nixon told her. "Twenty-one dead over two jurisdictions? The NCA's taking this one."

Cooper lifted her eyes, but before she could speak, Nixon continued. "I know you, Cooper. I know you like closure. But play nice with the NCA. They'll free up our resources to focus on the incident in Roker and the double murder come political assassination in Times Square."

Much to Cooper's annoyance, Nixon's words made perfect sense. She could use the time to focus on their other cases and attempt to bring some peace to Newcastle.

"NCA will need a dedicated contact from Northumbria," Nixon said.

Gesturing to the newest addition to their team, Cooper said, "Sir, this is DI Daljit Singh. He'll be perfect."

Singh extended a hand to Nixon and introduced himself respectfully, "Detective Inspector Daljit Singh, honoured to meet you, sir."

Curious, Cooper asked Nixon, "Did Police Scotland say if any children remained? Or did they all flee?

He confirmed her suspicions. "No witnesses remained."

Everyone in the room remained grimly silent until Nixon left the room. The second he did, all hell broke loose.

"Another seven dead?" gasped a PC from the back of the room. "Another mass murder?"

Boyd looked shell-shocked. "How often are these sick gatherings going on? We only knew about these two because someone murdered all the attendees? Otherwise, all that abuse would have occurred, and we'd have been none the wiser."

An old-timer in uniform commented that it was somehow worse that a woman was there. Keaton quickly called him out.

"Sexist much?"

He huffed. “I’m just saying, it’s not right for a woman to do owt like that?”

“But it’s right when men do it?”

“No, it’s just—”

Keaton stood right in front of him. “It’s just the bar is set so fucking low for men that shit like this is expected?”

He pointed a finger at her. “Divint swear at me like that, lass.”

“Lass?”

Whyte quickly flanked Keaton. “Get your finger out of her face.”

Cooper banged her hand on her desk. “Everyone back in your seats.” When no one moved, she shouted, “NOW.”

Order restored, she took a breath and directed her next comment to the huffy old-timer. “Just because something is statistically less likely does not make it worse. A woman is less likely to speed or drive drunk. Does it make it worse when she does? No. It’s the same crime and deserving of the same punishment.”

The room was unsettled. Cooper knew she needed to defuse the situation before it escalated. “Let’s focus on the task at hand. DI Singh, please collate everything we have on Team Valley to hand to NCA.”

“Of course.”

“Keaton, keep working on making the final IDs.”

Cooper looked around the room. “Let’s not forget the other cases we have on our plate. The Mayor of Newcastle was brutally beaten, and her neck slit wide open.”

Everyone swallowed or shifted their weight, remembering the gruesome crime scene photographs of Hope and Catalina East.

"The ramifications of the Mayor's murder are playing out throughout the city. Newcastle is on the verge of descending into civil war. I will not tolerate infighting within our department. Is that clear?"

- Chapter 24 -

Shortly after nine a.m. on Monday, Newcastle's Central Station was at its busiest. The station was alive with activity, a hectic and vibrant hub of everyday life. People from all walks hurried about, each with their own destination and purpose.

Daljit Singh navigated the station's busy concourse, his gaze drawn to the arrivals board. The next train from London Kings Cross would arrive at platform four, albeit slightly delayed. Some things never change.

While he waited, Singh grabbed a bottle of water, blending seamlessly into the ebb and flow of the diverse commuter crowd.

He crossed the bridge spanning the tracks just as the train pulled in, its breaks screeching. As the doors opened, hundreds of passengers spilled from the carriage. Amidst the commotion, Marianne Grange of the National Crime Agency stepped onto the platform, rolling a small suitcase behind her. Her striking red hair was tightly secured in a bun; she wore a navy suit and a serious expression.

As passengers scurried past, jostling for first position in the race for the taxi rank, Singh's eyes locked onto Grange. He welcomed her to the northeast with a warm smile and a friendly wave.

"I'll be acting as your primary contact. Rest assured, Northumbria Police will assist in any way we can."

Grange's expression lightened slightly. "Thank you, DI Singh. It's good to know we have your support."

Singh waited for the crowd to thin, then gestured towards the bridge. "Would you like help with your case?"

"No, thank you," said Grange. "I travel light."

As they walked to the main concourse, Singh couldn't help but share some good news amidst the daunting circumstances. "I have an update for you. We've made the final IDs and now have the names of everyone killed in Team Valley."

In a cut-glass voice, she responded. "That is good news, DI Singh. But why do I suspect your next words will be bad news?"

She was right. The NCA must be teaching mind-reading now.

"Amongst the dead was an eminent heart surgeon."

"Hmm."

"And the other," Singh paused to take a breath, "worked for child services at South Tyneside Council."

A DRAGONFLY HOVERED OVER wildflowers, its iridescent wings shimmering in the sunlight. Cooper tried to snap a photo of it but was too slow. It zipped away towards the pond.

She and Keaton strolled along the tree-lined old waggon way close to HQ and followed the track through a tunnel under the A19.

Cooper crinkled her nose at the graffiti. "*God hates gays. Burn in hell—*" She couldn't bring herself to say the slur that followed out loud.

Shrugging, Keaton said, "Original. Not that the other lot are any better."

She pointed to thick red spray paint on the roof of the tunnel. "*Shoot fascists, stab the cis and eat the rich.*"

"The irony of wanting to shoot people who disagree with you, then having the nerve to call them fascists?"

Keaton gave a dry chuckle. "Yeah, that's some twisted hypocrisy."

"Or complete lack of self-awareness."

They emerged from the tunnel on the other side of the motorway, continuing to a bench with a small plaque dedicated to a former colleague.

Keaton patted the bench and said, "Hey, Jack," before taking a seat.

"I got an update on the case this morning," Cooper said. She paused while a young mum jogged past while pushing a pram.

Keaton's attention sharpened. "And?"

"Remember the texts from the mysterious Patrice."

"Yeah," she said. "He'd been harassing Catalina, begging her for a date."

"Becky's worked some of her witchcraft and found the number in an old email sent to Catalina a few years back. The email was from a P Ndiaye."

There was a beat while Keaton pieced the two names together in her mind. Cooper waited for the penny to drop.

"Wait!"

Ding. The penny dropped.

"Patrice Ndiaye? Of Harlequins fame?"

"The very same."

"But why would a rugby player be texting—"

Cooper cut her off. "Catalina wasn't an estate agent. She was a sports agent. My bad. I think the sight of their bodies knocked me for six. I didn't take in all the background info when it was given to me."

Keaton's eyes widened. "He never played for the Falcons, though."

"No. But he moved up here when he semi-retired. He has some coaching franchise now, teaching rugby in schools."

Cooper unlocked her phone and brought up an image of the franchise's logo. "I'm texting you his address. Can I trust you to bring him in without going all starry-eyed?"

Cooper was teasing. Paula Keaton was the last person who'd be influenced by someone's fame or fortune.

Keaton snorted. Given her upturned nose, she appeared somewhat porcine. "As if I'd *fan girl* over Patrice Ndiaye. Six years he was at Harlequins and they never won the Premiership until he transferred to Sale."

Keaton had lifted the Premiership trophy when she'd played for Saracens. She crossed one strong leg over the other as if waiting for Cooper to mention it. Cooper caved.

"Say, didn't you win the Premiership?"

"Why yes, I did," Keaton said, her round face filling with pride and happy memories. But just as quickly, her face hardened. "You really think all this could be a story of unrequited love? You think a former rugby star killed his agent because she wouldn't return his texts or leave her wife for him?"

A cyclist sped by. The first leaves of the season to fall were churned into the air, fluttering in tiny vortices.

"It's a possibility, Paula. As much as Catalina and Hope's death could be a hate crime or a political assassination, we have to acknowledge the statistics when it comes to female murder victims."

One of the leaves landed on Keaton's knee. She picked it up and held it between her thumb and index finger. "We can spitball about motivation all day; it doesn't change the end result. Two women lost their lives because some bloke couldn't handle rejection." She crushed the leaf in her fist. "I've read those text messages; Patrice didn't like being told no."

"Nor did Chen Long," said Cooper, thinking of the Dragon's email to the mayor.

"Any news from Chardonnay?"

She shook her head, got to her feet, and rolled her shoulders back. "It's not like *no* is that difficult a word. It's only two letters."

Keaton smirked, a playful glint in her eye. "I dunno. You seem to forget what it means whenever Nixon tells you *no*."

She was right.

"That's different," Cooper said, trying not to laugh. "Now get up and find me a love-sick rugby star."

Keaton saluted.

"And Paula?"

"Yes, boss?"

"Be careful."

- Chapter 25 -

Keaton tapped her fingers impatiently on the steering wheel while waiting for the lights to cycle from red to amber and finally green. In the passenger seat, Martin gushed about Boyd, prattling on about how sweet she was, how clever she was, or how pretty she was.

She had nothing against Martin and Boyd's relationship. She was happy for them. But Keaton was single and still wounded from a brutal breakup. The lovey-dovey stuff got on her wick.

She made a left onto Church Road in the village of Stannington in Northumberland. They pulled over and parked outside a two-story stone cottage with a small but fetching front garden filled with fruit trees.

"Did you ever play against this Patrice bloke?" Martin asked as they got out of the car.

Keaton gave him a trademark *are-you-for-real* look. "You're asking if I played against Harlequins' men's team?"

"Ah." He laughed at himself. "Sorry. It's just you're..."

"What?"

"Never afraid to take on men at work. I guess I just pictured you—"

"As a bloke?"

"No," Martin said quickly. "Just as strong as one, I guess."

Keaton locked the car using the fob. "Okay, you've saved yourself with some flattery there. And no, I never played against Patrice Ndiaye. Never met him. But if his crush on Catalina East is anything to go by, I'd say he has a thing for lesbians. Let's see if I can charm him into coming quietly."

She froze, cheeks flushing red.

"Pretend I didn't say that."

Martin laughed. "Too late. Way too late."

IT WASN'T TO BE. After much knocking on the cottage door, Keaton and Martin returned to the car in the knowledge that Ndiaye wasn't home.

"Do we wait?" asked Martin?

Keaton, ever the strategist, dialled the number listed on Ndiaye's rugby coaching website. Alas, no one answered.

"*Press one to book a coach for your school. Press two to enquire about becoming a coach...*"

"Worth a try," Keaton said, searching the website to see if it gave any indication of where the rugby ace would be teaching that day. It didn't."

"Ahem."

In the passenger seat, Martin looked smug. Too smug.

"What is it?"

He smiled. "In social media, we trust."

He held his phone up for Keaton.

"Someone just tagged him in a selfie."

"Where?" she demanded, grabbing the phone.

"Outside the Percy Arms."

"When?"

"Five minutes ago."

Keaton started the ignition and turned the car on a sixpence. "Now, we're talking."

Granted, the photo could have been taken ages ago and only posted now, but Ndiaye had harassed a woman, and that woman was found murdered. They needed to speak to him, and if there was a chance Keaton could get her hands on him today, she would take it.

PERCY STREET WAS ONE the main thoroughfares funnelling traffic into the city. On one side, a bus interchange backed onto M&S and the rest of Eldon Square shopping centre. The other side fed side streets to Newcastle Uni, St James' Park and the Royal Victoria Infirmary.

After a quick scan inside the Percy Arms, it was clear Ndiaye wasn't there. Keaton sent Martin to check the loos while she made enquiries with a bartender. Martin returned, shaking his head. Thankfully, the skinny male behind the bar had good news for them. A man matching Ndiaye's description had left only minutes earlier.

"Big bloke? Yeah, he was sat over there." He nodded to a table beneath a flat screen. "He was chatting sports with a geezer with cauliflower ears."

Stepping out onto Percy Street, Keaton glanced around, blinking in the autumnal sunshine. If they couldn't find him, they'd head back up to the stone cottage, but they might as well wander Newcastle for a while. See if they got lucky.

She felt Martin's elbow nudging her ribs. "Well, well, well."

Across four lanes of traffic, unaware of their presence, Ndiaye knelt, tying the laces on his trainers.

His bright orange trainers.

"Son of a baguette."

In her mind's eye, Keaton saw herself sprinting through Jesmond Dene, hopping the fence at the petting zoo and becoming lost in a crowd of joggers. Moreover, she felt the sting of losing the chase.

"I bloody said that tangerine trainer-wearing thief wasn't your average meth head."

She watched the traffic. Waiting for a gap between the constant stream of cars and buses.

Martin edged into the first lane. "No wonder you couldn't catch him."

Keaton hardly heard him as she stepped onto the road. Her ears filled with the pulsating thrum of increased blood pressure; her eyes dilated, adrenaline filling her muscles.

Ndiaye finished tying his shoelaces and rose to his feet.

Keaton and Martin strode purposefully across the second and third lanes. They'd just stepped into the fourth when Ndiaye clocked them, briefly making eye contact. Without hesitation, he broke into a sprint, fleeing toward a nearby multi-story car park.

They gave chase, their footsteps echoing on the concrete ramps as they pursued their prey up the spiralling levels. He edged ahead. If he reached the fourth floor, he could take the bridge into the shopping centre, and they'd surely lose him.

Again.

A car reversed from its space, narrowly missing Ndiaye. A ping to Keaton's left indicated the lift doors opening. A woman pushing a double stroller laden with shopping bags got out.

In a swift decision, Keaton veered left, a gleam of determination in her eyes. *Work smarter, not harder,* she told herself as the lift doors closed and the sound of Martin's footsteps and laboured breathing disappeared.

She rode the lift to the fourth floor, praying no one on two or three pressed the button. Her heart pounded in anticipation while she willed the metal box to rise faster.

Bing.

Keaton stepped out and listened. She could hear running, could hear Martin yelling for Ndiaye to stop. Was it coming from the left or right? Had she missed them?

She turned right just as Ndiaye rounded the bend, practically running headlong into her. Reflexes sharp as ever, Keaton lowered, braced for impact and drove her shoulder into Ndiaye's midsection. Her arms engulfed his thighs and he fell to the concrete with the impact of a Mont Blanc avalanche.

Not too far behind, Martin came to a stop. He doubled over, hands on his knees, breathing deeply. Gathering himself, he panted, "You might not have played him, but at least you can say you tackled him."

Keaton rubbed her shoulder. It had been like tackling a tank, and her shoulder hadn't been quite right since an incident the previous year ripped it from its socket. She looked down at Ndiaye, who seemed to have almost knocked himself out in the fall.

"Wakey wakey, sunshine," she said, helping him sit up. "We have some questions for you."

- CHAPTER 26 -

COOPER STARED AT THE hulking man across the metal table. Ndiaye's cool, dark skin was dewy under harsh fluorescent lights. His shoulders stretched the seams of his t-shirt; a vein pulsed in his forearm.

"This interview is under caution," Cooper said sharply. "You have the right to remain silent..."

Ndiaye slumped in his chair, eyes downcast. He mirrored her, reciting the caution in perfect time with her.

"Off by heart," Cooper said. "You've clearly heard these words before."

"Not in the way you're thinking," he said. "I watch a lot of cop shows."

"Well, unfortunately for you, this is no cop show. This is serious."

Cooper flipped open a manilla file and fanned gruesome crime scene photos from Times Square across the table.

"Want to tell me about the night Catalina and Hope East were murdered?" she asked.

Ndiaye shook his head, refusing to look at the images.

She tapped one of the pictures with her index finger.

"It wasn't me. I'd never hurt Catalina."

"But you would harass her?"

Ndiaye squirmed. "No. I—"

Beside Cooper, Whyte leant forward, folding his arms on the table. "April last year. You sent two hundred texts in one day."

"Including three dick pics," added Cooper.

"I'd never hurt her," he repeated, eyes darting briefly to one of the photos.

Whyte cleared his throat. "Your messages would imply otherwise. *I saw you today; you looked delicious... It's me again, just wondered why you're ignoring me...I'm a nice guy, Catalina.*"

Nice guy. The words grated in Cooper's mind. In her experience, nice guys never had to keep insisting they were nice. They just were.

"Shall I go on?" Whyte asked.

"No," Ndiaye said.

"Think I will. For my own amusement." Whyte glanced back at his notepad. "*Why won't you answer me? This is your last chance... You're being rude, Catalina...* and my personal favourite... *I know where you live. Perhaps I should just come over.*"

"How tall are you, Patrice?" Cooper asked, hoping the quick subject change would throw the suspect. "Six feet?"

"Five-eleven."

"We have a witness who saw a heavily built man running from the scene. The witness estimated their height to be five-ten to six feet."

He took a slow breath before answering. "All eyewitness testimony is unreliable,"

He was right, which irked Cooper more.

Whyte placed the blurry still from the traffic cam on the table. Ignoring Ndiaye, he addressed Cooper. "I think it looks like Patrice. What do you think?"

"I think so, too."

Ndiaye tried to look indifferent but couldn't help glancing at the grey-scale photo. "That's not me. I wasn't there. I didn't kill anyone."

"Okay, Patrice," said Cooper. "Say we believe you. Say we believe you weren't in Times Square on fight night. We know for a fact you were obsessed with Catalina. And we know that you were in the Easts' home the morning of her murder. Unless you want to claim that I myself am an unreliable witness?"

"Maybe you imagined things?"

"Cut the crap," Cooper spat, her mouth curling. "You were in their house. You fled through the dene, and you took their laptops and tablets with you."

"You can't prove any of that."

"Oh, but I can." Cooper gathered the crime scene photographs and filed them away. "Here's how it's going to go, Patrice. DS Whyte is going to arrest you for trespassing, unlawful entry and theft. We might even throw in a malicious communications charge for good measure. We will take fingerprints and a DNA sample, and those samples will prove you were at the Easts' home. We will obtain warrants to search your home and places of work for Catalina and Hope's laptops. We will find them."

Cooper sat back, folded her arms and waited.

EIGHT HOURS.

It took eight hours of stewing in a cell before Ndiaye decided to cooperate. He was a stubborn man, but Cooper had a teenage daughter, stubborn she could deal with.

Ndiaye leant forward, his massive frame crowding the small table between them.

"I loved Catalina," he said softly. "Maybe more than I should have."

He looked down at his hands, twisting them together nervously.

"She was a married woman," Cooper said. "And nowhere in her messages does she give the slightest inclination that she was interested in you. She was your agent. You were the talent. She never once wavered from that. Not once."

Cooper studied his face. He hesitated, finally meeting her gaze; his brown eyes pleaded for understanding.

"I know it seems creepy. But I wasn't stalking her, not really. I just...I wanted to be near her. Make sure she was okay. I'd watch her sometimes through the windows. While she ate breakfast or got ready for work."

Cooper suppressed a shudder.

"There's a spot in their back garden. It's a bush of some kind with pink flowers. From behind it, I can see into the house."

As a victim of stalking, Cooper fought to keep her emotions in check. She flexed her fingers, realising she'd been gripping the armrests on her chair so tightly that the pads of her fingers had gone numb.

"I was there that morning. I thought something was wrong because neither of them were there. Then I heard Hope's mother banging on the front door and windows."

He choked up for a moment before continuing. "I went online, and you know what the internet's like. The murders in Times Square were already news. I— I don't know how I knew it was them, but I did. I knew. Something told me my beautiful Catalina was dead."

He began to cry, unable to continue. Cooper waited, stone-faced. After several minutes, Ndiaye composed himself.

"I swear, I didn't hurt them."

Cooper took a sip of water. "I just heard from the search team. They found two laptops and an iPad in a cupboard under your stairs. Want to explain?"

Ndiaye flushed. "I panicked, okay? But only because..."

"Because why?" Cooper prodded.

"Because of the emails," he said, mumbling. "Between me and Catalina. They're private. Embarrassing."

Cooper raised an eyebrow. "More embarrassing than the texts DS Whyte read earlier?"

Ndiaye stiffened. "Poems."

"Cute," Cooper said sarcastically. "*Roses are red, violets are blue. Reject Patrice, and he'll murder you?*"

"I want a lawyer."

"And I want to know who killed Hope and Catalina East."

"It wasn't me."

Ndiaye glowered at her silently. Cooper slumped back in her chair, frustration simmering. Something told her Patrice Ndiaye wasn't their murderer, but it didn't change the fact he was a dangerous man. A stalker. They'd digitally comb every nanobyte of the Easts' electronics to see if anything pointed at the killer, Ndiaye or otherwise. In the meantime, he wasn't going anywhere.

A knock interrupted her thoughts. Whyte stood, opened the door and chatted with Boyd. He closed the door before whispering in Cooper's ear.

"Rebecca Hogg's here to see you. She found some documents on Hope's work computer that she thinks you'll want to see."

Cooper felt the familiar thrill of a lead. She glanced at Ndiaye, still sullen and silent. She stood.

"We're not finished here," she told him coolly.

"Keep him stewing," she told Whyte. "And if you want to add tampering with evidence and obstruction of justice to his sheet, you have my blessing."

- Chapter 27 -

With a swipe of a finger, Rebecca Hogg sent Cooper a zip file containing multiple documents. Her hair was tied in two braids that poked out from a vibrant Pokemon beanie, a touch of geeky whimsy in stark contrast to the gravity of her work. While Becky the Techie helped on many cases, she was most often called upon to help find evidence of child trafficking and abuse. The strap of a heavy messenger bag filled with laptops and files dug into her shoulder, a literal and metaphorical weight she carried on her slim frame.

"Took me a while to crack the passwords," Becky said, her eyes tired behind her thin-framed glasses. "But I got there. Seems you lot aren't the only detectives in the city."

"What do you mean?" Cooper asked, checking her tablet to see if the files had arrived yet. A ping. She clicked on the red icon and began the process of downloading evidence that could lead to Hope and Catalina's killer.

"Hope East was running some sort of unofficial investigation at the Civic Centre. Several women working there complained about a councillor making them feel uneasy. She was gathering evidence. Emails, texts, photos. Anything to build a case she could then pass to the police."

"Uneasy?"

Becky nodded. "Standing uncomfortably close. *Accidental* groping." She made air quotes as she said the word accidental. "One woman – Jane Bailey – reported hearing a camera shutter when she was alone in the ladies' bathroom. Another – Kathy Welsh – said he was always trying to get her to stay late. And another – Sarah Sweetland – said he constantly referred to her as Sarah Sweet Cheeks. She'd joined him for drinks after work after weeks of being pestered about it. She doesn't remember getting home."

One of the names rang a bell: Sarah Sweetland. She was the young woman working on the reception desk when Cooper and Singh visited the Civic Centre.

Cooper could feel her blood pressure rising. She didn't need to guess who it was Hope had been collating evidence against.

Frank Bloody McKenna.

Cooper and Singh arrived at the Civic Centre shortly after lunch to be told McKenna had taken a half day. They returned to their vehicle and drove ten minutes north to McKenna's home in Kenton.

Saxondale Road was lined with former council houses. The dwellings were large and often double-fronted. Some were semi-detached, others in short terraces of three to four houses. McKenna's neighbour to the right tended a traditional garden with flowerbeds forming a square boundary around a central lawn. His neighbour to the left was more modern, with a perfect square of artificial grass, stylish tiles and geometric planters filled with herbs. Between them, McKenna's garden was nothing more than a concrete drive.

His car was parked outside the house, a small hatchback. Cooper and Singh strode confidently up to his front door. Strangely, it was ajar. Cooper could hear the sound of a television from inside but no other noise. She knocked loudly and called his name.

"Frank? Frank McKenna?"

No answer.

Singh rapped his knuckles on the window pane. "Mr McKenna? Hello? Anyone home?" Turning to Cooper, he said, "I'll try the neighbours."

The first neighbour told him to "Fuck right off," but Singh's winning smile worked on the other.

"Yeah, I've seen him," said an elderly man in a polo shirt, a shivering whippet hiding behind his legs. "I saw him get home about half twelve. He had a bottle of whiskey – drinking straight from the bottle. Disgrace. Acting like that in a nice street like this. He must have downed the lot by three because I could hear him talking to himself. Well, arguing with himself. He was effing and blinding, yelling the place down."

"What was he saying?" Singh asked.

"Ah, I couldn't make it out, really. Didn't want to snoop, ya kna? But we have adjoining walls, couldn't help but hear the swearing, like."

"Did anything happen after that? Have you seen him since?"

"Aye. 'Bout an hour later, he was staggering roond drunk as a skunk. Talking to himself like an absolute mental case. I've got the grandbairns over after school the morrow. He'd better have got his act together by then. Don't want him scaring my Harper."

When Singh returned, he asked Cooper, "You hear that?"

"I certainly did," she confirmed. She thudded the side of her first against the door again. "Frank McKenna, this is DCI Cooper. We met last week."

No answer.

"Should we enter?" Singh asked. "PACE seventeen?"

Cooper ran through the various subsections in her head. She could enter McKenna's home to arrest him, or she could enter to save life or limb. Knowing what she knew about Hope East's investigation into the councillor, she had grounds for arrest. She wanted McKenna in their care for the full twenty-four hours. He had a lot to answer for. Still, she chose the less confrontational approach.

"If he's pissed as a fart, he's more likely to be violent." Again, the image of Hope's mutilated body wormed its way into her mind. "Let's play nice."

Cooper pushed the door; it swung open silently. "I'm concerned for your well-being, Frank." Can you tell me if you're okay?"

No answer.

"Frank, we're coming in to check on you."

The house was dark and still, the air stale with neglect. Cooper's boots crunched on broken glass as she entered through the open front door. She stopped to inspect the fragments for blood but found none.

"Frank?" she called again.

Singh crossed the threshold behind her before moving ahead to inspect the downstairs floor, the torch on his phone cutting through the gloom.

"Let's just confirm if he's here," Cooper said. "And don't touch anything unless your tetanus is up to date."

"Kitchen clear," Singh said, rejoining her. "And by clear, I mean he's not there. Not clear as in clean."

"I gathered that by the smell," she whispered, nose wrinkling.

The living room was in an equally sorry state, with an empty whisky bottle filled with cigarette butts resting on a side table. The television was on, volume low. For all McKenna's bragging of sophistication and his fondness for fancy, designer suits, his place was in disarray.

Throat dry, Cooper climbed the creaking stairs, her steps in sync with Singh. She swept her torch over the stained carpet, larder beetles scattering from the light.

"Frank?" she tried again, checking the bathroom while Singh checked the bedroom.

"No signs of life," he said. "Unless you count the insects."

"He's not here." Cooper closed the bathroom door, not wanting to inspect it further. "Let's get out of here. We can secure the premises, but let's wait until he's in custody before we search the place for evidence."

They plodded back downstairs, planning to return before dawn to catch him off guard.

"Oh." Cooper came to a standstill, eyes firmly on the inside of McKenna's front door, the side she hadn't seen until now. "Well, that changes things."

A screwdriver was on the floor in the corner behind the door. It had been used to carve deep, angry lines in the back of the wooden door.

Cooper turned the torch off her phone and opened the camera app, snapping a couple of photos. Carved into the wooden panels were the words, *Fuck you, Mayor East.*

"Let's get back," she told Singh, pulse racing. "Rally the troops. I want everyone out searching for McKenna. Get his wandering hands in cuffs by the end of the day."

When Singh didn't respond, she turned to face him. He was watching the television.

"Did you hear me, Daljit? Find McKenna."

"I may have found him," he said, his voice low and weighty.

A journalist spoke into the camera, her face serious. Behind her, Cooper recognised Kingston Park Metro Station and level crossing.

"Just moments ago, we received word that a man in his forties tragically lost his life after stepping in front of an oncoming train. Emergency services are currently at the scene, but it's been confirmed that the gentleman died instantly."

The camera panned along the tracks where a train carriage was at a standstill, forensic officers crawling all over it.

"The incident occurred here at the level crossing, where commuters were left in a state of shock as they witnessed the tragic event unfold before their eyes. The train involved will remain here while authorities conduct their investigation."

The camera zoomed in on a group of onlookers, their faces a mixture of shock and disbelief. With wide eyes, a younger man shook his head. "It was deliberate. He jumped right in front of it."

The reporter resumed, "Services are suspended in both directions between South Gosforth and Newcastle Airport. As we continue to gather more information about this developing story, our thoughts go out to the deceased's loved ones during this difficult time. We'll be providing updates as they become available. For now, back to you in the studio."

- Chapter 28 -

As dusk painted the sky in shades of burnt orange, Cooper shivered and wiggled into a tight neoprene wetsuit. She felt ridiculous. Like a human-sized lump of pork mince being forced into sausage casing.

Atkinson's slender, lean body looked at home in the tight-fitting outfit. Before Danny was born, Cooper was used to seeing him run or cycle in leggings and aerodynamic t-shirts.

"Nice view," Atkinson said, ogling her backside.

Cooper slapped him playfully on the chest; Tina rolled her eyes.

Clinging to the last breath of summer, they'd decided to enjoy an evening on the water. Atkinson rented three kayaks while Julie pushed Danny around the coast in his buggy.

Some exercise would do Cooper good. She needed to switch off after the day she'd had. It hadn't taken long to confirm the man who'd jumped in front of the Metro was indeed the oleaginous Councillor Frank McKenna.

Zipped into their wetsuits, they picked up the red kayaks and plodded down the bank to Cullercoats, a pretty, half-moon beach encased by two piers. The icy water lapped at Cooper's feet. She grimaced. Who's silly idea was this anyway? Tina clambered into her kayak and began a gentle paddle out to sea. Atkinson helped Cooper onto hers before sorting himself out.

"So your suspect killed himself?"

Cooper adjusted her weight on the plastic seat and got her legs into a comfortable position. A gentle swell made her bob up and down in a peaceful rhythm.

"And brought half the Metro system to a halt."

"Case closed?" he asked, paddling in time with Cooper.

"He's not our only suspect. But between Hope's investigation into his behaviour, his obvious hatred of her, the message carved into his door... It all points to him being guilty. Looks like he killed the mayor and her wife, then killed himself."

Behind his glasses, Atkinson's brows raised.

"What?"

"I know you, Erica. You don't look convinced."

She shrugged. The suicide made McKenna look guilty for sure, but it didn't sit quite right with her.

"It's all a bit convenient," she said. "I met the man. He didn't seem the type to be deeply affected by allegations against him. It wasn't like the allegations would harm his marriage. He was already divorced."

"Divorced? Estranged from his kids? Maybe his career was all he had left."

A seagull landed nearby, a small fish jerking erratically in its beak, squirming for its life. The seagull tipped his head back and swallowed.

"Perhaps," Cooper said. "Maybe you're right. Maybe the threat to his career was enough to make him want to end it all. Some of the things he's accused of... Hope would have reported him to the police sooner or later."

She paused to watch two teens on the pier. One pushed the other off the end; he fell like a stone into the water, resurfaced, laughed and dared his friend to jump in after him.

"You don't think..."

Atkinson shook his head. "It was definitely suicide, Erica. It was all caught on CCTV as well as the camera in the driver's carriage. Eyewitnesses too."

Cooper gazed out at the dark water, mind churning. If McKenna had done all the horrible things she thought he'd done, then part of her wished him good riddance. Still, part of her wanted to sit across from him at the station and pull at the threads until the whole sorry thing unravelled. She wanted to cuff him, charge him and see him found guilty in court.

A thudding noise pulled her from her gloom. Tina was slapping the water with her paddle. "Come on, you two. Last one to the cave buys ice cream."

Atkinson quickly accepted the challenge and took off at a rate of knots. His long limbs gave him a lengthier stroke, and he soon caught and overtook Tina.

"Show off!" Tina yelled after him as his kayak slid swiftly through the waves.

Cooper, though she could be competitive at times, knew a lost cause when she saw one. She'd rather pay for ice cream than exhaust herself trying to do the impossible. Instead, she took her time, enjoying the way the water reflected the kaleidoscope colours of the sky.

Up ahead, Atkinson whooped as he paddled into the sea cave, his voice echoing off the rocky walls.

"This is brilliant!" he called back to them.

Cooper manoeuvred her kayak into the cave entrance. Jagged rocks jutted up on either side, looming dark and menacing. She paddled slowly, letting her eyes adjust.

At the back of the cave, Atkinson pointed his paddle towards the cave's walls, his wide grin visible even in the dim light.

"Check out the scoured sandstone. Isn't it beautifully abrasive?"

"So beautiful," said Cooper, mocking him. As far as she was concerned, once you'd seen one rock, you'd seen them all.

"So beautiful," said Tina simultaneously but without a trace of sarcasm.

Once again, Cooper wondered if there'd been a mix-up at the hospital. Her daughter took after neither Cooper nor Kenny. When it came to her father, she thought, thank goodness for that.

They stayed in the cave for a while longer, Tina wondering if it had ever been used for smuggling,

Atkinson examining the stratification. When their time was almost up, they paddled back to shore, squinting against the dying sun. The teens from the pier were gone. Julie and baby Danny were the only other people around; they waved from the promenade up above.

Cooper's feet were now numb and slightly blue. She couldn't wait to change back into dry clothes and turn the heating up to full whack during the drive home.

They pulled the kayaks to the ramp by the marine biology lab, then hoisted them into the crooks of their arms to carry them up towards the Watch House.

As Atkinson strode ahead, Tina turned to Cooper. "Everyone at school is really upset about the mayor. I know she wasn't Mayor of North Tyneside, but..."

Hope East was young and progressive, and she used social media in a way that had been lacking in politics until recently. She posted short-form video reels talking directly to the people of the northeast, not just Newcastle, acknowledging that what went on in Newcastle had knock-on effects in other areas of Tyne and Wear and Northumberland.

"The year thirteens are organising a vigil for her on Friday," Tina continued, water dripping off the ends of her black hair. "The whole school's invited, but I get the feeling there'll be trouble."

"It's the same all over at the moment, T. It seems every group is trying to hijack the narrative."

"Really?"

"Unfortunately. Some say Hope and her wife were killed because they were gay, and whoever did it was doing God's work." She rolled her eyes dismissively. "Others say those who hold such homophobic views should be deported. Some say those who hold such Islamophobic views should be jailed or cancelled. The old guard wants to take us back to the *good old days* when only men could vote and only one sort of lifestyle was tolerated. A time when babies born out of wedlock were an abomination."

"Like me?"

"And your brother," said Cooper with a tired smile. "The new guard wants to drag us forward but don't know where to go or how to communicate it without it turning into a slanging match. Everyone wants free speech as long as no one says something they disagree with and one man's terrorist is another man's freedom fighter. It's tricky. And don't get me started on the little shits who are rioting and looting just for the hell of it."

Having returned his kayak, Atkinson jogged back to help Cooper and Tina carry theirs. While they peeled themselves from the wetsuits, Cooper wondered how her attempt to disengage from work had failed. She'd spent the entire time talking about or thinking about the case. She couldn't help it; there was something she was missing. She could feel it in her gut, and the Easts deserved justice.

Newcastle deserved justice.

By the time they got back to the car, it was dark and they were shivering. Julie fastened Danny in the baby seat. He began to cry, not stopping until Cooper took the seat next to him and offered him her finger to hold in his little hands.

"Ice cream?" asked Atkinson.

Shuddering, Tina said, "It's too cold. How about fish and chips?" she asked Cooper.

"Of course. Anything for my little abomination."

- CHAPTER 29 -

TUESDAY MORNING AND THE hot glare of camera lights burned Cooper's eyes. As she stepped up to the podium, part of her cherished the warmth. She still hadn't thawed out from the previous night's kayak expedition. The other part of her felt dirty; she was speaking to the press not because she wanted to but because Nixon had made her. She was the young, camera-friendly female DCI. In short, she was Northumbria Police's Hope East.

Microphones jostled towards Cooper. She glanced at the expectant faces crammed into the small press room – this was it.

"Yesterday evening, a man was hit by a Metro train near Kingston Park level crossing. He died instantly. We can now confirm that man's identity as Newcastle Councillor Frank McKenna."

A respectful hush fell across the room.

"Mr McKenna became known to us in our investigation into the murders of Hope and

Catalina East. He was a suspect who we now believe was responsible for their murders."

The room erupted into shouted questions and flashing cameras. Cooper raised her hand for silence. She took a breath, mainly because she didn't believe that. Not fully. Ninety per cent, perhaps. But it wouldn't be one hundred per cent until Chen Long showed his face, and she could rule her other suspect out.

"Mr McKenna first came to our attention because he was witnessed arguing with Hope at her home in Jesmond and acting in a threatening manner," Cooper said, her voice steady as cameras clicked and flashed. "It has since come to light that Mayor East was collating evidence alleging Mr McKenna of harassing behaviour and a series of sexual assaults."

Cooper could see Nixon lurking in the shadows to her right, ensuring she stuck to the script.

"Prior to his death, Mr McKenna scratched a message into the door of his home, a message showing his hatred for the mayor."

"Has the murder weapon been found?"

"Not as of yet."

"Will he be charged posthumously?"

"We hope so."

"For for the sexual assault allegations too?"

"That's less likely," Cooper said. "That's all for now. We'll update you in due course."

She left the room, more questions bombarding her as she stepped away and moved quickly to CID where she was greeted by the pacifying smell of coffee.

"It's cold," Keaton apologised, "but it's the good shit, not the vending machine crap."

Cooper toasted her cup against Keaton's. "Cheers."

She looked round. The department was bustling with officers sharing information and tapping away on computers. Stacks of paper covered desks, filing cabinets lined one wall, and a giant map of the area hung over the main desk. Despite how occupied everyone was, there was a lack of energy. Tiredness seeped from each of them. They were the walking, talking embodiments of a long yawn.

"Whyte," she called. "Find Boyd and get over here."

The dark man with brooding eyes left, returning a few minutes later with Boyd, petite and well-dressed. Both their faces were lined with frustration.

"I take it you're no further forward on the Roker case?" Cooper asked, perching on the edge of a desk and sipping cold caffeine.

Boyd made an apologetic face. "Forensics came back. The only DNA on the victim was his own and that of an unknown female."

"Probably the woman he followed down the embankment," said Whyte. "No further CCTV despite our appeals to local drivers and businesses. And no further witnesses. Apart from our unknown female."

Cooper sighed. "What's your next step?"

Whyte and Boyd shared a look, then Whyte said. "We're going to extend the CCTV search. See if we can find any footage from further afield."

"And we'll continue trying to trace the woman," Boyd said. "But other than that, we've hit a bit of a wall."

She cast her eyes downwards.

"This might not have been his first time," Cooper said, sipping her drink. "Maybe he didn't leave any DNA at Roker because he's well-practised?"

"There might be other unsolved attacks?" Whyte asked, scratching his jaw. "We'll scour the database. See what we can find."

The pair looked defeated, eyes dull and unresponsive. Their body language spoke of exhaustion, shoulders slumped, heads low.

Cooper patted Whyte on the arm. "Keep at it. You'll get there."

"And if we don't?" he asked.

"You've been around as long as I have. You know you can't win 'em all."

"But we can try."

"Exactly." Cooper smiled encouragingly. "Now get back to work."

They headed for a free computer at the far side of the department, looking as dejected as ever. Behind her, Cooper heard the double doors swing on their hinges. She turned to see Singh with a slim woman in a striking maroon suit that emphasised her pale skin and vibrant red hair.

"Boss," Singh said. "Allow me to introduce Marianne Grange of the NCA."

The two women shook hands. Cooper led them to a smaller room where they could have some privacy and asked Keaton and Martin to join them.

Singh, ever the gentleman, pulled out a seat for Grange. She thanked him before turning her attention to Cooper. "And thank you to Northumbria Police for the hospitality. Between yourselves and Police Scotland, I've been made most welcome. As always, it's a shame none of us met under better circumstances."

Noting the upper class inflexion, Cooper asked, "How are you handling the accents?"

"With great difficulty," Grange admitted, her serious demeanour cracking with a slight chuckle. "I asked a young constable downstairs how he was, and he responded that he was *canny canny.*"

"It makes sense if you're from up here," Cooper assured her. "First canny means *quite* or *rather*. Second canny means *good*. He was saying he's fine."

Language barrier cleared up, the team discussed the massacres at Team Valley and West Lothian.

"At first, the powers that be wanted me to look into organised crime," Grange said. "The hypothesis was that another trafficking gang was taking out the opposition."

Keaton blew a raspberry.

"My sentiments exactly," Grange said. "Large quantities of cash and drugs were found in the warehouses. A rival gang wouldn't think twice about taking that."

Cooper agreed. "Especially when they wouldn't think twice about a mass murder."

"Exactly."

Grange pushed her chair back a touch and crossed her legs. "They also left the most valuable items behind."

"Valuable items?" Martin asked.

"Yes," said Grange. "The— How should I say it? Assets? Merchandise?"

"Children," said Cooper sternly. Semantics aside, she agreed with Grange – and with Keaton's raspberry. "We always suspected the killer was making a point. This wasn't about sex, drugs or money. This was about sending a message. Abuse kids, and you'll end up dead."

"The question is," Keaton said, "who's sending the message, and how do they know where and when the parties are happening?"

"We've nothing concrete yet. But the level of precision suggests someone with tactical experience. Military, perhaps." Grange tilted her head to the side. "The pathologist working in West Lothian agrees with Dr Swanson. It looks like the cause of death is strangulation. A blood choke, to be precise."

Martin looked up from his notepad. "What's a blood choke?"

"Rather than stopping a person from breathing, a blood choke cuts off oxygen to the brain," explained Grange.

"Like Eric Garner?" Cooper asked, casting her mind back a few years to when an NYPD officer killed a man with a prohibited hold.

"Precisely." Grange glanced at her wristwatch, checking the time. "A blood choke works by compressing the carotid arteries or the jugular vein. Applied correctly, one would be unconscious in under ten seconds."

"And dead within minutes," finished Keaton. She clicked the top of her pen a few times before staring out the window.

"Wait?" Martin leant forward. "Like that – what was it called? Blackout challenge?"

"Tap-out challenge," Cooper said, correcting him. Recently, the deaths of several children and teens had been attributed to social media challenges. Tina's school had issued a warning to parents after two year tens had been caught playing it at lunchtime. "The blackout challenge involves choking yourself. The tap-out challenge involves being choked."

Martin shook his head. "The things people will do for likes and attention."

Next to Cooper, Singh interlaced his fingers and rested his hands on his notepad. "I know we're concerned with catching the killer. But what about the children? Have any of them been found?"

"A few." Grange confirmed, sighing deeply. "Some are too traumatised to talk. The others speak very little English. We're working on identifying them, getting them the help they need."

There was a moment of collective silence as everyone acknowledged, but didn't say, how they could have all the therapy in the world, but it would never fully fix those poor souls.

Eventually, after another glance at her watch, Grange pushed her chair back and got to her feet. "I'm sorry to have to cut this short. But my train to Edinburgh leaves in forty minutes. Forensics have released the scene, and I'd like to take a look today. I appreciate we're all concerned about the children. But so far, none of them have been able to provide a description of the killer or killers. My job is to determine who would have the means and motive to commit such audacious crimes."

Keaton waited for Grange to leave the room before pulling her gaze from the window and fixing it on Cooper. "I can think of someone."

- Chapter 30 -

The A19 stretched south through suburban South Tyneside before houses and shops morphed into lush green belt and tree-lined fields. The countryside didn't last long, and soon Cooper passed the mega Nissan manufacturing plant and crossed the Wear. She turned the steering wheel, eyes fixed on the tarmac as they left the main road, following a country lane enclosed by thick bramble. She'd only been driving for half an hour, but the local accent had already changed, and the stripes on the footie shirts were red instead of black.

"So," said Cooper, pulling Keaton's concentration from the sat nav. "Want to tell me why you waited for Marianne Grange to leave before telling me your little hunch?"

Keaton smirked. "Probably the same reason you waited until she was on the train before passing my hunch on."

Fair enough.

"We're very naughty girls," said Cooper. With deceased Councillor Frank McKenna seemingly guilty of murdering the Easts, this was an opportunity to get out of the office.

"So naughty that Nixon might have to put you over his knee and—"

"Finish that sentence, and I'll leave you here to walk home."

Keaton snorted. She pressed her thumb and index finger together and dragged them over her mouth, zipping her lips closed.

"Means, motive, opportunity," Cooper muttered, slowing and yielding to allow oncoming traffic to pass. Mick Hunter, the man they were going to see, had all three.

Hunter, a former UFC fighter, had been in Vegas with his family in the run-up to his heavyweight title fight. While Hunter was busy with training and media commitments, his youngest son disappeared. Hunter dropped out of the fight to help look for him, but five days later, his son's body was discovered in a shallow grave in Red Rock Canyon. Joseph Delaney, a paedophile recently released from San Quentin State Prison, was charged with his murder.

"He was never the same after MJ's death," Keaton said. "Take the next left. It was years before he fought again. He signed to some bare-knuckle league down in the sticks of Alabama but got viciously knocked out. Then he failed a drugs test."

Cooper didn't know what to make of Hunter. She guessed she'd wait until she met him face to face before casting judgment, but the story of his son tugged at her heart, and she found her hands tightening on the wheel. She couldn't help but think of her own children, one at school, one at home with his father.

When the GPS announced their arrival. Cooper turned down a long dirt road past yellow-overgrown fields. At the end loomed a sagging farmhouse, paint peeling.

You have reached your destination.

The Hunters' home was big and isolated. It would be worth a decent chunk of change if it weren't so neglected. But with tiles missing on the roof, cracks running through a couple of windows, and stuffed bin bags stacked by the front door, the house was firmly in fixer-upper territory.

They unbuckled and climbed out, walking through weeds towards the house. Silence.

The noiselessness lasted seconds before it was punctured by the noise of barking dogs.

Big dogs.

Big, angry dogs.

Cooper and Keaton made it back to the car, jumped in and locked the doors just as the first dog rammed the side of the BMW.

"Jesus!" Cooper said, almost squealing. Her heart pounded in her chest.

The dogs, two American pit bulls by the looks of it, jumped at the car, drool slavering from their jaws. Relentless, they barked and snapped at the two women inside.

Keaton, who was trying to keep a brave face, shouted, "Bloody hell," as one dog hit his front paws off the passenger window. The glass flexed and bowed. "He's going to break the fucking window. Let's get out of here."

Cooper fumbled, dropping her keys in the footwell. She slid her chair back, her hands scrambling over the floor for her keyring. She straightened up to see the other dog on the driver's side. Its powerful jaws clamped around the wing mirror and tore it from the frame.

"Christ."

It was like a scene from a horror film. The car shook violently from side to side as the dogs, seemingly possessed, jumped up repeatedly, scratching and clawing at the vehicle.

A piercing whistle split the air.

The dogs froze. So did Cooper.

Teeth still bared, they retreated toward a beefy man emerging from the house. His cold eyes assessed the strangers in his drive while the pit bulls circled him before sitting, one on either side.

The man rested a shovel-sized hand on one of their heads. "Who are you?" he growled towards the car.

Cooper could barely move. Keaton lowered her window a fraction and called, "Mr Hunter. I'm DS Paula Keaton. This is DCI Cooper. We're from Northumbria Police."

Silence, other than the low snarls coming from the dogs.

"We'd like to ask you some questions."

Cooper gathered herself, steadying her breathing. The dogs were scary enough, but Hunter was a different matter. It wasn't just his stature that intimidated her; it was the look in his eyes. She'd never seen someone so cold and yet haunted.

Pull yourself together, woman, she told herself. She'd stared down harder men than this before. The Blackburns, a notorious criminal family, could attest to that.

Cooper ran her tongue around her mouth, trying to regain some moisture. She lowered her window an inch and spoke as calmly but as confidently as she could manage.

"Mr Hunter, as my colleague says, we'd just like to ask you a couple of questions. Please restrain your dogs so we can talk with you."

Hunter blinked his dark, tormented eyes at her before taking each dog by the collar.

"I'll put the kettle on," he said.

- CHAPTER 31 -

THE INSIDE OF HUNTER'S property was coping better than the outside. It was homely. Dark, dusty and a little damp but homely all the same. In the hallway, Cooper stopped to look at some family photographs. Three tiny faces smiled out of a faded picture, the turrets of Cinderella's Castle rising behind them. A happy memory untouched by the years of sorrow that followed.

Hunter's hulking frame seemed to fill the hall, casting a moody shadow over Cooper and Keaton. Thick ropey veins netted over ageing arm muscles. But there was something else. A fragility that pulsed beneath the surface.

"Uriah," he said, pointing to the eldest boy. "Catherine. We call her Cat. And that's Michael Junior. MJ." His gruff voice cracked. "Cuppa?"

In the kitchen, Cooper studied his weathered hands as he fumbled with the mugs, his knuckles like knots on an ancient tree.

"Thanks." She took the tea, steam rising between them.

"I'm guessing this is about MJ." His thick fingers gripped a wooden kitchen table. "If that bastard's up for parole or wants some restorative justice crap, he can stick it where—"

Cooper raised her hand to signal for him to stop. "No, Mr Hunter."

"Mick."

"No, Mick."

"Been stabbed by some other inmate?"

"Not as far as I'm aware."

"Pitty."

Cooper felt the warmth of the tea seep through the porcelain and into her palms; they were still sweating from her encounter with the dogs.

"You know about my boy, though? You know what happened to him?"

Cooper met his gaze. Saw the ferocity simmering behind the pain and powerlessness of a man who couldn't protect his child.

A frail woman, so thin she resembled a toothpick, entered the kitchen, her tanned forty-something face lined with anguish. She gave the detectives a once over and approached Hunter.

"This is my wife. Kim."

Kim wore shorts and a vest top. Her hair was tied back, and her cheeks flushed pink from a recent workout. Cooper discretely cast her eyes over her bare arms and legs.

Not discretely enough.

"If you're looking for bruises, you won't find any," Kim said, folding her skinny arms over her chest. "My husband's no wife beater."

"I wasn't," said Cooper.

"Liar."

Hunter pulled out a chair for Kim. She sat. He laid an arm over her shoulders, his massive hand engulfing her tiny frame. "Have some tea, love."

Cooper studied their body language. Kim leant into him, tension draining from her.

Hunter used his free arm to pour another cup from the teapot. "If this isn't about MJ, what is it? Has something happened to my parents? Kim's parents?"

There was an uneasy silence before Cooper, choosing her words carefully, asked, "Are you aware of the incident at Team Valley?"

"Incident? You mean mass murder?" He raised his heavy brows. "Aye. I'm aware. And judging by the fact you're here, in my house, that the rumours are true."

"What rumours," Cooper asked.

"That the place was full of fucking nonces."

Cooper nodded slowly.

Hunter's massive hands curled into fists, knuckles whitening. "And because of what happened in Vegas, because I'm a fucking fighter, you think— You think—"

"We don't think anything," Keaton said, opening her palms in a gesture of peace. "But they died by blood chokeholds. Expertly executed." She held his fiery gaze. "Like the one you're famous for."

Hunter went still. Somewhere in the house, a dog barked. The room crackled with tension until Kim, shaking with rage, said, "*Was* famous for. Now all my husband is known for is losing a son."

"Did you know what was happening in Team Valley?" Keaton pressed. "Maybe you heard, went there to see for yourself, lost control—"

"Lost control?" Kim's colour faded. "He's not the bleeding Hulk. That man..." she pointed a thin, quivering finger at her husband. "Never hurt anyone outside of the ring."

"What the hell is going on?"

A young woman stood in the doorway, a textbook under her arm and headphones hanging from her neck.

"Cat, it's okay," Hunter said. "Go back to your coursework."

Cat looked more like her father than her mother. Tall with sad eyes and a square jaw. Still, she was a handsome woman with her long blonde hair secured in a neat plait.

Hunter's voice cracked again.

"Dad?" Cat ran to her father just as he collapsed over the table in a fit of desperate sobbing. "Come on, Dad. Sit with me in the living room." She supported him from the room. "Let me tell you about what we did at college today. Take your mind off things."

Kim stood, her fragile body as tense as steel. "I think it's time you left, Chief Inspector." Her voice permitted no argument.

- Chapter 32 -

Cooper's legs felt like lead as she opened her front door. The house was silent; she knew instantly that she had the place to herself. She boiled the kettle and made a cup of herbal tea, collapsing into a chair at the kitchen table. Neither the warmth of the cup nor the scent of lemon and ginger calmed her nerves.

She didn't know what had upset her more. So much had happened in the past few weeks. Images scrolled through her mind. Each time she dismissed a dark thought, it was replaced by something just as sinister. Or worse.

The abandoned holiday to Mexico. Hope and Catalina. Hate crime or assassination. Throats slit. Crushed by a Metro train. Fourteen bodies. A terrified Moroccan boy. Mick Hunter's indestructible body. Mick Hunter's destroyed soul. His wife. Their dogs. Their dead son. A shallow grave in a desert.

She let go of the teacup, hands shaking. The whole thing had her frazzled. It was too much, and she couldn't turn to wine or beer to numb the intensity of it all. It was only Tuesday.

Tuesday.

"Shit."

Cooper glanced at her watch and cursed. Tina's first game of the season, and she was already late. Tearing upstairs, Cooper threw on jeans and a clean top. No time to fix her make-up. No need to fix her hair. Grabbing her keys, she sprinted to the car, guilt coursing through her.

She'd missed too much of Tina's childhood. Granted, she was trying to build a career to provide a better life for her daughter, but still, she'd missed school plays, sports days and PTA meetings. Catching as many netball games as she could before Tina left for uni wouldn't make up for all the times she hadn't been there, but it was a start. It was her daughter's first outing for her new team and her first time playing as goal attack.

Speeding out of Latimer Terrace and headed for the Coast Road, Cooper made it to the away game venue just as the third quarter started. She hurried to the sidelines, scanning the court until she spotted Tina. The red uniform was striking against her pale skin and sleek black hair, and a bold GA on her chest denoted her new position. Her daughter looked focused, bouncing lightly on her toes while waiting for the whistle.

Not wanting to distract her, Cooper skirted the edge of the sports hall until she reached Atkinson, who cradled baby Danny. Beside him, her mother,

Julie, cradled a hot chocolate. She kissed all three and, at the sound of the whistle, turned her attention to the court.

"What's the score?"

"Seventeen–eighteen," Atkinson answered before a cheer and a blow of the whistle caused him to correct himself. "Eighteen all."

The game was fast and physical. Elbows flew; warnings were issued. Cooper winced as a defender knocked Tina to the ground. She bounced back up, eyes blazing.

It was neck and neck going into the final quarter. Twenty-two a piece. Cooper's heart raced as she watched Tina dart across the court, her movements precise and calculated. As the opposition took possession, Cooper couldn't help but feel a sense of dread. She'd seen this scenario play out countless times before – a loss in the final minutes of the game.

"Damn it," she growled as Tina's team dropped behind, quickly followed by, "Yes!" as they equalised.

The opposing team had a reputation for playing rough, and their goal defence was no exception. Luckily for Cooper, Tina was unfazed. Her daughter considered the no-contact rule more of a suggestion and met every shoulder nudge with one of her own. Still, with two minutes to go and after one particularly vicious clash of bodies, the two girls stood nose to nose, snarling insults at each other.

Cooper hardly recognised the girl on the court. At home, Tina avoided conflict, despised eye contact, and could be quiet to the point of mutism. On the court, she was a different person. She refused to back down, her jaw set as she stared out the opposition.

The whistle sounded, the ref warning them both.

One minute to go.

The referee turned her back, blowing her whistle for the game to continue. Then, as Tina moved to walk away, a foot shot out at her ankle, tripping her. Tina fell to the floor. Hard.

"Ref!" Cooper shouted in time with Atkinson.

Julie was beside herself, her hot chocolate spilling on the linoleum floor. "Foul!"

Play went on. Undeterred, Tina pushed herself to her feet, bleeding from both knees, blood trickling down her shins. In the final seconds, a short powerhouse playing centre lobbed the ball high in the air towards the goal circle. Tina made her move. The ball sailed overhead, and Tina leapt, suspended for a split second as she stretched for it. Snatching the pass from midair, she pivoted smoothly and shot in one motion before her feet hit the ground.

Cooper punched the air and Julie squealed as the ball sank through the net.

Tina's teammates mobbed her, but her eyes searched the court until they found the opposition's goal defence. She looked incensed. Tina smirked, blowing her a kiss as the final whistle sounded.

LATER THAT NIGHT, COOPER slept deeply, exhausted from the emotional rollercoaster of the day. But the dream that came was far from peaceful. Vivid and real, it plunged her into a world of fear.

Cooper was in an unfamiliar room with no exit, the walls of her prison surrounding her on all sides. A man appeared in front of her, brandishing a cruel-looking metal collar. His face was hidden in the shadows, and he grinned maliciously as he advanced towards her. As Cooper tried to back away, she felt the wall behind her close in, trapping her.

The man stepped closer, his face morphing into that of a former colleague, then into Kenny, Tina's father. He held up the heavy metal collar with its cold, sharp edges and laughed menacingly as he slowly tightened it around her neck, clamping down so tight she could barely breathe. Cooper screamed, but there was nobody to hear, all hope for escape fading away.

After what seemed like an eternity, Cooper awoke gasping for air, her pulse racing, and her whole body cold with sweat. She reminded herself that it was just a dream. But the feeling of suffocation lingered, and she couldn't shake the terror of the nightmare.

She got up and padded down to the hall to Danny's room. She admired him in his crib, his tiny feet twitching as he slept, before gently lifting him into her arms. She sat on the floor in the dimly lit room, watching her son sleep, feeling his soft breath on her cheek. The warmth of his little body against hers was comforting, and she felt a sense of calm wash over her. She swore a silent oath to herself, vowing to protect him at all costs. Never would her children face the same horrors that MJ Hunter had. Never would they endure a motherless childhood like Brandon East.

Cooper took a deep breath, holding Danny tight. She checked the time: two thirty-eight.

AT TWO THIRTY-EIGHT, EIGHT miles south in Sunderland city centre, Lexi Jones prepared to head home from the hell hole kebab shop where she worked.

The shop was clean, with a five-star hygiene rating. The food was prepared to a high standard, earning it a top ten ranking on Tripadvisor. But still, Lexi hated it there. She despised the drunk customers and their rude demands. She hated the staff, how they talked about her like she wasn't there and gave her all the worst jobs because she was the new girl. Most of all, she hated cleaning the toilets and floors before closing up.

Lexi grabbed her bag. It had been a particularly taxing shift with a queue out the door. The night had been full of problem customers. There was the guy who threw a raging fit because his kebab didn't have enough chips and the couple who argued over who would pay for their taxi home.

A group of lads came in yelling and swearing, singing offensive songs as they waited for their food. Despite her best efforts, she left feeling frustrated that she had to weather such behaviour.

Sighing heavily, Lexi took a deep breath and stepped outside into the cold night air, ready to walk home. The streets were quiet as she passed a bookies and an Asian supermarket. She quickened her pace as she turned onto Bridge Street, fumbling in her bag for her phone. She sent a text to her mum, saying she was on her way and swore as it slipped through her fingers, skittering across the pavement.

As she crouched to grab it, a dark sedan crawled up beside her. The passenger window slid down.

"Need a ride, hinny?" The driver leered at her, his eyes crawling over her body.

"No," she mumbled, pushing the phone back into her bag. She grabbed her keys, gripping them between her knuckles as she straightened up.

The car kept pace with her as she passed St. Mary's and scurried across the main road and onto Wearmouth Bridge, a green arched bridge spanning the Wear.

"Come on, darling. It's not safe out here at night."

When she didn't respond, the driver mounted the pavement and opened his door, blocking her path.

"Don't be like that," he said, getting out of the car.

As the man reached for her, a dark figure seemed to materialize from the shadows. Before either could react, the vigilante's fist connected with the driver's temple. He crumpled to the ground, cursing.

Lexi staggered back, her keys cutting into her palm when she saw his knee pads and black mask.

The masked man turned to Lexi. "Run. Now."

She didn't need to be told twice.

- CHAPTER 33 -

COOPER BLINKED AWAY THE grit in her eyes as she strode into the station. No amount of coffee could erase the nightmare, its claws tearing at her psyche even in the reassuring light of day. She undid the top button on her blouse and tugged at her collar.

Focus, she told herself. *Hunter. The case.*

She rapped her knuckles on Superintendent Howard Nixon's open door.

"Come in, Cooper." Nixon set down a pair of reading glasses she'd never seen him wear before. "Mick Hunter. Tell me about him."

Cooper sank into the chair opposite his desk and gave him an abridged version of Hunter's life story, his career, and his youngest son's death. "He's certainly capable. Aside from special forces, he's probably the best man in the country when it comes to applying a blood choke. And as for his motivation, well..."

"It's not evidence, though, is it?"

"No, sir. It's not. And the NCA would agree. As would the CPS."

He rested his elbows on his desk. "You could arrest him for having a banned breed of dog. Then, with a warrant to search the house, you could see what else you accidentally stumble across."

Cooper had already considered this. "We could. And we definitely need to handle the dogs. I'd prefer seeing them adopted abroad rather than destroyed, but that's likely out of my hands."

Nixon made a rare sympathetic face. "I can't make any promises there, Cooper. Can you arrange for someone to seize the dogs by the end of the day?"

She agreed she could, but Cooper pitied whoever had to confiscate the beasts. She didn't know who would put up the bigger fight, the dogs or the Hunters.

"We'll take the dogs, but let's not bring him in. Not yet. He knows we suspect him. If he's our guy, it might spook him into doing something that gives him away."

Nixon studied her face, then nodded. "All right. We'll keep eyes on him for now. Anything else? How's DI Singh settling in?"

Cooper paused, thinking. "He's very capable, sir. He's trying to fit in with the rest of the department, and no one's giving him a hard time. It's just... He's not..."

"He's not DS Daniel," Nixon finished.

"Exactly."

Cooper forced a smile before bidding the superintendent farewell and heading for the incident room where she found Boyd discussing Mick Hunter with two other constables.

A woman with a deep tan and golden hair swivelled on her chair, a pen in her mouth. "We're talking about someone who was able to find out details for a secretive, underground, illegal event. Someone who knew how to cut the power to disable the door locking mechanism. Someone who killed fourteen men and didn't leave his DNA all over the shop. Does Cooper *really* think this Mick Hunter's clever enough for that?"

The other constable, who Cooper recognised as Lewis Haig, was hunched over a keyboard, typing with two fingers. He looked up. "Let's not underestimate someone because they punch people for a living, Emily."

"It's more that he *gets* punched for a living," Emily said. "I watched his last bare-knuckle fight on YouTube last night. He took some serious brain damage."

Boyd tidied a stack of paper on the table. "You're not the only one who did some research last night." She stopped when she saw Cooper approaching.

Cooper sat and folded her legs, giving Emily a pointed look. "Don't mind me, Saff. Where's Paula? And what did you find out?"

Boyd blushed. "DS Keaton and DC Martin went to meet Chardonnay Long. I erm... I found out that brains and brawn aren't mutually exclusive. There are plenty of boxers and UFC fighters with university degrees." She ticked off on her fingers. "Chuck Liddell, degree in accounting; Randy Couture, degree in foreign languages and literature; Rosi Sexton, PhD in theoretical computing; Roxanne Modafferi, degree in Japanese and linguistics; and our very own Abdul Ahmed – The Tyneside Terror – has a degree from the Open University in environmental science."

Emily nodded, chastised. "You're right. We shouldn't judge."

Cooper, grouchy from lack of sleep, felt defensive about her own lack of further education. "A degree isn't the only mark of intelligence."

"Book smarts versus street smarts," said Lewis.

"And the rest," said Boyd. "As well as academic intelligence, there's social and cultural intelligence, music and creativity, emotional intelligence."

Lewis grinned at Boyd, earning him a look of disapproval from Emily. Cooper wondered if Boyd and Martin weren't the only couple in the department but dismissed the thought, realising she didn't give a monkey's.

"Besides," said Cooper, "a degree's no guarantee of aptitude. There are plenty of prize idiots who went to university."

Lewis saved his work and pressed *Print*.

"Agreed," Boyd said quietly. "Most of them work in Downing Street."

Cooper laughed. Moments of levity were fleeting these days but sorely needed.

A cough interrupted them, causing Cooper's smile to fade as quickly as it had arrived. Whyte held a piece of paper, his dark eyes burning.

"Sorry to interrupt, but you asked me to look for cases with a similar m.o. to the Roker murder."

"And?"

He waved the sheet of paper. "And I got a hit."

- CHAPTER 34 -

COOPER STRODE DOWN THE hall, her heels clicking sharply on the floor while Boyd and Whyte trailed behind.

"Sorry about Emily, ma'am. She's new," Boyd said, voice low. "I think she's trying to prove herself. Going about it the wrong way, though."

Cooper grunted, eyes fixed ahead. New detectives were always trouble.

"You shouldn't be apologising for other people—"

"Sorry."

"And Emily would do well to remember that around here, the walls have ears."

Whyte moved ahead and pulled open the door to the conference room, holding it for Cooper and Boyd. Cooper swept inside, the smell of air freshener and dry-erase markers greeting her. She took a seat at the head of the table.

Whyte passed them each a thin folder. "Two other deaths in the past year. Vikram Sharma, twenty-four, of Hetton-le-Hole, and Jamie Brown, thirty-nine, of South Hylton. Both died from falls from a height. Their autopsies indicated head wounds that may have been sustained separately to the falls, but it's not conclusive."

Cooper flipped through the pages, scanning the details. Sharma died in the first few days of the year; Brown died in March.

"Sharma had two allegations of sexual assault made against him." Whyte's face was as serious as ever, but his eyes glinted excitedly. "And eleven years ago, Brown was found guilty of rape. Released after five."

Cooper glanced at a newspaper article documenting Brown's sentencing at the time. She took in the man's round face and flat nose, the dismissive expression as if the thought of jail didn't bother him.

It wasn't concrete, but a pattern was emerging.

"There's more."

Cooper met his eye, willing him to continue.

"Early this morning, a car was abandoned on Wearmouth Bridge."

"Abandoned?" Cooper asked, eyes narrowed, wondering if and how this connected.

"The driver was found in a crumpled heap on the footpath that runs under it." Whyte pointed to an old police photograph of a bearded man with beady eyes. "His name's Grant Salcombe. Five years ago, he was accused of luring girls into fake taxis. But nothing stuck."

"Suicide?"

"That's just it, Coop. The bastard's not dead. He's in a coma, but the doctor I spoke to thinks he'll make it."

Whyte looked pleased with himself. And so he should. He'd found a pattern, and now, he potentially had a witness. They just had to wait until he woke up.

Cooper, delighted, reached across the table to shake his hand. "Good going, Whyte."

She was about to ask him to trace where the car had been, get it to the lab for testing, and do a sweep of CCTV in the area when she was interrupted by the door banging open.

DI Daljit Singh burst in, face ashen.

"It's Martin. He's hurt."

Cooper was on her feet in an instant, chair clattering to the floor behind her.

"It's the Dragon," he said. "Long's back, and he's got Martin."

SIXTY YEARS OF STEEP decline had taken its toll on Blyth. First, the railway closed, and then the shipyards. The collieries weren't far behind, and by the 1980s, only one remained. Yes, renewable energy companies were investing in the town, and there was talk of a gigafactory to bring jobs back to the region, but it wasn't fair. It wasn't fair that in the past six years, most of Northumberland Council's money had been spent in the wealthiest areas of the county – Ponteland, Morpeth and Hexham. Blyth, a town that proudly built the navy's first aircraft carrier, was losing its income and identity. Blyth South was fairing better, but still, some areas of the town felt forgotten. Areas where the only industry growing was the drug trade. Thanks in part to the man Keaton found herself pleading with: the Dragon.

The terraced street of pebble dash, peeling paint and boarded-up windows was a far cry from the idyllic countryside a mere five miles away. Overgrown weeds choked small front gardens, abandoned fridge freezers and old mattresses smothered backyards. The house at the end of the terrace faired the worst of the lot. This was a cuckoo's nest: a house belonging to a vulnerable person that was taken by force or coercion by drug gangs and used to house their product or hide their cash.

In the front garden, young DC Oliver Martin struggled to crawl away from the menacing figure of Chen Long, the Dragon. Pain contorted his face, and blood stained the concrete tiles beneath him. His Achilles tendon was severed. He gripped the loose flesh on the back of his ankle, trying to stem the blood flow.

"Chen!" Keaton begged from behind a squad car. "Let him go. He needs medical attention."

Long staggered in the shabby garden, a machete-style knife in one hand, a gun in the other. His eyes were dilated and wild, his movements jerky and robotic. He wore black joggers and gold chains. No shirt. No shoes.

He tilted his head as if Keaton's words had come from behind him, somewhere in the house. He listened, then giggled.

Keaton's heart pounded in her chest as she watched Long move around the garden, waving the knife so casually he could hurt himself as much as further injure Martin. Guilt and fear clawed at her conscience. She blamed herself for getting Martin into this mess. She thought she'd done everything right, arranging backup before following the tip-off. She didn't know Long was armed, but she should have assumed it. *Where the hell were armed response?*

"Hang in there," she muttered to herself, hoping the words somehow reached Martin telepathically. He'd need surgery and months of physio to repair the tendon, but the most pressing issue was the bleeding.

So much blood.

"Chen," she called again.

This time, Long seemed to hear her. He paused, swaying slightly, looking up at the sky as if considering his next move.

"Drop the weapons," Keaton said firmly, her voice stronger now. Though she forced herself to sound confident, her body was shaking uncontrollably.

"Let me help him."

She could try to bargain with Long, say he didn't want a murder charge added to the trouble he was in, but she didn't want to frighten Martin by suggesting he might die from his wounds.

But he might, the pessimistic voice in her head told her.

She felt helpless. If Long was unarmed, she wouldn't hesitate. She didn't care how many of his goons were inside, she'd have rushed him and got Martin the hell out of there. But against a knife of that size, she knew better. Against a gun, it was suicide.

A uniform to her right made eye contact. He was just as lost, seeking leadership she couldn't provide. "Hold back," she mouthed. She couldn't risk someone else getting hurt.

Keaton's ears strained for the sound of sirens. She needed tasers, dogs, guns, or preferably all three. The only sounds she could pick out were a stereo blasting rap music within the cuckoo's nest and a car alarm a few streets away. A curtain flickered further down the terraced street where residents had been told to get inside and lock their doors. With Long waving a gun around, she'd instructed the locals to stay away from doors and windows, but self-preservation proved less important to nebby neighbours.

Keaton stepped forward, determined to draw Long's attention away from Martin and onto her. If she could keep him preoccupied, perhaps he could crawl to safety.

"Chen," she called again. "Let's talk. You've been away from home for a while now. You don't look well."

That was an understatement. Whatever he'd taken, he'd taken a lot of it. His skin had a grubby sheen to it, and he smelled repugnant. She motioned towards the squad car. "I can make sure you get the help you need, but only if you come with me."

Keaton paused, her mind racing as she frantically searched for the right words to convince Long to put down his weapons. He was clearly in an altered state of mind, but something in his gaze told her he could understand what she was saying; it was almost as if he wanted someone else to decide what he should do next. She had no way of knowing how long he would keep them there like that or when armed response would arrive on the scene – and even then, it might be too late for Martin. And still, the only sound was that blasted car alarm.

Long sucked in an audible breath. He stared at her, his swollen pupils tracking her as she took a few steps forward, palms open. "Put down the weapons," she repeated, softly this time.

Long twitched, looking over one shoulder and then the other. "What?" he hissed, speaking to an invisible voice.

He spun, the machete screeching along the rough, stoned wall of the Blyth terrace. The sound of metal on pebbledash grated down the street like a siren's wail, pebbles popping and scattering like hail. Long took two thundering steps, snatched Martin by his arm, and pushed the blade dangerously close to his neck.

"Up!" he barked.

When Martin failed to comply, Long jabbed him with the tip of the machete, forcing the young DC through the open door into the cuckoo's nest.

Long scanned up and down the abandoned street before slamming shut the door and locking them both inside.

- Chapter 35 -

THE CAR TORE THROUGH the gloomy countryside, patches of weak sunlight breaking through the clouds. Cooper gripped the wheel tightly as the car bumped along a road pockmarked with potholes. Singh sat beside her, jaw clenched and face pale.

"What the hell happened?" Cooper asked, frustration evident in her voice. Her focus was entirely on getting to Keaton and Martin, but the situation appeared to be spiralling out of control.

Singh swallowed. "Chardonnay Long made good on her promise to inform on her husband. He turned up at their home this morning. It was the first time she'd seen him since he fled Bamboo Grove. Long grabbed some of his clothes, told Chardonnay he loved her and left. She overheard a phone call where he said he needed to check on production at the house up the coast. She guessed it was an address in Blyth where she'd been once before."

"Cooper flicked him a look."

"She told Keaton she'd waited in the car while Long spoke to a business associate. That was about six months ago."

Cooper scoffed at the words *business associate*. "A cuckoo's nest?"

"I imagine so. The house is owned by Mr Miles Lowestoft, fifty-three, no criminal record. Rented to Miss Fiona Peters, twenty-three, also no criminal record. Lowestoft described Peters as – and I quote..." Singh checked his notes. "...Thick as sugar, but pays her rent on time."

"He didn't say *sugar*, did he?"

"No. But I don't wish to swear."

"Well, he sounds like a delight." Cooper took a left at Old Hartley. To her right, the sea looked rough and grey, smashing off the rocks at Collywell Bay.

"I take it Long's using a burner phone?" she asked.

"That's right. Nothing's pinged on his business mobile, the one he uses for Longevity Building Solutions. My guess is he ditched that after he fled Stowell Street."

Entering Blyth, they passed through a series of modern, new-build suburbs, the streets named after birds: Kingfisher Way, Sandpiper Close, and Osprey Driver.

Five minutes and a few turns later, they were on an entirely different side of town. Empty crisp packets and soda cans rolled along the curb. Cigarette ends and the occasional needle littered the depressing-looking streets. What few shops there were had long since boarded up their windows to prevent yet another smash-and-grab.

The car came to a halt outside the cordoned-off area. Cooper and Singh exited the vehicle and were met by the sight of a group of uniformed police officers looking anxious and fidgety. She could see Keaton, pale and tense, her lips sucked into her mouth, her eyes red.

No sign of Martin.

"Boss, thank God you're here. Where the fuck are armed response?"

Cooper surveyed the house, seeing movement behind a net curtain on the first floor. "It all kicked off in town. It's Hope East's funeral tomorrow, and things are getting heated."

"We've got a hostage situation. Long's got Martin. Put a machete to his throat and locked themselves inside. He's got a gun too. Might be imitation, but I wouldn't risk it."

"Me neither," Cooper said, feeling the chill of dread cloak her body like an icy blanket.

"Martin's badly hurt. His Achilles tendon's been slashed through. He can't put any weight on his right leg at all, and he's lost a lot of blood."

"Have you tried negotiating with him?"

"I've been trying, but he's not listening. He's out of his mind on something and won't let Martin go."

Cooper's heart thumped. Each beat the ticking of a clock, reminding her they were running out of time. Voice hoarse, she told Singh to call Nixon. "We need that back-up. Armed back-up," she qualified. She ran a hand over her jaw, feeling it shake. "And we need a hostage negotiator."

While Singh made the call, Keaton made another call, praying her informant would pick up. After a few tense rings, Chardonnay's voice crackled through the line.

Keaton pressed speaker so Cooper could listen in.

"I've already helped you. Leave me alone."

"Chardonnay, please listen," Keaton pleaded. "The situation here is dire. Your husband has weapons and has taken one of our men hostage. We know he's using a burner phone. Do you have the number?"

Chardonnay hesitated. "No."

"Chardonnay?"

She sighed heavily. "Is that bastard there with another woman?"

Keaton looked at Cooper, shrugging. Cooper knew the house was occupied by a female. Whether Fiona Peters was in the house, she had no idea. Whether she and Long had some form of sexual relationship, consensual or coerced, was anyone's guess. Cooper nodded.

"Yes," said Keaton. "There's another woman here. But this isn't about your husband's infidelity. Lives are at stake."

"Damn right they are," said Chardonnay. "I'll kill the bastard myself. Right after I cut his dick off."

Chardonnay spat out several possible phone numbers, one angry digit at a time, and hung up.

Singh hurried over, shoving his phone into the inside pocket of his blazer. "A unit's on their way. Canine too. Five minutes. Ten max."

"Negotiator?"

He shook his head.

Keaton dialled the first number on the list, placed the phone to her ear and closed her eyes. She leant on the roof of the squad car, using it as support.

Cooper knew exactly how she felt. They'd both lost a dear friend and colleague that day in Kielder Forest. Neither of them had fully recovered, and the sad truth was that they probably never would. They'd never be the same without him. If Keaton lost Martin, Cooper didn't dare wonder what she'd do.

"No answer," she said, hanging up and trying the next number on her list, letting it ring a painfully long time.

Cooper put a hand on Keaton's shoulder. "He'll be okay."

She shrugged it away, her body stiffening.

Next number. Nothing.

The next number. Nothing.

As the sound of sirens heralded back-up in the form of guns and dogs, a call connected and Keaton's eyes widened.

Long's voice cackled as he laughed and shushed people in the background like a child making a prank call. "I'm sorry, the Dragon can't come to the phone right now—"

Cooper held out her hand for Keaton to pass her the phone, but she refused.

"Listen up, you piece of shit—"

"Paula, give me the phone."

Keaton turned her back. "You're going to be less dragon and more gecko when I get my hands on you, matey. Do you hear that?" She held up the phone, the sound of sirens growing louder. "That's the sound of a power shift."

"Paula," Cooper snapped, trying to grab the phone from Keaton. "Give me the goddam phone."

Keaton brought the phone in front of her face, her lips forming a tight snarl. "You're not in charge anymore, Long. We are."

Blue lights filled the street. Men in tactical outfits carrying MP5s burst from van doors, surrounding the cuckoo's nest.

"You have a simple choice, Chen," Keaton said. "One, you give us the casualty. Or two, you die."

"Paula!"

There was a moment's silence, a giggle, then, "Please leave a message after the beep."

The Dragon hung up.

- Chapter 36 -

Cooper had to press redial sixteen times before Long answered again.

"Domino's pizza, can I take your order?" he chuckled, taunting her.

Cooper kept her tone even. "This isn't a game. Release the hostage."

"But we're having too much fun, aren't we buddy? He's going to braid my hair. I'm going to paint his toenails."

Cooper gritted her teeth. "My colleague wasn't lying."

"Huh?"

"You will die today."

"I don't think so."

"I do."

Cooper's eyes burned holes in the windows of the dirty, pebble-dashed terrace, willing them to see something, anything, that would help resolve the situation.

"Listen, Chen. The place is surrounded. There are only two ways out. One is in handcuffs; the other is in a body bag."

Silence. She let it stretch, pulse pounding in her ears.

"We need to get DC Martin to hospital. We will force entry if you don't allow us to take him in the next twenty minutes. If you are holding a weapon, if you reach for a weapon or conceal a weapon, they will open fire. If you try to prevent us from getting to DC Martin, they will open fire."

More silence. She wondered if he'd put the phone down somewhere, accidentally hit mute, or even understood what she was saying to him. Alternatively, her words could be getting through. Perhaps he was rapidly sobering up, realising the gravity of the situation.

"Chen?"

"I'm thinking."

"You don't want to die today. Let us get DC Martin out of there, and then we can talk."

"Give me ten. I need to think."

He hung up; Cooper swore.

It was a painfully slow ten minutes while Cooper paced behind a row of squad cars, her eyes constantly moving from the house to the phone in her hand, willing it to ring. She was staring at the phone when she noticed Keaton's body stiffen; the front door was opening.

"Drop the weapon! Drop the weapon!"

Armed police shouted their demand on repeat. Long edged around the doorframe, one bare, muscular arm supporting Martin's fragile frame, his other holding the machete. There was no sign of the gun.

Cooper's breath caught at the sight of Martin's ghostly skin. A crude bandage of loo roll and string was tied around his ankle, shirt sleeves soaking with blood. He limped along, wheezing, as Long shoved him forward. Martin slumped to the ground and began crawling towards the gate.

"Not so fast," Long sneered. He pointed the machete at Martin. "You're not going anywhere just yet."

Long was sober enough to know Martin was his bargaining chip; he wasn't willing to give him up just yet.

Long glanced around at the guns, eyes as bright as they were mad. Each weapon pointed at his chest. "I want immunity."

"Not a chance," Cooper said, then to Martin, "How you doing?"

The question sounded so stupid, so casual.

"Where's Saff?"

"Waiting for you."

Cooper hadn't let Saffron Boyd come to the scene. It was the right call but she could tell Martin wanted to see her. "I'll have her meet us as soon we get you out of here," she assured the young man.

"Immunity," repeated Long, sweat glistening off his torso.

"Not a chance," repeated Cooper. "Best you can hope for is some sort of deal, and you'd need something pretty special to make a judge look favourably towards you."

"Like what?"

"The answer to the biggest questions going at the moment. You keep your ear close to the ground, Chen. Team Valley. Who organised the event? Who committed the massacre?"

Long blew a raspberry, spittle flying from his lips. "I don't know. I don't trade in people or sex. Especially kids."

"Don't act so insulted, Chen. You have kids running drugs throughout the county."

He squinted. "That's different."

"You exploit children, give them supposedly free samples, then tell them they have to pay it back by moving your gear. You threaten to hurt their families if they don't comply, you..."

While Cooper continued to rant at Long, Martin edged away from him, moving towards the gate.

"...get them addicted so they become trapped in your viscous claws. Even if they escape having to work for you, they still need to buy from you. This is your lottery ticket, Chen. You tell me everything you know about Team Valley and—"

"I don't know anything. No one does. Everyone's talking about it, but no one has a fucking clue." He wafted the blade around as he spoke, coming close to injuring himself a few times.

Martin moved closer still, pain clearly written on his face. Keaton, shoulders rounded, weight forward, was ready to sprint ahead and drag him to safety at the earliest opportunity.

"Right, no lottery ticket," Cooper said. "Scratchcard then. Did you kill Hope and Catalina East?"

"No." Long crossed his arms over his chest, letting the blade hang beside his ribs. "Wish I had."

"Why?"

"That bitch hindered Longevity at every turn. That was a legitimate business."

Cooper tried not to blow a raspberry of her own. She settled on a scoff. "It's hardly legitimate. Inflated invoices, payroll manipulations, encouraging clients to pay cash. I could go on." She took a breath, watching Martin wincing. "Did Frank McKenna kill Hope and Catalina East?"

"No."

"And how would you know that?"

His mouth formed into a thin smirk; he licked his top lip. "Well, detective, it just so happens I know th—"

A woman's shrill cry split the air. "Chen! You bastard. You cheating piece of—"

Chardonnay came from nowhere, breaking through the police barrier and dodging the tackles of nearby officers. She flew at Long, her dagger-like, red nails raking his face. "Where is she? Where's your tart?"

Keaton made her move, grabbing Martin in the chaos. Singh ran to help, and together, they pulled him free from the front garden and behind a police car. Keaton bundled him into the backseat and commanded another officer to drive.

Long seized his wife's wrists, spinning her against his chest. A flash of silver and the knife was at her throat.

Pop. Pop.

Two shots rang out. Long staggered back, a look of surprise on his face as he sank to the garden path.

The Dragon had been slayed.

- Chapter 37 -

The red-bricked facade of terraced houses, now primarily split into flats, stretched before GA's view. This was an unassuming street in an unassuming suburb, its anonymity its most striking feature. The hum of a street light punctuated the stillness. A smoky aroma drifted from a nearby takeaway, mingling with the crisp chill of salty September night air. The distant murmur of city life droned like a faint echo.

Amber light poured from a first-floor window, casting a warm square on the neglected lawn below. The rhythm of approaching footsteps disrupted the quiet, reverberating off the uneven, gritty pavement. A man, absorbed in a phone call, paced closer, his shadow stretching towards the house.

"I'm 'ere," he said with a slight Yorkshire accent. The door swung open, and he slipped inside, vanishing from view.

"That's the sixth, right?" Justice asked. "Six men. Two girls. Wanna go with plan A or plan B?"

GA tilted his head in contemplation. Plan A, they stuck to their usual routine: cut the power, force entry and use darkness as their friend. But this time, they wouldn't have to force entry unless they wanted to. Justice had found GA a way in: they had the password.

"Plan B," he said, flexing his fingers, feeling both excited and repulsed. He rolled his shoulders and loosened his elbows and wrist joints, limbering up. "Let's change things up."

"You know it's more risky. They'll see your face, and I don't like you going in without me."

GA understood, but his mind was made up. "I want to look the bastards in the eye before I choke the life out of them. And we don't need to worry about them seeing my face. None of them will live to tell the tale."

"And the girls?"

"They won't say owt."

Justice sighed but said nothing.

"It won't be for long. I'll get in and start making small talk. Soon as the opportunity arises, I'll get started. Wait in the back lane, but stay out of sight. When the time's right, I'll open the back gate for you, and you can come join the party."

GA inserted coloured contact lenses, blinking furiously as he adjusted to them. He pulled a pair of spectacles from a baggy blazer pocket and put them on. Checking his reflection, he noted how they changed the shape of his face. He looked older. Thinner. He'd found the blazer in a charity shop. Its mustard fabric faded and coarse. It was a few sizes too big and had the effect of making him appear frailer. He pulled on leather gloves, then jutted his neck forward and folded his shoulders inwards, adopting a posture that suggested a sedentary desk job.

"How do I look?"

"Like the sort of bloke who volunteers at the Scouts for all the wrong reasons."

He laughed, but it was an empty one, tinged with nerves. "Perfect. Let's get on with it then."

As Justice departed for the back lane, GA activated a burner phone and dialled the provided number. With a feigned limp, he approached the house, his heart pounding. The phone connected.

"User six-three-two. I'm outside."

A SICK FEELING CHURNED in Cooper's stomach as she awoke on Friday. She rubbed her tired eyes and glanced at the clock. It was time to get up and dressed.

She brushed her teeth before showering and choosing something sombre to wear. Standing before the mirror, she took in her appearance. A knee-length black dress with three-quarter sleeves contrasted against her pale skin, briefly reminding her of the tan she should have had after two weeks in Mexico. Cooper's short buzzcut accentuated her striking features, but the fatigue etched into her face hinted at the toll recent events had taken on her. Today, she would stand with her colleagues and pay her respects to Hope East, the former Mayor of Newcastle – a woman who championed good causes and gave a supportive hand to society's most vulnerable, a woman whose murder had the city teetering on the brink of chaos.

The smell of coffee and bacon wafted up the stairs, pulling Cooper out of her thoughts. She found Atkinson at the stove, preparing breakfast while Tina gathered her things for school. He looked dishevelled, his usually neat appearance replaced by an unshaven face and wrinkled pyjamas. Cooper couldn't help but miss seeing him in a sharp suit and polished shoes. Danny gurgled happily in his crib, blissfully unaware of the heavy mood hanging over the house.

"Morning," Atkinson greeted her, handing her a steaming mug of coffee.

"Thanks," she replied, taking a sip and letting the warmth spread through her. "You didn't have to make breakfast, you know."

"Least I could do since I'm off this morning," he said, flipping the bacon in the pan, his casual demeanour contrasting sharply with Cooper's formal attire, silently highlighting the disparity in their current roles.

Tina threw her backpack over her shoulder, ready to leave, her black hair secured with a rainbow ribbon, the only item of colour in her otherwise monochrome outfit. Cooper pointed at it, "For the vigil?"

"Yeah. It's at lunchtime," she said. "The headteacher's giving a speech, and a few students are reading poems and stuff. Think the school choir are performing too. We're not allowed candles, so the year thirteens have bought a load of fairy lights."

Cooper thought it sounded like a fitting tribute to a woman who encouraged young people to vote and engage in politics. As Tina left for school, Cooper sat down to eat, the conversation turning to the unavoidable topic of Chen Long's death.

"How's St. George?" Atkinson asked. "Any investigation?"

Cooper took a bite of a bacon sandwich, careful not to get crumbs or grease on her dress. The armed officer hadn't even left the scene when he'd been given the nickname he'd never shift.

"None," Cooper said. "As justified a shooting as there could be. Chardonnay'll be in hospital for a while. She lost a lot of blood and will have a nasty scar, but she'll be okay."

"And Martin?"

"Back home and on crutches. He's coming to the funeral, but I want him to take at least a week off, preferably two. And he needs to see a psychologist."

"You seen this?" Atkinson placed a copy of the morning's paper on the table. *Frank McCreeper: More misdeeds alleged at Mayor's murderer.*

Cooper skimmed the article, her brows furrowed. With both suspects – McKenna and Long – dead, she didn't know what to believe.

McKenna's suicide pointed at his guilt, but Long had implied someone else was to blame. Unfortunately, he was shot in the head before he could reveal who. Not that Cooper could take Long's word at face value, a man who dealt drugs and beat women, a man known to have threatened the murder victim.

The truth would come out eventually – she hoped – but for now, all she could do was finish her sandwich and offer condolences.

- Chapter 38 -

The protesters were out in full force at West Road Crematorium. Cooper eyed them warily as she parked and stepped out of her car – the hate-filled bigots praying loudly, trying to recruit lost souls to their misguided causes. Across from them, counter-protesters were shouting and holding signs, using fear and control of language to apparently fight fascism. The irony.

Cooper sighed. She didn't have the energy for this today. All she wanted was to pay her respects and get back to work before finishing for the weekend. The former mayor had poured her heart into this city, working tirelessly to unite people. But now, seeing the division and anger on display outside the railings, Cooper wondered if Hope's dream for a caring, harmonious city died with her.

She approached an arcaded cloister with a central clock tower and a chapel at either end. She followed mourners into the eastern chapel.

Unsurprisingly, the inside was packed with friends, family, and colleagues. Cooper slipped into a pew near the back, not wanting to draw attention. The service was simple but moving. Whitney Chambers, Hope's grieving mother, spoke about her daughter's love for Newcastle and its people. Her voice trembled, and tears flowed.

Cooper's throat tightened when she saw Nick Chambers, Hope's father. He sat in the front row, holding hands with a woman to his left. Occasionally, he'd turn his head, look around and smile, seemingly unaware of where he was or why he was there. When Whitney talked about Brandon, Hope's young son, Cooper shed her own tears. Absent from the service, she wondered where he was now. In foster care, waiting for adoption? Would his new parents tell him about Hope and Catalina? Would he ever know what an extraordinary person his mother had been?

Though Cooper wasn't religious, and the ceremony had been a humanist one, she still found herself saying a silent prayer for Hope and Catalina, Whitney and Nick, Brandon, and Newcastle. She prayed for Danny and Tina, hoping they understood why she worked long hours and wasn't always there, her heart aching with the wish that she could be home more, especially on days like this. Before she knew it, Tina would be heading off to uni, and Danny's infancy would have passed in the blink of an eye. He seemed to grow and change every day. Would he grow to resent Cooper for her choices?

As the final words of condolence echoed through the crematorium, Cooper's phone vibrated in her pocket. She glanced around, hoping no one had heard it. A quick look at the screen showed it was Marianne Grange of the NCA.

Cooper slipped out of the pew, her movements quiet and respectful. She walked towards the exit, discreetly answering the call as she stepped into the cool autumn sunshine, feeling the contrast against the crematorium's sombre warmth.

"Any news?" she asked, skipping a greeting and strolling through the cloisters to the garden of remembrance.

"Sorry to disturb you, DCI Cooper, but I've tried contacting Daljit. He's not picking up."

"His phone will be on silent," Cooper told her. "How can I help?"

"Mick Hunter. Do you know if he left town last night?"

"Not that I've heard. Why? What's happened?"

"Six dead in Blackpool."

Cooper stopped in her tracks. "Same m.o.?"

"Not exactly," Grange told her. "But there are more than enough similarities to connect it with Team Valley and West Lothian. I'd appreciate it if you or DI Singh met me at the scene. You saw the bodies in situ at Team Valley, and I'd like your opinion."

Cooper hesitated. She wanted to stay in the northeast, but duty called. "All right. Daljit and I will be there as soon as we can. I'll find out where Hunter's car has been in the last forty-eight hours."

"Thanks, Cooper." There was the briefest hint of gratitude in Grange's voice. She continued, telling Cooper something most intriguing before ending the call.

With a heavy heart, Cooper returned to the chapel where mourners had gathered outside. She offered her condolences to Hope's mother, then messaged Singh to meet her at her car.

The cacophony of protesters seemed louder than before, but Cooper pushed through the noise, her mind already racing ahead to what she would find in Blackpool. She unlocked her car and started the engine; Singh arrived a few minutes later.

"That was—" he looked like he was about to say *nice*, searched for a better description and settled on, "moving."

"It was," she agreed. "The chaplain did a great job."

"Do funerals ever get any easier?"

"Not for me," Cooper said before asking the new DI, who she still knew very little about, "What's your wife's name again?"

"Amrita."

"Call her. You're going to be late home. We're going on a road trip."

"Where?"

Cooper checked her mirrors, indicated, then pulled away from the curb. "Blackpool."

Singh fastened his seatbelt, peered at the DCI and asked, "Why do I have the feeling we're not going for a donkey ride and a stick of rock?"

"Because Grange just called. She's got six dead, and get this," Cooper said, her voice lowering as they headed towards the A1, a grim determination settling in. "There's a witness."

THE LONG DRIVE SOUTHWEST had taken its toll on Cooper. By the time they reached the seaside town of Blackpool, her eyes were weary, and her throat parched from dehydration. They drove past a social club and took the first parking space on the right. It was a permit zone, and no doubt, a ticket would await them when they returned.

"Check it out," Singh said. He pointed west. The very tip of Blackpool Tower poked above the terraced rooftops. Piercing a clear blue sky with a spear of red.

"As close as we'll get to sightseeing today," Cooper said. "Let's go."

They turned left, stopped at the police cordon and introduced themselves. The officer signed them in and led the pair to Marianne Grange, who shook their hands. Her red hair was pulled back in a tight bun, but a few strands had escaped, wafting lightly in the breeze. She took in Cooper's black dress and Singh's black suit and tie.

"Funeral," Cooper explained.

They were handed protective clothing. While Cooper pulled on booties and gloves, she looked around the street. Residents peered from upstairs windows, and others gathered beyond the police tape, phones out, recording the drama. She could hear music playing, a dull baseline from a song she knew but couldn't name. The front window of one house glowed purple, the sign of a home sunbed.

"He didn't cut the power?"

Grange shook her head. "No power outages reported this time."

"But you still think it's the same guy?"

Grange hovered by the door to a plain-looking house with a small patch of grass out the front. "We won't know until we get autopsies, but we've got a bunch of dead paedophiles with no stab wounds or bullet holes."

"How do you know they're paedophiles?" Singh asked.

"Because our witness is eighteen, and she says she's been involved with some of them for four years, maybe five."

Cooper clenched her jaw and followed Grange inside, with Singh trailing a few steps behind her, his expression grim. The house, a relic of bygone times, was draped in dated decor and faded floral wallpaper. Police officers and SOCOs swarmed through the house, combing over evidence and trying to find a sample of the killer's DNA – the needle in the haystack that would solve these brutal murders.

"First one's in here," Grange said, pointing to a door leading to a living room.

They waited for a photographer to leave before entering. An elderly man lay supine on beige carpet, the familiar petechiae marks speckling the grey skin around his eyes. Heavy drapes hung from the windows, their once vibrant colours now dulled by years of sun. The furniture was a mismatch of styles, and a bulky television sat in one corner, its screen a black mirror of the gruesome scene. A lamp had fallen from a side table, but other than that, there was no sign of a struggle.

They ascended a narrow staircase, Grange cautioning them to watch their step. The upstairs hallway was cramped, the air stale and heavy. They weaved their way past several SOCOs to get to the bedrooms where a further two bodies, both in a state of undress, had been discovered. One lay in a crumpled heap on the floor at the foot of a double bed. The other was in a small box bedroom, naked and face-up on a single bed. Cooper watched a SOCO taking samples from under the man's fingernails.

After inspecting the upstairs, they descended back to the ground floor, where the final three bodies lay in the kitchen. Cooper's stomach stirred at the chaos that greeted them.

"More of a struggle in here," she said, taking in shattered glass, spilt drinks, a toppled chair and a large blood spatter stain on the wall.

A corner of the table was coloured red, viscous blood dripping down the leg to linoleum flooring, patterned with faded geometric shapes. The DB on the floor next to it had a hole in his face where his right eye once was. Cooper could picture someone grabbing his head and thrusting it into the sharp, right-angled corner of the table. Another victim appeared to have two dislocated shoulders and two broken knees, his limbs twisted as if someone had played a cruel game of human origami. A final DB remained seated, his forehead resting on the table, red marks visible on his neck.

"I never saw the bodies in situ at Team Valley," Grange said. "I'd appreciate your honesty, DCI Cooper, DI Singh. What do you think?"

Cooper and Singh exchanged a look, their eyes communicating a shared understanding. Singh didn't have to say a word for Cooper to know he felt exactly the same way she did.

"There's no doubt in my mind," she said. "Same killer."

- Chapter 39 -

Blackpool beach was a ten-minute walk away. There, tourists and locals enjoyed the September sunshine, breathing in salty air and listening to the sound of waves rolling against the sand. But for Cooper and Singh, all they breathed in was the grim perfume of death and the slight ammoniacal scent of luminol reacting with haemoglobin.

"Where was the witness?" Cooper asked, thinking of Tarik, the Moroccan boy hiding in the wardrobe.

"Right where you're standing," Grange told her, gesturing across the kitchen towards her. "When the first responders arrived, she was here in the kitchen, raiding the fridge and eating breakfast like nothing had happened."

Cooper briefly glanced at the three bodies. "Jesus." She looked at Singh and saw a flicker of disbelief in his eyes. "Where's she now?"

"Blackpool HQ," Grange said, leading the detectives back towards the entrance. "I'm heading there now. Care to join me?"

"We came all this way," Singh said.

"Yes," Cooper said, her mind racing with questions. Working with Grange and the NCA was the best of both worlds. She had time to focus on other tasks but still got to feel part of the investigation. "We'll meet you there."

GRANGE ARRIVED AT BLACKPOOL HQ fifteen minutes later. Cooper and Singh took an additional twenty minutes, taking a cheeky detour along the promenade. They drove past Blackpool Tower, the central pier and Blackpool Pleasure Beach. While Singh quickly jumped out of the car to grab three sticks of rock, two for his girls and one for Tina, Cooper called home.

"Hey, handsome?"

"I don't feel handsome," Atkinson told her. "I'm covered in baby vomit."

"Beautiful image. Is Danny okay?"

"He's fine. Just drank his milk too fast. How was the funeral?"

"Sad," she said, though it was an understatement. "I got called away towards the end. I'm in Blackpool."

She was met by confused silence.

"I'll be back tonight, but not before Danny's bedtime."

"What happened?" Atkinson asked. There was a cool, nervous undertone to his voice.

"Team Valley all over again. Six of them this time."

Atkinson let out a long, low breath. "Another one? Christ, Erica, I don't know what to say. Part of me is disgusted."

"Disgusted that they've been murdered or disgusted that they were ever alive?"

"The latter."

Cooper could hear noises. It sounded like he was loading the dishwasher. After a few seconds, Atkinson sighed and said, "As a SOCO and the partner of a DCI, I probably shouldn't say this. But honestly, I think this bloke's doing the world a favour."

Cooper couldn't agree more.

Of course, she could never say that in public. She could never publicly endorse vigilante justice and would do whatever it took to catch the one responsible, be that Mick Hunter or otherwise. But deep down, she approved.

As Singh trotted back to the car waving sticks of rock, she said goodbye to Atkinson and hung up, her thoughts turning to her son and daughter. She didn't have the skills needed to choke someone to death, nor did she have the strength. But she knew people who did. Would she make such a call if her loved ones were groomed and abused? She pondered the question as she turned the key. In the second it took for the ignition to growl, she knew the answer.

"SORRY," SINGH SAID TO Grange when they finally arrived at HQ. "Sat-nav took us the wrong way."

Dark horse, Cooper thought. She hadn't pipped Singh as being able to lie so easily. Still, she backed him up, remembering how pleased he'd been to be able to grab a treat for his daughters.

Officially known as Lancashire Police West Division Headquarters, Blackpool HQ was a modern building that had only been open a couple of years. The three-storey building featured floor-to-ceiling windows, but it was only after stepping into the airy atrium that the coloured panels of glass came to life. Sun shone through, illuminating thin, vertical panes of vivid colour. Glowing pink, blue and orange, the bars resembled the sticks of candy currency hidden in Cooper's handbag.

They were offered tea or coffee and followed Grange and a moody, local DI named Johnny Wilson to meet their young witness. As they approached the interview room, Cooper wondered what sort of girl could eat breakfast surrounded by twisted, bloodied bodies? The answer was a starving one.

"Willow, this is Erica," Grange said. "She'll be joining us."

After discussing it in the corridor and wishing to avoid overwhelming the young woman, Singh and his local counterpart decided to observe from the other side of the one-way glass.

Willow looked up from a bag of crisps. Cooper couldn't blame her for continuing to eat; she was disturbingly thin. Downy hair and self-harm scars covered her stick-like arms. Her cheeks were hollow, and her eyes appeared enlarged in her skeletal face, giving her a childlike, alien quality.

Grange took the lead. "Willow, we'd like to ask you some questions about last night. If you find it distressing or upsetting, let us know, and we'll take a break."

Willow blinked her enormous green eyes. "Distressing? I find it fuckin' hilarious," she said, though she neither smiled nor laughed.

"Hilarious?" Grange asked.

"You know why those dirty bastards were havin' their little meet-up? Aside from the obvious with me and Billy?"

"Who's Billy?" Cooper asked.

"Belinda. The other lass who was there."

This was news. They'd wrongly assumed Willow was the only girl at the house.

Cooper gripped her pen. "How old is Billy? Where did she go?"

Willow crunched a crisp, the smell of salt and vinegar filling the room. "Dunno. Younger than me by a couple of years. Fifteen? Sixteen? Never asked."

"Was she there this morning when you called the police?"

Willow shrugged and ate another crisp. "Didn't see her. Reckon she took off when whatever 'appened last night started 'appening. She'll be back, though."

Cooper sipped her tea. "What do you mean?"

"She'll be back. She'll go back to Gary. Well, not Gary. He's dead." A slight smirk crossed her lips as she said this, but it vanished just as quickly. "Yeah, she'll find a new Gary. It's all she knows, and there's always another fuckin' Gary."

The stark reality of Willow's words resonated with Cooper, who could see all her experiences etched into every line on her young face. In the dimly lit room, the shadows emphasised the gauntness of her cheeks and the darkness beneath her eyes.

Grange took out some photographs from the crime scene. "Sorry, Willow. These might be difficult to look at, but—"

Willow pulled the images towards her, salt-covered fingertips marking the pictures as she shuffled them around. "I'm not bothered by the photos. I caught the live show, remember? Aye, that's Gary." She pressed her index finger into the face of the man they'd found in the bedroom.

Grange made a note, then asked, "How long have you known Gary?"

"Dunno. Since I was thirteen, fourteen, something like that. He used to buy me things. Food, treats, little gifts. Next thing I know, he's saying he's my boyfriend even though he was like thirty-five or something and that I owed him for all the nice things he'd bought me."

She dropped her gaze.

"Yesterday, he rang me up, told me he and his mates were having a little get-together and that I had to get there at nine to... I dunno... make sure they had a good time."

Cooper felt for the young woman whose eyes remained fixed on the table. She hated herself for having to ask, but for the purposes of getting an accurate record of what happened that night, she said, "He didn't drive you there? You went willingly?"

Willow's eyes flicked to meet hers. Fire burning behind her pale green irises. "Willingly? Technically, you could call it that. But I learned long ago that what Gary wants, Gary gets. The last time I said no to him, he beat the shit out of me. Broke my—" She pointed to her brow. "What's this called? Orbital? Yeah, he broke my orbital and said the next time I disobey him he'd pay my mother a visit. I didn't know if he meant he'd beat her too, set fire to her 'ouse or what, but either way, I don't say no to Gary."

She picked up the photo of his corpse. Another brief smirk. "Well, maybe I do now?" She paused, then screamed at the photograph. "No. No. Fucking NO!"

She put the image down and ate another crisp. "That felt good. So anyway, yeah, I went to the 'ouse. The other men came one by one. Billy and I were in the kitchen drinking vodka. Helps you forget. Know what I mean? And the men – oh, I didn't tell you – you got me all distracted talking' about Billy and Gary. Yeah, they were in the living room discussing what happened in Gateshead and

Scotland. Talking about how they had to be more careful online and off. How they should tighten their security."

Willow tipped her head back and emptied the remaining crumbs of salt and vinegar crisps into her mouth.

"Tighten security?" she laughed, swallowing. "On the night they all get what's coming to them? Like I said, fuckin' hilarious."

Cooper and Grange exchanged glances, both disturbed by the bleakness of Willow's life.

"Right," Willow said, folding the empty crisp packet into a tiny square. "Gary took me to one of the bedrooms, but I was pretty far gone from all the vodka on an empty stomach." She paused, her eyes distant. "Billy was in the other room with him." She pointed at a picture of the man on the single bed. "That's Simon. They think I don't know much about them, but I'm not an idiot. I listen. Simon lives in Bolton; he's a pub landlord. His missus is called Isabelle, and she's a hairdresser. That'll help you find her, right?"

Grange nodded. "It's very helpful, Willow. Thank you. Please go on."

"Right. Yeah. I was in Gary's room. Barely conscious like, but I remember someone else coming in and askin' *mind if I join you?* Dunno who. I passed out after that. Next thing I know, it was mornin'." Willow's voice took on an eerie calmness. "It was dark since all the curtains were drawn. So I got up and fell over something on the floor. Really hurt my knee, like. When I turned the lights on, I thought I was dreamin' or hallucinatin' or something cos it was Gary I'd tripped over, and he was dead as a dodo. I was scared for a bit 'cause I thought the others might think I'd hurt him, but when I left the room, I saw all but one had gone the same way. I checked for Billy, but she must have legged it. I thought about doin' the same, but then I thought, nah fuck it, I'll do the right thing and phone you guys. Meant I could get some of this off my chest. Know what I mean?"

Cooper studied her face, trying to gauge how much pain she might be hiding beneath her tough exterior. Willow seemed weirdly unperturbed by the horrors she had witnessed, but Cooper suspected it was shock. It would hit the poor girl in time. All of it would.

"Wait," Cooper said. "All but one? You said all but one had gone the same way?"

Willow spread the photographs out before her. "Yeah. There were seven of them. Like I said, that's Gary, and that's Simon. I can't pronounce his name, but everyone calls him Vik. And that one, that's Perry. He has a restaurant on the seafront. I don't know them two," she said, pointing at the pictures of two of the men in the kitchen, one with the hole where his eye once was. "And I didn't know the seventh man either. Figured he either got away or he was the one who killed 'em all."

Cooper felt adrenaline filling her limbs; her toes and fingers tingled. She rifled through her bag for her phone and brought up an image of Mick Hunter. "Is this the seventh man?"

Willow wiped her salty fingers on her trousers, then took the phone, studying it briefly before handing it back. "Nah. He looks like a bouncer or something. This bloke looked like a librarian. Proper geeky as owt with glasses and elbow patches on his jacket."

Grange asked Willow to speak with an e-fit specialist so they could make a likeness of the seventh man.

She nodded. "Yeah. No worries. But can I get some more food first?"

Cooper left the undernourished young woman with a promise that she was safe now, but as she walked away, Willow's earlier words echoed in her mind, leaving a heavy feeling in her chest.

There's always another Gary.

- Chapter 40 -

After reuniting with Singh, they returned to the airy, stained-glass atrium of Lancashire Police West Division Headquarters. Sunlight filtered through orange and pink glass, casting the room in warm, sunset hues. Cooper helped herself to a black coffee, the aroma strong and inviting. She took her first sip and winced slightly; it was boiling hot. Singh, opting for mint tea, stirred it thoughtfully with a silver spoon, the scent of mint wafting gently. They sat silently, their minds undoubtedly wandering to the same dark places.

How many Willows, Billys and Tariks were out there?

Singh drummed his fingers on the table, looking contemplative, his face creased with concern. Finally, he broke the silence.

"Have you ever known anything like this?"

She shook her head. "Never. I've been on some dreadful cases, but this one... It's a whole different level. The world's a dark, dark place, Daljit."

Singh took a sip of his tea and let out a long breath. "The things humans are capable of inflicting on each other never cease to amaze me."

"Same." Cooper dug her phone from her bag and dialled Whyte's number.

"Do we have ANPR results for Mick Hunter's car yet?"

"It's in Kim Hunter's name," Whyte said, referring to Hunter's wife. "Results are in, but there aren't any hits. It hasn't been on any major roads in the last forty-eight hours."

Cooper thanked Whyte and gave him a quick update from Blackpool, telling him she and Singh wouldn't be back that day, but they'd see him Monday morning. He wished her safe travels, then hung up.

Grange was approaching with Johnny Wilson, the local DI. Unlike Grange, who always looked healthy, well-presented and stern, Wilson was scruffier. His shirt wasn't tucked in fully, and he'd loosened his tie a couple of inches. He looked like a stranger to both exercise and sleep.

"How's the e-fit coming along?" Cooper asked.

"Slowly," said Grange, joining them at the table. She crossed her legs and sat with perfect posture and poise.

Wilson slouched in the chair with his knees wide and said, "So, neither Northumbria Police nor Police Scotland could stop this nutter, and now I've got six bodies to clean up."

"Sorry to inconvenience you," Cooper said dryly. "But if you don't want someone killing your local grooming gangs, maybe do something about it and jail the groomers."

"I could say the same to you; the numbers were more than double in Team Valley."

Singh cut him off before neighbouring tables began to stare. "We should work together rather than cast blame." He shared his winning smile with the others. "We're dealing with a methodical, highly-trained individual who left no trace at either Team Valley or West Lothian. Perhaps we'll have more luck with forensics here."

"I do hope so," said Grange. "Some forensic evidence and an e-fit would really aid the investigation."

Cooper cupped her coffee. "Are we working with the theory that this mysterious seventh man is the killer? He's not another abuser who escaped?"

Grange pursed her lips, considering it. "I think so. He's never been careless enough to let anyone escape so far."

"That we know of," Singh said. "They're unlikely to come forward."

The coffee was decent. Better than what the vending machine offered back at Wallsend but not as flavourful as Cooper's favourite from Starbucks. She took a deep inhalation, savouring the aroma. "What I want to know, is how he's always in the right place at the right time. He must be part of this world somehow."

"Agreed," Wilson said, voice low, eyebrows lower.

"Maybe he spends time on the dark web," suggested Singh. "He might have infiltrated some groups."

"Which would explain why he didn't cut the power this time. If he was the seventh man, he must have been invited. Meaning he hasn't just been watching these groups; he's become part of them. And that's not easy," said Cooper, remembering some conversations with Becky the Techie. "These groups are suspicious of new members for obvious reasons. You often have to buy your way in with images." She didn't have to say what sort of images. They all knew.

"But it's possible," Singh said, smoothing his black tie. "If he managed to fake or hack his way in and monitored the groups, he'd know where and when the gatherings were happening."

"Isn't this the sort of thing your lot do?" Wilson asked Grange. "Doesn't the NCA have people undercover in these groups?"

Grange's restrained demeanour almost cracked, but she reigned it in. "Are you suggesting someone at the NCA has gone rogue, travelled the length of the country and killed, what is it now, twenty-seven people?"

"Or they leaked it to someone who did," he said, sinking further into his chair, knees widening.

"First," Cooper said, "let's wait for the e-fit. I don't know about you, but glasses and a blazer with elbow patches sound like a disguise to me. Maybe SOCOs will find some fibres from the jacket on the victims. It will at least give us something to work with. Second, I'll echo DI Singh's words and recommend we work together. If someone at the NCA has leaked information to the killer, it's even more important that we remain focused and avoid infighting. We know the perpetrator is getting their info from somewhere, and that's an avenue we should keep exploring. And third," she paused to sip her coffee. "Third, DI Wilson, kindly cease your man-spreading; we've seen enough gruesome things for one day."

- Chapter 41 -

Nippy, northeastern air bit Cooper's cheeks as she stepped out of her car, exhaustion and dehydration weighing her down. As she dragged her feet along Latimer Terrace to the front door of her Tynemouth home, she could hear the hum of chatter from inside. Unlocking the door, she was greeted by the welcome scent of the home-cooked meal she had missed.

"Hello, dear," Julie, her mother, called from the kitchen while washing up. "How was Blackpool?"

Cooper wilted into a chair at the kitchen table and removed her shoes. Her mother's question was so casual in tone that it irked her. Julie sounded as if Cooper had been on a pleasant day trip rather than attending the scene of a mass murder. She'd spent the afternoon speaking to a young woman whose past was as traumatic as her future was bleak.

"Long day," Cooper replied, rubbing her temples. She could hardly believe Hope East's funeral had just been that morning. It felt like a week ago. She put her annoyance aside, reminding herself that her mother knew not of the ghastly things she'd seen or heard that day and was simply making polite conversation.

"You must be starving," Julie said, retrieving a plate from the fridge. "I'll get this heated up for you."

Cooper salivated, eyeing a plate of what looked like shepherd's pie. She pushed herself to her feet, weary bones protesting, and hung her handbag on the hook by the back door. She hugged Julie. "Thanks, Mum."

In the living room, she found Atkinson, baby monitor in hand, engrossed in conversation with Tina. He was dressed in joggers, his faded t-shirt stained with what appeared to be baby vomit. Cooper loved that Atkinson relished being a hands-on dad, but that didn't stop her from missing his smart suits and intellectual conversation. Replaced now with slippers and babytalk.

"Did you see it?" Tina asked, turning to her mother as she entered the room.

Her daughter's eyes sparkled, her hands flapping with excited energy.

"See what?" Cooper asked, trying to shake off the fatigue long enough to engage with her daughter. She kissed Atkinson and stole a glance at the monitor; Danny slept soundly.

"My goal! It's gone viral!" Tina could hardly contain her excitement. "Someone put it on Tiktok and Instagram, and it's had like half a million views." Tina unlocked her phone, eyes widening. "No. Wait. Three-quarters of a million. It's insane. Every time I look, there's another hundred thousand views."

"Really?" Cooper said, taking the phone to see for herself, pride swelling in her chest as she rewatched Tina jump, catch, pivot and score mid-air. The bubble of excitement encasing the living room seemed to cushion Cooper from the dark cloud that loomed over her life lately.

"One of the Roses made a reaction video," Tina said, referring to the England team. She bounced in her seat, her excitement contagious. "I've just got off the phone with Radio Newcastle, and BBC Look North are sending a reporter to training on Tuesday."

"We should celebrate," Atkinson said. "Tomorrow night. Tina's choice. What should we do? Where do you want to eat?"

Tina shrugged. "I can't think. I'm too excited. Maybe the cinema? Or there's a new burger joint in North Shields that everyone at school keeps talking about. Or Mum likes steak. We could try the new Miller and Carter?"

"It's your choice, T," Cooper insisted. "Wherever you like." She stood and gripped her daughter in a vice-like hug. "I'm so proud of you."

"Finally, some good news," Julie said as she emerged from the kitchen, a relieved smile on her face and a hot plate of food in her hands. "We could use some positivity around here."

Cooper couldn't help but agree as Julie handed her the plate, cutlery and a tea towel. She sat on the sofa beside Tina and watched swirls of steam spiral before her face.

Tina had faced so much in her short life. She'd dealt with an absent father and a sick mother; she'd lost her great grandmother and her grandfather; seen her mother kidnapped and stalked; looked the Tarot Card Killer in the eye; ruptured her ACL and miscarried. Cooper had always said her daughter was brilliant. It was about time the world saw it too.

With the mayor's murder and the ensuing riots and protests, the northeast was under a shadow of uncertainty. But for now, Cooper would bask in the sunny glow of Tina's success.

"Burgers," Tina said, glancing at her phone and gasping as the view count increased before her eyes.

Cooper cut into the shepherd's pie. "Then burgers it is."

MONDAY MORNING GREETED COOPER with the bouquet of autumn. Of damp leaves and smoky wood. The smell of woollen scarves pulled from the depths of wardrobes for the first time that year. Leaves crackled beneath her feet as Cooper walked Tynemouth's tree-lined streets, and although the sky was bright, the air was cold. She wrapped a scarf around her neck and started her BMW, the engine grumbling to life. The short commute from Tynemouth to Wallsend was familiar and passed as if she were on auto-pilot.

HQ fizzed with activity as people shuffled in, coffee cups in hand. Colleagues approached Cooper with cordial smiles and inquiries about Tina's newfound fame.

"Heard Tina on Radio Newcastle," Neil Fuller told her as they climbed the stairs. "She's a natural."

Pride surged within Cooper as she recalled all the times selective mutism rendered Tina silent for days on end. Now, she spoke to reporters as if they were old friends.

"Your girl's a star," Keaton said, meeting Cooper at the doors to CID.

"Tell me about it. People weren't this excited when we sent Eddie Blackburn to Frankland."

"Jealous?" Keaton teased, holding the door for her.

"Proud," said Cooper. "Ridiculously proud. Now, let's get down to business."

Inside the incident room, Daljit Singh and Elliot Whyte huddled around a table with Rebecca Hogg – Becky the Techie. As Cooper entered, all eyes turned to her, their expressions a mix of excitement and concern.

"Morning, everyone." Cooper pulled up a chair. "What have we got?"

"Quite a bit, actually," Singh said as Becky's fingers flew over her laptop, entering a password so long Cooper wondered how she ever remembered it.

"The laptops that were found at Patrice Ndiaye's house," Becky said. "I've been working on them..."

"And?" said Cooper.

While Cooper and Keaton wore casual office attire and Whyte opted for a rather dashing navy suit, Becky was more relaxed in black skinny jeans and an oversized Jurassic Park hoodie. Her glasses slid down her nose as she stared at her screen, the retina display lighting her face in shades of blue.

"And he told you he took them to cover up his infatuation with Catalina."

"I wouldn't call it an infatuation," said Cooper, thinking of Ndiaye's thinly veiled threats. "But go on."

"Looks like he had something else he wanted to hide."

"If he sent unsolicited dick pics, I don't need to see the evidence," Cooper said. "It's Monday, and it's not even nine a.m."

Becky sniggered, pushed her glasses back up her nose and turned the laptop to face Cooper. "I think he took Catalina's laptop to cover up evidence of match-fixing."

"Match-fixing?" Cooper leant back in her chair, her brow furrowing. "You're saying Patrice was involved in throwing games?"

"Exactly," Becky nodded. "And it doesn't look like it was just a one-time thing either."

Cooper's mind raced, trying to make sense of the implications. Why would Patrice, an accomplished athlete, risk everything for match-fixing?

Keaton made a disgusted noise, stood and began pacing the room. "Dirty, cheating bastard."

"All right," Cooper said, her voice steady and determined. "Let's start piecing this together. Firstly, what evidence?"

Becky cleared her throat. "We found emails between Patrice and Catalina discussing specific games. He was told to lose *by any means necessary.* I did some research, and on those dates, his team always lost. He missed penalty kicks, fumbled the ball at the worst possible moment, committed deliberate-looking fouls that got the opposition free kicks or penalties."

"Show me," Cooper demanded, her eyes scanning the screen as Becky pulled up the incriminating emails followed by a video montage she'd put together of Ndiaye playing. She watched the big man drop a catch even she could make, saw him slow down so the opposition could tackle him, and watched him drop the ball for seemingly no reason.

"But why?" said Keaton, arms folded as she lurked in the corner.

"Yeah. Why would Patrice compromise his integrity like that?" Cooper asked, voicing her thoughts aloud. "Yes, he was... *in love with* Catalina," she said, making air quotes, "but surely that's not enough to make someone throw a game. What sort of athlete would lose because a woman asked him to?"

"A horny one," said Whyte, grinning. "Maybe he was so desperate to sleep with her he thought he'd stand a chance if he did what she asked?"

"Pretend you're a pro athlete. Would you miss a penalty kick because someone you fancied asked you to?" said Cooper.

"I am a pro athlete," Whyte joked, flexing his biceps before looking disappointed in himself. He pondered the question. "In a dry spell, I'd cut my own arm off if it got me laid."

"And you?" Cooper turned to Singh. "Would you miss a penalty if Amrita asked you to?"

Singh's eyes sparkled. "Without a doubt."

Cooper glanced at Keaton but knew better than to ask the question. Keaton would sooner die than lose on purpose.

Reading her mind, Keaton said, "Let's be honest, there's nothing dumber than a horny bloke. But Catalina? Why would she do this? The better Patrice played, the more he earned from his sponsors. Catalina would have taken a percentage of every deal, so the better he did, the better she did."

"Because someone made her." Becky closed the laptop and returned it to its case.

"Who?" asked Whyte.

"You mean the mob?" Cooper asked, her instincts kicking in. "You mean Chen Long? The Dragon?"

Singh shook his head. "No, that doesn't fit Long's style. He was into drugs and money laundering, not match-fixing."

"Then who?" Cooper pressed.

"I don't know," said Becky. "Sorry. But whoever it was, they covered their tracks."

Cooper felt the puzzle pieces shifting but not yet clicking into place. "We need to find out who's pulling the strings here. Keep digging through those emails, Becky. See if there's any mention of a boss or contact. And look for any financial transactions that might lead us to them."

"I'll do my best," Becky said, putting her laptop in her shoulder bag. "But if everything was offline, in person and cash-based, there won't be a digital trail for me to follow."

Cooper sighed. "I know. But we have to start somewhere."

"We'll also have to interrogate Patrice again," said Singh. "See if he'll give up any information."

"Good luck with that," Keaton muttered. "He's not exactly been forthcoming so far."

Cooper knew Keaton was right. Ndiaye had been tight-lipped during his first interview. But Cooper had a feeling that they were missing something. She just needed to figure out what it was.

The door flew open. Boyd rushed into the room, wearing a tailored suit and smart heels. "Sorry to interrupt," she said breathlessly. "You won't believe it, ma'am."

"Don't tell me," said Whyte, getting to his feet. "Sleeping beauty has awoken from his slumber?"

When Cooper looked blankly at him, Boyd translated, "Grant Salcombe. The pervert who was pushed off Wearmouth Bridge."

Cooper sat up straight. "He's out of his coma?"

"He is indeed," said Boyd. "If you can spare DS Whyte, I think we should head over to the hospital right now."

That was a turn-up for the books.

"He's all yours," Cooper said with a smile. "But I'm sure his doctors will want you to go easy on him."

Whyte brushed his hair back, his intensely dark eyes fixed on hers. "And I'm sure you want us to do no such thing."

- Chapter 42 -

DS Elliot Whyte and DC Saffron Boyd pulled up to the modern facade of Sunderland Royal Hospital. Pale brick and glass, the emergency department loomed over them. A row of ambulances were parked outside, protected from the wind by a shard of blue jutting from the building, thick white letters spelling *Emergency.* Situated in a bustling pocket of Sunderland, the hospital was a short drive from the city centre and Wearmouth Bridge – the very bridge where Grant Salcombe's car had been found abandoned.

"Here we are," Whyte muttered as he exited the car, his swarthy, stoic features set against the cold.

Boyd, her blonde hair styled in a simple French plait, gave him a silent nod and followed suit. A shiver ran down her spine, her nerves prickling with the same unease she always felt when confronted with men like Grant Salcombe.

Salcombe had survived being pushed off the bridge but had been lying comatose ever since. Whyte and Boyd suspected he was the latest target of a vigilante who attacked men who attacked women. A vigilante who watched potential predators stalk their prey, then struck with all the mercy of an executioner.

As they strode through the sterile corridors, the sharp smell of disinfectant filled their nostrils. They reached the ward where Salcombe lay and were met by a stony nurse who greeted them curtly. Whyte and Boyd showed their badges, and the nurse led them to Salcombe's room. He was hooked up to various monitors and machines, some beeping, some whirring. He looked sickly and powerless, but Boyd pushed aside any sympathy she might have had for him. Salcombe was a predator, and he deserved whatever punishment came his way.

His eyes fluttered open at their approach, revealing pain and annoyance in equal measure.

"Mr. Salcombe," Whyte began, his voice clipped and icy. "We want to talk to you about what happened in the early hours of Wednesday morning."

Salcombe hesitated, his gaze darting between Whyte and Boyd. "I— I don't remember much," he stammered, avoiding direct eye contact.

"Try," Boyd prompted gently. His stocky build and broad face reminded her of her old DCI in West Yorkshire. "You were driving along Bridge Street at two forty-five a.m."

"Was I?"

Boyd didn't know if Salcombe's amnesia was genuine or convenient, but she continued to prod. "Yes. Your car was seen on CCTV on the corner of Bridge Street and High Street."

"Then I guess I was," he said, wincing slightly as he tried to adjust his body in the hospital bed. Both of his legs were in plaster casts.

"Why did you stop your car on the bridge?" Boyd asked.

Salcombe glanced at Whyte before answering. "I'm not sure. I'm struggling to remember."

"You don't remember pulling onto the curb? You parked at an odd angle. You were completely blocking the pavement."

"Erm. There was a bang. A loud noise, like. I thought I'd run over something, so I pulled over to check me tyres."

Boyd didn't believe him. "Then what happened?"

"Some fella ran at me. Punched me in the face, proper sucker punch, like. If I'd been ready for him, I'd have— Well, I would've defended myself, wouldn't I?" He screwed his face up as pain took hold of him. After a moment, he added, "He pulled a baseball bat oot and swung it at me so hard I went over the railing. Next thing I know, I'm in here and being telt the police wanted to speak to me."

"Can you describe him?" Whyte asked, his tone conveying that he too wasn't buying Salcombe's act. And with good reason.

"Uh, he was a big bloke. I can tell you that for nowt. And he was wearing this creepy mask."

"A mask?" Boyd's pen hovered over her notepad. "Like a balaclava?"

"No, pet. Like a—"

"My name's DC Boyd. I'm not your *pet*."

Boyd could feel her chest tightening.

Salcombe wrinkled his nose. "Nah, luv. I didn't mean it like—"

"I'm not your *luv* either," said Boyd.

"You treat all your assault victims like this?" Salcombe muttered. "I was punched in the face, hit with a baseball bat and fell off a bridge."

"What kind of mask?" Boyd asked, ignoring his objection.

"Like one a superhero would wear."

"Superhero?" Boyd questioned, raising an eyebrow. "Like Batman?"

"Sort of..." Salcombe admitted reluctantly. He moved to fold his arms but evidently was in so much pain he changed his mind and hit the morphine button instead. "But without the ears. And there was nee cape before ya ask."

Whyte and Boyd traded glances.

"Anything else you can remember?" Whyte asked.

Salcombe shook his head, his expression guarded. "That's all I've got."

"Right then," Whyte said tersely. "Was anyone else around at the time? Did anyone witness you being attacked?"

Salcombe was quiet, his eyes searching Whyte's face. "No. I don't think so."

"No one at all?"

"No. Just me and the psycho."

"That's very strange," said Whyte. "Isn't it DC Boyd?"

"Very strange," said Boyd. "Because we found a witness who was on the bridge that night. A young woman who not only saw you being attacked but saw everything in the preceding minutes. She said you followed her in your car and pulled across the pavement to block her path."

Salcombe swallowed. "That's nonsense. She's probably in cahoots with that masked bastard. Probably his girlfriend."

"Let me make this clear," Boyd continued. Her delicate features hardened as she cast her eyes down his body, her gaze lingering on his broken legs. "You're not going anywhere for a while, and while you're enjoying the comforts of the NHS, we'll be busy gathering evidence. Evidence against your attacker, but also against you. Get some rest, Mr Salcombe. We'll see you again soon."

They left Salcombe to his thoughts and walked through the hospital's hallways, their steps in sync. The polished floors gleamed under fluorescent lighting, their shadows shifting across the walls like net curtains in a breeze. The place was busy but quiet, with concerned patients and relatives waiting for X-rays and blood tests.

"Bloody hell, Saff." Whyte unlocked the car and jumped in. "Remind me never to call you *pet*."

She sat next to him, her cheeks flushed. "I'm still shaking," she said, holding her hands out before her.

"You really let him have it. Good for you. I bet he's squirming all night now."

Boyd smiled coyly, feeling a glimmer of the person she'd been a long time ago. She was getting there. Slowly.

"As if you'd call me pet," she said, tucking her shaking hands under her armpits.

"My dad would," said Whyte, starting the engine.

"Yeah, but he's not a creepy sex pest."

"No," said Whyte. "He's a gentleman. You'll have to meet him one day, you and Oliver. Come for Sunday dinner."

"I'd like that. Count us in."

Whyte left the car park, turning right and then left. "So what do you make of this mask the attacker was wearing?"

"We've got someone dressing like a superhero and saving women who are being attacked or are about to be."

"What would drive a person to do that?"

Boyd thought about it while they waited for a gap in the traffic to join the A183.

"A messiah complex, maybe? He might believe he's on a special mission to help others. He might perceive himself as some sort of saviour."

Whyte scoffed. "Maybe he just likes hitting people round the head with a baseball bat."

"I'm sure he does," Boyd said. "He might have some past trauma he's trying to work through, or he might even be narcissistic, doing it for the attention he'll no doubt receive when this all comes out."

"Maybe he's hoping to score with the women he saves."

Now Boyd scoffed. "You might be on to something there." She sighed before unfolding her arms and wiggling her fingers in front of the air vents. "Sunderland's own superhero."

Whyte took a left. "The Masked Mackem."

- CHAPTER 43 -

SIXTEEN MILES NORTH, DI Daljit Singh approached Camperdown Industrial Estate. The roller-shuttered units brought back memories of Team Valley. The images rushed through his mind, but he fought them one by one, not allowing nausea or weakness to take hold. He shook off the clammy chill and focused on the task at hand.

"Unit five," he muttered to himself, scanning the numbers on each door until he found the one he was looking for. After Frank McKenna's suicide, a search of his home found bills for a self-storage facility. He and Cooper doubted McKenna's guilt, especially after what was found on Catalina East's laptop. Still, they didn't want to leave any stones unturned, and if something in the unit pointed to McKenna's guilt or innocence, it was Singh's responsibility to find it.

After speaking to the facility manager, Singh was shown the unit. He thought of his new home in CID at HQ and wondered what the team thought of him. He hoped he'd made a good impression but knew they were silently comparing him to Daniel, the man everyone called Tennessee. Cooper seemed nice enough, but he'd spotted a vague look of surprise and sadness on her face on occasions when she glanced at Daniel's old desk and saw him sitting there instead. He'd heard she was a determined, driven woman and a good boss. From what he'd witnessed so far, that was true. He'd also heard she was a bit of a rocker and that she'd given birth in jail. He didn't know how true that was.

The manager rolled up the metal door, revealing a dimly lit space cluttered with boxes and assorted items.

"I'll leave you to it," the manager said. "I'll be at the front desk if you need me."

Singh thanked him and stepped inside, a sense of foreboding enveloping him. He took a deep breath and, with gloved fingers, began opening the boxes methodically.

Old clothes, tools. Nothing out of the ordinary. He opened an old, dusty box to find video cassettes, DVDs and vinyl records. He closed it again and moved it to one side. At the far end of the unit, tucked in a corner, he spotted a cobweb-covered golf bag and trolley. Singh eyed the clubs carefully, noting their worn grips and scratched faces. He removed them one by one until he saw it – a baseball bat hidden at the bottom of the bag.

"Well, well, well. What do we have here?" he whispered, heart racing.

He picked up the bat, feeling its weight. "Liar, liar, pants on fire."

Although, now he thought about it, now he remembered being in McKenna's office, watching the man with his puffy face and fancy suit. Had he lied? They'd asked if he owned a baseball bat. He'd said he didn't play baseball. He never actually answered the question.

Councillors, politicians, all the blooming same. Can never answer the blooming question.

Observing the scratches and dents covering the surface of the bat, Singh wondered if it could be the weapon used to beat Hope and Catalina East before their throats were cut? He needed to know.

Singh pulled out his phone and dialled forensics. Cooper's boyfriend answered. "Mr Atkinson? My name is DI Daljit Singh... Yes, that's right. Yes, recently joined the team... Thank you, Mr Atkinson... Thank you, Justin."

"What can I do for you?" Atkinson asked.

"I found something in McKenna's storage unit. A baseball bat. I need it tested for the Easts' DNA. ASAP."

"Understood. I'll send someone to pick it up straight away."

"Thank you." Singh disconnected the call. If Hope or Catalina's DNA was on this, it could change everything.

As he stood alone in the square, breeze block room, lost in thought, Singh couldn't help but wonder what other secrets McKenna might have hidden in the unit.

COOPER LEANT BACK IN her chair, fingers patting the desk as she waited for the rest of the team to return. The office buzzed with murmured conversations and ringing phones, but it all felt like background noise compared to her mind, which raced with ideas and theories about the three cases they were working on. Her brain was filled with images of Hope and Catalina, their little boy, and the riots that followed their deaths. She tried to shake the sense of walking through Team Valley, seeing the house in Blackpool and the empty look in Willow's eyes. She closed her own eyes and inhaled deeply, trying to clear her head. But when she opened them, she found herself facing the murder board, and all the same imagery returned to her once more.

She needed that bloody holiday.

As if on cue, she heard the familiar sound of Whyte's low voice. Cooper looked up to see him and Boyd walking towards her desk, chatting like old friends. She had to admit, when the pair first joined her team during the Blackburn case, she assumed Whyte would hit on Boyd, chew her up and spit her out. Cooper had unfairly judged him on something he did when he was barely out of his teens.

Guilt punched her in the stomach. Whyte and Boyd were a great pair. She could see the way Boyd was building in confidence around him and the way Whyte was developing his soft skills. She straightened in her seat.

"Any news?"

"Boss," Whyte greeted as they approached. He looked pleased to see her. "You should have seen Saff. She was brilliant. Thinks we're dealing with someone with a messiah complex or – what was the other one?"

Boyd blushed. "Hero syndrome."

"Or some plain old narcissism," he added. "But here's where it gets interesting. We marked all the Masked Mackem assaults and deaths on this map—"

Cooper's eyes widened. "The Masked what?"

"Mackem," said Boyd. "Someone from Sunderland."

"I know what a Mackem is," she said, laughing. "What do you mean by the Masked Mackem? It sounds like the world's shittest comic book."

Whyte sat beside her. "I'd buy it."

"Yeah. You would," said Cooper dryly. "I feel like I'm a few steps behind. Fill me in."

"Salcombe told us his assailant was wearing a mask. Like Batman but without the ears."

"And without the cape," added Boyd.

"Yeah. No cape." Whyte clasped his hands in his lap. "I know it sounds ridiculous, but we have someone who's either following vulnerable women around and waiting for them to be attacked so he can jump in and save the day, or he's stalking men who have form in this area and waiting for them to strike so he can jump in and kill them."

"We nicknamed him the Masked Mackem," Boyd said. "But this is a dangerous man. He's killed at least three men, and he almost killed a fourth."

Whyte stirred. "Or we could look at it that he's saved at least four women."

"It can be both," Cooper said. "But we need to find him. You said something about a map?"

"Yes." Boyd opened a folder and retrieved four sheets of A4 that had been sellotaped together. She unfolded them to show a printout of Google Maps. "It's a bit messy, but I couldn't find a physical map. Had to print one out."

She spread it on the desk and pointed to where they'd drawn circles in red marker pen. "Here's Roker, where Lee Edwards was killed. Not too far away from Wearmouth Bridge, where Grant Salcombe was attacked. Down here," she moved her finger southwest, "is Hetton-le-Hole, where Vikram Sharma died. And over to the east is Seaham, just over the Durham border. Jamie Brown lived in South Hylton but was discovered at the bottom of the cliffs at Nose's Point."

Cooper examined the map, studying the red circles. It was hard to ignore the way they seemed to radiate around a specific area. An area she recognised all too well.

She placed he index finger on a patch of green between Doxford Park and Ryhope. "This is where Mick Hunter lives," she muttered, voice sceptical and yet curious.

"Exactly," Whyte said. "Maybe we've been looking at him for the wrong crime. All these crime scenes are within a twenty-minute drive of his house."

Cooper ran her fingers over Ryhope, Silksworth and Farringdon. "No," she said. "There must be fifty-thousand people living in that general area."

"But how many of them are big, strong men?"

Cooper did some quick maths. "One in ten might fit the bill physically. That's still five thousand."

"And how many of those could have the narcissism of having once been famous and the hero syndrome of someone who lost a son? He used to fight for fame and fortune. Now he's fighting for a purpose."

She shook her head at Whyte. "I can see why you're both excited by this. But no, it's tenuous at best, and if we go rushing over there making accusations, he'll shout police harassment and rightfully so."

Disappointment flickered on Whyte's face. "Isn't it worth a conversation? Maybe we could pay him a visit for another reason. We could take his statement regarding the pit bulls, make chit chat, ask if he's been to Roker Beach recently, see if he flinches."

Cooper pinched her nose and felt like she was arguing with Tina: a losing battle. She sighed. "Can I trust you to be subtle?"

Whyte and Boyd nodded enthusiastically.

"Oh, Jeez," Cooper said, fearing the harassment claim already. "I'll go. You two can't even nod subtly."

- Chapter 44 -

The lowering sun coloured the sky an eerie blend of purple and orange as Cooper and Keaton pulled up to Hunter's house. The wind howled through the trees, and dark shadows flittered across his unkempt garden.

"Can't believe we're back here," Keaton muttered, eyeing the isolated house suspiciously.

"We're just here to talk about the dogs," Cooper replied, her gut churning uneasily. "And to make small talk."

Keaton unbuckled and stepped out of the car. "Remind me again how we casually drop all this into the conversation. *Hey, Mick. Long time no see. Remember how we had your dogs confiscated? Yeah, no hard feelings, mate. Now, while we're here, did you happen to throw anyone off Wearmouth Bridge recently?*"

"Something like that," Cooper said with an empty laugh.

As they approached the front door, it burst open. Then out they came – the same two hulking American pit bulls that should have been seized a few days earlier. They bounded down the steps with an eagerness that raised Cooper's fight or flight response.

"Back in the car," she yelled.

They barely had time to scramble in before the dogs were upon them.

Snarling and baring their lethal teeth, the dogs clawed at the car's doors and snapped at the tyres. Making eye contact with the one on the driver's side, Cooper thought she was looking at a hound from hell. Behind it, she spotted Mick Hunter taking off on foot, sprinting through the fields surrounding his home.

"Oh, here we go," Keaton said, flinching as a dog pounded against her window. "Set the bloody dogs on us while he legs it. Does that look like an innocent man to you?"

"And why the hell weren't the dogs seized when I reported it? They're a banned breed."

"Budget cuts," guessed Keaton, cowering away from the window.

The dogs' muscular bodies tensed like coiled springs before pouncing at the car, unleashing pent-up fury.

Cooper revved the engine and edged the car forward. As much as she knew the dogs would likely be put down, she didn't want to be the one to kill them.

"Oh, get out the way," she urged, beeping her horn. Eventually, the dogs withdrew, allowing

Cooper to accelerate along the shadow-laden country lane, her tyres spitting gravel behind them.

"Where's he going?" Keaton asked, leaning forward, shading her eyes from the low sun as the lane wound through overgrown hedges and tall, whispering grasses.

Cooper kept her eyes on Hunter's form as he ran in the distance. "No idea, but we're going to find out."

They followed him through the narrow roads, braking for every blind turn. They lost Hunter when he hopped a fence and traversed a field, only to find him again minutes later around another bend. "He's not looking back," Keaton said after a minute.

"I know." Cooper slowed, then accelerated again. "It's like he's running towards something rather than running away from us."

Eventually, Hunter led them to a small, quiet cemetery on the outskirts of Ryhope. It was dusk, and the air was heavy with humidity. Rain was coming.

"What's he doing here?" Cooper whispered.

She pulled up not too far from where Hunter had come to a halt. He stood by a grave, his broad shoulders slumped, and his fists clenched.

His son's grave. MJ's grave.

Cooper showed her empty palms as she stepped out of her car. "We came to talk about your dogs," she said, but the lie tasted bitter in her mouth.

Hunter sensed it, flicking her a dismissive look. "Aye, right."

He reached forward and touched the grave marker shaped like a teddy bear. He rested his large hand on the stone, stroking it with his thumb. Eventually, he said, "When I was fighting, MJ was too young to understand. We used to tell him I was a superhero and had to fight the bad guys. What sort of superhero can't even save his own son?"

Cooper watched as Hunter's shoulders shook. She could feel his grief radiating from him.

Keaton stepped forward. "From what I've seen and read, you're a great father. Look, I had a real arsehole for a father, the sort who'd... Put it this way, he didn't hit other consenting adults like you did. He preferred to hit his wife and kids."

Hunter's face seemed to both soften and harden at once. Cooper could see his pity for Keaton and his repulsion at her father, and though they looked nothing alike, it was a look that reminded her so much of Tennessee that it hurt.

"So, yeah," said Keaton. "I know a crappy dad when I see one, and you're not it."

He lowered his eyes.

"Why did you run?" she asked.

"Because I know you didn't come to talk about my dogs. You think I killed all those people."

"No," said Cooper. "We think someone as skilled as you are did."

"Any idiot can learn a choke. You've got school kids doing it on their lunch breaks."

"Not against man after man after man," Cooper said. "Not with such extreme force and accuracy that their victims can't scream for help or fight back. Not with such brutality that they render them completely helpless. But we're not here to talk about that, not exactly anyway."

Hunter's cold eyes met hers.

"We wondered where you were on Tuesday night and Wednesday morning."

"Why? And don't give me any bullshit about my dogs."

Cooper took a breath and decided Mick Hunter would likely prefer straight talking over vague insinuations and beating around the bush.

"Someone, possibly the same person who committed the Team Valley massacre, seems to be on a mission to protect the people of Sunderland from potential rapists." She watched his expression as she spoke. Still. Confused. Drained.

"And you want to catch him? Sounds to me like you should hire him."

"He's killed at least three that we know of. A fourth is in hospital," Cooper said. "All four attacks are within a twenty-minute drive of your house. We have reason to believe the perpetrator thinks of himself as..." She hesitated, knowing the hurt she might cause. "...as a superhero."

Hunter's eyes were now red-rimmed and wet. "It wasn't me," he said. "I rarely leave the house these days. I go out to walk the dogs, and that's pretty much it. And a twenty-minute drive, that's what, a two-hour walk?"

Hunter wiped his eyes with the back of his huge, callused hand. "I don't drive, detective. I can't." He pointed to his left eye. "One too many retina tears. No depth perception. So unless you think I walked two hours there and two hours back to..."

His words faded as a car pulled up. A young man got out. He looked like a slimmer, clean-cut version of Hunter. The same square jaw, the same sorrowful eyes. Cooper remembered standing in the Hunters' hallway, staring at the photograph of their happy children at DisneyWorld. Elijah, was it? Uriah?

"Dad?" he called as he approached.

Hunter took a shuddering breath and wrapped his ginormous arms around his son.

"Why won't you leave him alone?" he asked. "If you knew what he'd been through, if you knew all he sacrificed for us. This man's a hero."

"This is my eldest," said Hunter. "Uriah."

"Uri," said the son. "Did you know Dad was only seventeen when Mum was pregnant with me? He didn't run away from his responsibilities. He married her. How many seventeen-year-olds would do that?"

Not many, thought Cooper. Thinking of the absolute waste of space that Tina had to call her father.

"All he ever wanted was to give us a better start in life than he had. He took up one of the most dangerous jobs going to make sure we didn't live in poverty, and he was bloody good at it too."

Uri gently supported his father's weight, holding him around the waist in a comforting embrace.

"Almost won it all," said Hunter with a sniffle. "But what's the point of winning it all only to lose one of the most precious things in life?" His knees almost buckled as he stared down at MJ's grave. "I'm so proud of all my children," he said, hugging his son tighter. "You know that, don't you?" He looked at Cooper and Keaton. "Uriah's going to be a chef. He's at catering college. And Cat's learning a trade. Going to set up her own business when she graduates."

"We're a reflection of you, Dad," Uri said, tears in his eyes as well. He pressed a finger into his father's chest. "It's because of you we want to make something of ourselves. You're the one who taught us about hard work and discipline."

A distant owl hooted, its melancholic call momentarily drawing their attention to the dusky sky.

Uri swallowed. "You set a good example for us, made us do our rounds every morning, made sure we stuck in at school."

As the owl took flight, swooping low over the cemetery, Uri pulled a key fob from his pocket and unlocked the car. The beep-beep sound of the fob symbolising their conversation was over; he was taking his father home.

"Come on, Dad."

Hunter straightened up and composed himself, his features becoming impassive, concealing his inner feelings.

"I don't know anything about those murders, detectives. But I'm not surprised you came knocking on my door. Everyone in town thinks I'm some sort of savage."

As he walked away, the fading light seemed to soften his frame, disguise his hard edges. Hunter looked like neither a villain nor a hero. Just a broken man searching for the missing piece of his soul.

- Chapter 45 -

Cooper's morning had been a blur. It was Tuesday, and though Tina tried to hide it behind a facade of pale foundation and heavy kohl, her excitement was palpable. She was positively hyperactive over the idea of a camera crew coming to watch her train that evening. She sprinted out to school with far more enthusiasm than her new gothic look should allow. Julie had come by to watch Danny while Atkinson worked the next three days. Her bar in the Canaries was doing well but still had no buyer, and she was considering taking it off the market for the time being.

As Cooper sat in the car outside headquarters in Wallsend, she felt the familiar pang of working mum guilt. As she'd left for work, Danny had uttered what sounded like *Mama*. She knew it was just baby babble at this age and didn't really count as his first word, but still, she ached to stay home with him, to witness each of these fleeting moments. Not all day, every day, of course. She loved being a DCI, but on days like today, the weight of missing these small yet significant milestones settled heavily in her heart.

She also couldn't escape her remorse over her preconceived ideas about Mick Hunter. Just because the man was trained to kill didn't mean he was a killer. He was a man in the worst pain imaginable, spending every day in the living hell that comes with losing a child.

Shaking off her thoughts, Cooper walked into HQ, ready for the morning briefing. The air was cold, and the ground was wet from the previous night's rainfall. Small puddles formed by the curb, and Cooper's shoes splashed as she walked towards the entrance. The building was busy as usual, with officers hurrying to and fro and the sound of phones ringing non-stop. She made her way upstairs to the briefing room, where she'd wait for the troops to assemble.

"Morning, everyone," Cooper said as she entered the room. Keaton was already there, sipping coffee and flipping through a file. Cooper sat near the front of the room, trying to shake off her lingering shame.

The room filled up quickly. Cooper checked her watch; Singh wasn't there yet. Disappointing, she thought. She expected punctuality from a DI, and he'd shown good timekeeping so far.

"Alright, let's get started," Cooper said.

She began to go over their current cases and what she expected from the team going forward. She covered the developments in the Masked

Mackem case and asked that his nickname stay within those four walls. She updated the team on Oliver Martin's recovery and how he'd be returning to work in a few days. He'd require crutches for a few weeks and physiotherapy for a few months, but he looked forward to seeing everyone again.

Cooper was about to inform the group that Billy – Belinda – the girl from Blackpool, had been located when Singh arrived carrying an evidence bag filled with old VCR tapes.

"Look who brought the 80s back," Keaton joked, raising an eyebrow at the outdated technology.

"Sorry for my tardiness," he said to Cooper, then turning to Keaton, "I am rather partial to some Stock, Aitken & Waterman."

"I didn't have you pipped as a Bananarama fan," said Keaton."

"You can't go wrong with a bit of Kylie and Jason."

Cooper, unsure if Singh was serious or pulling their legs, steered the conversation back to the task at hand.

"Good find at McKenna's storage locker, DI Singh. Any word when the test results will be in."

"Thank you, boss," Singh replied, placing the evidence bag on the table. "The baseball bat is in the queue to be processed. I'll update you as soon as I hear otherwise."

"And what's with the VCRs?" Cooper asked.

"I found these in Frank McKenna's storage locker," Singh explained, holding up the bag of videotapes. "It took me a while to locate a

VCR player. Did you know Panasonic stopped manufacturing them over a decade ago?"

The room fell silent as Singh continued, a collective curiosity taking hold of them.

"They contain footage from a hidden camera in the women's toilets at the Civic Centre."

"You're shitting me?" said an officer near the back. Realising his unintended pun, he covered his mouth with his hand.

"I kid you not," said Singh. "McKenna's creepy behaviour had been going on for a long time. Mayor East recorded that a lady called Jane Bailey had heard a camera shutter while in the women's toilets. He must have changed to video at some point after that."

"Now we have proof," Keaton said. "We can get justice for Jane Bailey, Sarah Sweetland and the other women who'd put their faith in Mayor East."

"Brief the press," Cooper told Singh. "Everyone will know the accusations are true. McKenna can't escape it, even in death. Well done, Daljit."

He replied with a formal nod followed by a wide smile.

"But do we really think McKenna killed Hope and Catalina?" Keaton asked.

"The baseball bat in his storage locker's pretty damning," said someone from the back.

"Surely he would have disposed of it better than that if he was guilty," Keaton countered.

Cooper agreed. "We'll wait for the results."

"Besides," Keaton continued, "Chen Long said he knew who killed them, and it wasn't McKenna."

"Can we really believe anything Long said?" Cooper asked, sceptical. "I've seen zeppelins that weren't as high as he was."

"Good point." Keaton tightened her ponytail and slumped down her seat.

Cooper glanced around the room, noting the serious expressions on her team's faces. Saffron Boyd absentmindedly played with a dainty silver chain around her wrist, her mind probably on her injured boyfriend. Cooper wondered if McKenna could be guilty of the mayor's murder. If not, why kill himself? Were the accusations about this behaviour enough to push him over the edge? Unless the mayor's real killer had seen McKenna as a good scapegoat and thought his death would solidify his guilt. But Cooper has seen the CCTV from the level crossing herself now. He wasn't pushed.

A phone ringing interrupted Cooper's thoughts and cut through the tense atmosphere. Boyd picked it up, putting a finger in her free ear to hear the caller better. She listened momentarily, then said, "Sorry to interrupt, boss." Boyd covered the receiver with her hand. "It's Mick Hunter. He wants to speak to you."

- Chapter 46 -

Cooper scanned the crowd of shoppers in The Bridges, a shopping centre in the heart of Sunderland. She could smell an odd mix of perfume and pastry, the former coming from Boots and the latter coming from Greggs. Laughter and conversation could be heard throughout the shopping centre as consumers moved between the various stores. For a Tuesday morning during term time, the place was still relatively busy. Stay-at-home parents and those out of work mixed with students and the odd waif strung out on spice who had nowhere else to be.

It didn't take long for her to spot Mick Hunter. The burly man stood out like a sore thumb amongst the throng of shoppers.

"Mick," she said, shaking his enormous hand and feeling years of calluses and scar tissue. "I could have met you at your house."

"Kim dropped me off," he said. "She's got a pilates class nearby. And after what I said last night, I figured I should give leaving the house a go."

Though his words were friendly, his tone was guarded. He looked about nervously, shifting his body to avoid the slightest contact with anyone passing by. "Cuppa?"

"Sure," Cooper said, scrutinising her options. "It's on me. Are you a Starbucks or a Caffé Nero guy?"

"Neither," he said. "This way."

Hunter led her to Waterstones. Once inside the bookstore, they passed tables offering half-price reads and climbed the stairs to the first floor, where a cosy-looking café awaited.

"Wanted to pick up the new Lee Child," he muttered, then, almost defensively, "I can read, by the way."

Cooper winced inwardly at the judgement the man must face daily: His build and appearance, his job, the brutal knockouts and injuries sustained, his accent and working-class roots. Then, there was the loss of a child and the pitying glances that came with it. It wasn't fair, but she had to remind herself that she hadn't ruled him out of her investigation.

They ordered their drinks – Americano for Hunter, hot chocolate for Cooper – and settled into low, cushioned seats amidst the quiet hum of bookworms absorbed in literary escapes. It was a calm haven, with the soft murmur of page turns and the gentle clink of cups on saucers creating a hushed backdrop to their conversation.

Sipping cautiously at her hot drink, Cooper studied Hunter's creased brow. "You said you wanted to talk in person. That you had information."

Back to the wall, his voice barely above a whisper, Hunter said, "I think I know who's behind the massacre."

Cooper put her cup down, aware her hands had started to shake.

"Who?" she asked.

He squirmed, apparently wrestling with what he was about to say. He leant towards her, eyes fixed on his coffee.

"Someone I used to train. Private lessons," Hunter confided. "About four years ago, maybe five, someone got in contact with me. Remember that youth football coach in North Yorkshire? Ian Preston?"

Cooper shook her head.

"The club made a big song and dance about ensuring everyone was properly vetted and all that. But that's the thing with these DBS checks: they can't predict the future. If you've never been caught, you have a clear DBS. Anyway, Preston's in jail now."

"Who did you give private lessons to?"

"One of the dads," Hunter said. "His twin boys were coached by Preston. His boys were young. I often wonder if, in time, they'll completely forget what happened. Might not, you know, but I hope they do. Anyway, their dad needed an outlet. He was going mad. You do, like, go mad. You feel powerless, and so consumed with hatred... He contacted me. He thought some combat training would give him something to focus on, and he... He knew my story. Knew I'd understand."

They waited for two teas to be served to the table behind them before continuing. Cooper stirred her drink and took a sip. The hot chocolate was delicious. Another sip.

"I didn't want to take the job at first. To be honest, I didn't want to play therapist. Didn't want to hear about someone else's problems. This is going to sound pretty effin' heartless, but his boys were alive. MJ was dead."

He wiped his face, avoiding Cooper's stare. "Aye, that sounds cold. But I had bills to pay. After getting knocked out so badly, I didn't get many fight offers, so I decided to train him. Kim would drive me down three times a week, and we'd train for hours at a time. Hours. Turned out... Well, I got as much out of it as he did. It was restorative, like. I felt needed again. Realised I still had something to offer the world. That's why I feel a bit shit telling you this."

Hunter's large palms wrapped around his cup, steam coiled towards his face. He blew it away.

"You think he's capable of this?" Cooper asked, her voice hushed yet urgent.

"More than capable," Hunter admitted, his jaw tense. "I trained him to a damn high standard, just like everyone I train. If he was ten years younger, he could have competed. He was a natural. A real grafter. He put the hours in, and he certainly had the aggression. He would, after what happened."

"You taught him the sort of chokes—"

"Of course. It was my speciality."

"Why didn't you tell me this yesterday?"

He shrugged. "I'd like to say it only just occurred to me, but I think it was in the back of my mind. Dunno. Some sense of loyalty?"

Cooper's heart raced, and her hands shook. The dark, chocolatey liquid in her cup rippled in response.

"Who is it?" she asked urgently. "Give me a name, Mick."

Hunter's eyes darted around the café as if he expected the man in question to materialise right there. "His name is George. George Anderson."

"Where can we find him?" she pressed. "North Yorkshire?"

Hunter hesitated, his eyes clouded with inner turmoil. "I don't know," he said finally. But Cooper suspected he didn't want to cross some invisible line in his head. Hunter had provided a name; giving her an address was a step too far for the big man.

"Fine," Cooper said. "You've given me a name. I'll do the rest."

- Chapter 47 -

I hate this

GA – 22:42

???

Mingling in their filthy world to get intel. Pretending to be one of these people. It's disgusting.

GA – 22:46

Don't call them people. They're not human. Not even animals.

True.

GA – 22:51

So, where's our next target?

There's a bloke you can take out in Whitehaven tonight if you're up for it? I've been lurking in chat rooms, posing as a thirteen-year-old girl. Got a few sickos more than willing to chat. The usual playbook. "You sound so mature for your age… You're not like other girls… Bla bla bla." One idiot's already given out his address.

GA – 22:54

No.

??? Why not?

GA – 22:57

He hasn't committed a crime.

He invited a thirteen-year-old girl over to his house.

GA – 23:01

Except he hasn't, has he? He's invited you over.

Same thing.

GA – 23:02

It's not.

GA – 23:40

You there?

Yeah.

GA – 23:44

I'm not killing some bloke because he thought he was chatting to a kid. We take out organised gangs, and we catch them in the act. That's the deal.

GA – 23: 51

You got anything bigger?

Whispers about a meetup at a secluded holiday let next week.

GA – 23:53

Now you're talking. Where?

Somewhere out past Hexham.

GA – 23:54

Northumberland? Thought we sent a clear message at Team Valley.

I thought so too. Maybe they think lightning won't strike twice.

I'm sending you the screenshots, but I'll have to keep digging to get the details. The organisers are being even more cagey than usual.

GA – 00:02

You can do it.

I'll never get used to pretending to be one of them. It's just vile.

GA - 00:07

Stay strong.

IT WAS A GREY, miserable Wednesday morning when DS Paula Keaton's fingers tapped out a message on her phone. *Morning, pretty boy. How are you holding up?* She hit send, knowing that Martin would appreciate the jest.

His reply came quickly. *This brace is driving me mad. I'm bored out of my brain.*

Keaton dressed. She'd been through many rounds of rehab because of various injuries and knew exactly how Martin was feeling. Resting was the worst.

I'll get Whyte to drive you over to mine at the weekend, she typed. *We can hang out. A pizza and a few cans will do you the world of good.*

Martin had been there for her when she was wallowing in self-pity. The least she could do was fill him full of carbs and alcohol. Speaking of carbs – she put two slices of bread in the toaster, filled the kettle and grilled some bacon.

The bacon was sizzling when her phone buzzed. *Aww, thanks. That'll be ace. Already sick of these four walls.*

Keaton demolished her bacon toasty in four bites. She put the tea in a takeaway cup to savour en route to HQ.

You're worth it, L'Oréal, she teased.

Arriving in the incident room, Keaton was tasked with finding George Anderson, the man Mick Hunter had tipped them on to. Keaton pulled up the court records from Ian Preston's trial and skimmed through the list of witnesses and statements, her eyes scanning for George's name like a hawk searching for a mouse. There, buried in the sea of names, was George Anderson.

A bit of cross-referencing here, a search through a database there, and Keaton had a decent profile of the man.

"Inspector!" she called out, catching the attention of the new DI. He approached her desk, and despite the dark bags under his eyes, he seemed happy to be called upon.

Keaton was prepared to give Daljit Singh a fair crack of the whip; she knew others were unfairly comparing him to Tennessee. After Sutherland and Tennessee, she briefly wondered if the position was cursed. Hopefully, Singh could break that bad luck and bring some stability to the role and, in turn, the department.

"Good morning, DS Keaton. Found something?" he asked, his voice as smooth and polite as ever.

"George Anderson," she said, pointing at the screen. "The guy Mick Hunter mentioned. Full name: George Anthony Anderson, forty-six. He lives in Harrogate, but according to his socials, he's been in Morecambe for a few days, staying at the Travelodge in the town centre. He's doing a charity walk there starting later today."

"Morecambe?" Singh's eyebrows knitted together as he brought up Google Maps on a tablet. "That's not far from Blackpool."

"Exactly. The site of the last massacre."

Singh tapped a finger to his lips while he thought. "What else have you found?"

Keaton opened her notepad and pointed at her scrawling writing with the tip of her pencil.

"The charity walk. It's his charity. He set it up after what happened to his kids. It helps survivors of abuse, funds therapy and excursions, that sort of thing."

"How many people are attending?"

"That's just it. I think it's just him. People sponsor him to climb hills and mountains or walk long distances. Sometimes, he does something different, like carrying a fridge on his back or dragging a sledge, but usually, he just walks. Alone mostly, sometimes with a bloke called Yoshihiro."

"What's he doing this time?" Singh asked, taking a seat opposite Keaton.

"Walking from Morecambe to Bradford without stopping."

Singh glanced at the map again, his pupils dilating as he took in the distance. "You'd have to be pretty fit to do that."

"You'd have to be pretty fit to kill twenty-seven people with your bare hands," Keaton said. "And yeah, it'll take him nearly twenty-four hours, and a lot of that will be in the Forest of Bowland in the dark."

"And we know whoever carried out Team Valley and West Lothian is quite accustomed to working in the dark," he said. "Family?"

"Divorced. His twin boys live with his ex. They split up after the court case. From what I can tell, he leads a lonely life. Lives alone. Walks alone."

Keaton showed Singh Anderson's Instagram account. It was an endless scroll of bleak landscapes and empty horizons. Comments seemed to alternate between motivational quotes and depressed references to the black dog, the empty well and the endless night. Occasionally, he'd tag Yoshihiro – his new training partner – or give a shout-out to a corporate sponsor.

"His Facebook is exactly the same. His personal page anyway. The charity's page is more active. He interacts with people thanking him for his work and those offering to help with time, money or resources."

Anderson's online life suggested a man haunted by memories, seeking solace in the open air and the online company of the strangers who reached out to him for help.

"What do you think?" she asked.

The corners of Singh's mouth turned down. "I think I'm going to call DCI Cooper and Ms Grange. Then I think I'll be going on another little road trip."

Keaton put on her best *please-let-me-out-the-office* face and asked, "Can I come? I'll bring snacks."

COOPER WAS DRIVING IN Northumberland when Singh called. She was turning down a lane that led into woodland somewhere between Alnwick and Cragside. Facing another long day, she reminded herself that her holiday would be all the more relaxing when she and Atkinson finally got to take it. *Delayed gratification.*

She turned her headlights on as trees encroached on the narrow road, cutting out what little light was in the dull, cloud-covered sky. She pulled up at the security gates to a manor house surrounded by high stone walls. A camera angled around to view the car, and she lowered the driver's side window to stare into the lens without saying a word. After a tense moment, the gates creaked open.

Her BMW rattled over a pebbled drive, and she brought the car to a stop in front of the imposing Morshaw Manor.

"Let's hope he's feeling chatty," she muttered, killing the engine and unbuckling. Because if anyone knew about Catalina's ties to organised crime, it would be the head of this house – the notorious crime boss with a finger in every nefarious pie.

A butler-come-security guard showed her into the study. She took a deep breath as she crossed the threshold, like a mouse walking into a cattery. A tall, broad-shouldered man sat at a desk, surveying her, his tailored suit unable to hide the muscles beneath. He stood, revealing his full height and dipped his misshapen head in a curt nod.

Cooper was once again face-to-face with Dylan Blackburn.

- Chapter 48 -

"Detective Cooper," Dylan said, his voice dripping with false warmth. "To what do I owe this pleasure?"

"Hello, Dylan," Cooper said, doing well not to allow her anxiety to show in her voice. "How's the family?"

His face hardened. "Dead," he said. "Or in jail."

There was an unspoken *thanks to you* that hung in the air.

"What brings you here?"

Cooper ran her tongue around her mouth to moisten it. "The enemy of my enemy is my friend," she said.

Dylan raised his good eyebrow. "A belief my late father prescribed to. But you already knew that."

He gestured for her to sit, opened the lid on a porcelain teapot and stirred.

"Camomile?"

"Please."

Dylan poured and sat back in his seat, the china cup looking like it belonged in a doll house compared to his fearsome frame.

"So," he said, "what have my enemies done now?"

Cooper took a second to take in her surroundings. It was familiar and yet different. The study bore faint echoes of the past but had undergone significant changes since her last visit. The exquisite antique desk was still the centrepiece of the room, but the decor had been revamped. The walls featured a more modern, vibrant print. The old white carpet, which had been irreversibly bloodstained, had been replaced with a luxurious shade of navy.

Behind Dylan, a dramatic floor-to-ceiling window revealed the manor's well-tended garden. Still, it was the ancient yew tree, lopsided from multiple lightning strikes, that drew her attention. It mirrored Dylan in some ways – bearing the scars of life's brutality while still standing tall. Few knew the dint in his skull came from his father's boot. Even fewer knew the injury was sustained while Dylan was still in his mother's womb.

Cooper held her tea cup close to her nose and inhaled. The brew carried a herbaceous aroma with soothing hints of honey and citrus.

"Match-fixing," Cooper said. "What do you know about it?"

"Not as much as the Roker Bastards."

"You mean the Roker Boys?"

"I know what I said."

Cooper smirked. Little love was lost between the Blackburns and the Roker Boys, the gang controlling much of Sunderland. Despite their name, one of the head honchos was a woman.

Dylan tapped the nail of his index finger against the china teacup, creating a soft, musical *ding, ding, ding*. "The Roker Bastards have been making a song and dance about coming into some big bucks lately."

"Forgive me, Dylan. But how do you know that has anything to do with match-fixing?"

"Because they're about as subtle as a kick in the teeth. Two days after that golfer missed an absolute sitter, they were all online posing with their new Maseratis."

Dylan gave a dismissive cackle. "Fools couldn't even wait a week for it to be out of the papers."

"And?" Cooper sipped her herbal tea. It was the expensive kind that came in pretty pyramid-shaped bags.

"And they've suddenly gone to ground, haven't they? Haven't boasted about shit since the big fight two weeks ago."

Cooper swallowed, casting her mind back two weeks. Had it only been a fortnight?

Abdul Ahmed. The Tyneside Terror.

"Ahmed was the big favourite, right? Seven to one," Cooper said. "No one was surprised he won."

She touched her mouth, considering what she just said. "And that's the point. You don't make big bucks betting on the favourite, do you? You need to bet big on the underdog."

Dylan nodded as comprehension dawned on Cooper's face.

"The Yank was a massive underdog," he said, "despite having home soil advantage. Ahmed was supposed to go down in the fifth. He didn't. And you might not have noticed, but he hasn't been seen since."

Cooper stilled again, feeling her body chill from the implication. "Where is he?"

"Beats me. But when you find his body, it'll probably look much like Catalina East's."

The mere mention of Catalina's body caused Cooper to shoot to her feet. Blood pooled in her legs. She felt faint. She gripped the edge of the table for support, seeing all over again the look on the sickly first responder's face and the tears in his eyes. She recalled the fair-haired woman in her stylish outfit slumped in the alley like a grotesque, lifeless mannequin. Her gory, beaten head hanging limply, barely connected to her torso. Cooper had seen the inside of her neck, her bodily tissues, spinal bones and blood. So much blood.

The image would haunt her until the day she died.

She thought of Hope beside her wife, the caring mayor, with crushed features and a mouth missing multiple teeth. She thought of Abdul Ahmed, a man born with the deck stacked firmly against him, growing up in damp, crumbling poverty, attending inadequate schools. He used his childhood as fuel for discipline. He was a role model. She couldn't bear to picture him suffering the same fate.

"Sit down," Dylan told her. "Before you hurt yourself."

He manoeuvred his bulk from behind the desk and guided Cooper back into her chair. His hands felt heavy and firm against her shoulders, reassuring and terrifying. She knew what those hands were capable of.

A piece of art on the study wall caught Cooper's eye. A print of Newcastle at sunset; the Tyne Bridge silhouetted against a vibrant sky of purple and red.

"The city's been torn in two," she said, her voice cracking.

The same knife that had killed the Easts had slashed the city down the middle, with a chaotic sea of hatred and bigotry raging on both sides. Homophobic slurs were smeared on walls. Religious extremists blindly fuelled the fire. Opportunists took advantage of the chaos, looting and vandalising the city. Right-wingers spewed intolerance, while left-wing protesters used violence and intimidation, silencing any voice different from their own.

Newcastle had never been so dangerous.

Never felt so alien.

Cooper could barely believe it. "A goddamn culture war because they lost some money betting on sports?"

"Not *some* money," said Dylan, squeezing her shoulders before returning to his seat. "Fucking millions." He steepled his fingers in front of his chest. "And they killed Mrs East because she couldn't control her asset."

- Chapter 49 -

Under the watchful eye of the Blackburns' security guard, Cooper took a stroll around Morshaw's gardens before heading back to HQ. It was cold enough to need a coat, not cold enough to see frost on the ground. The old, scorched yew cast a long shadow across the lawn. Though the snapdragons and deadly foxgloves had faded with the summer, other plants still adorned the garden – chrysanthemums and various daisy-like flowers.

Cooper remembered walking here eighteen months ago. This was the place she and Atkinson discussed getting back together. If this house hadn't been the scene of a double murder, if they hadn't stood where she stood now, would they have ever rekindled their love? Would Danny even exist?

Fresh air, bird song and thoughts of loved ones soothed Cooper's soul. She relaxed her clenched fists and forced herself to breathe deeply. She'd considered political assassination, hate crimes and unrequited love for the death of Mayor East and her wife, Catalina. And yet, all the destruction and vandalism had been down to money.

Cooper vowed to give the Roker Boys hell for what they'd done to Newcastle.

She bid farewell to Dylan, a man she feared and pitied in equal measure, and returned to her car for the journey back to Newcastle, where she'd pick up Singh before heading west to find George Anderson and question him in relation to the massacres. When she reached Northumbria Police Headquarters in Wallsend, she was surprised to see Keaton ready to join them.

Keaton held up three paper bags. "I brought sustenance."

While Singh sat in the back, enjoying a McPlant burger with a side of veggie dippers, Keaton sat up front, feeding Cooper fries while she kept her eyes on the road.

"If we get pulled over, we're done for," she said, chewing and steering simultaneously.

"So chew faster," said Keaton, shovelling more food into her DCI's mouth before getting distracted by their eighties soundtrack. "Classic," she said, turning up a Sonia hit.

Cooper rolled her eyes at Keaton's music choice. She'd have preferred some Metallica, but the bubble-gum factory pop was a much-needed distraction from the weight of the investigation. Besides, Cooper suspected Keaton had chosen the music for Singh's benefit. As she glanced in the rearview and saw the DI nodding his head in time to the beat, she appreciated Keaton's efforts to make him feel welcome.

They were taking the scenic route past Hexham and Haltwhistle, avoiding the Tyne Tunnel and the A1(M). As they drove through the winding roads of the Northumberland countryside, Cooper zoned out, ignoring Singh's singing and Keaton's air guitar playing. Before they knew it, they'd made it to Carlisle and were heading south. That's when Marianne Grange called.

Keaton turned the radio off as Cooper pressed *accept* on her dash. "Cooper."

"I'm at the Travelodge with the local officers."

Grange's voice was as serious as ever, but it had an irritated edge today. Cooper could guess what she'd say next.

"He's already checked out."

Bingo. Three points to the lady in the BMW.

Keaton spoke up. "This is DS Keaton, ma'am. We don't know the exact route of Anderson's walk, but I know from social media that he'll cross the Lune using the pedestrian bridge. I suggest we intercept him there."

"How far are you out?" Grange asked.

Keaton checked the sat nav. "An hour. Forty-five minutes if we push it."

"I'll meet you north of the river in forty-five," said Grange before ending the call.

Cooper accelerated. "Guess I'm pushing it then."

HAVING MORE THAN PUSHED it, Cooper found a parking space in a residential area. They walked for five minutes, finding Grange on a marshy footpath sporadically flanked by tall deciduous trees. The sun shone on the western side of the UK today, casting creepy, mottled patterns on the ground.

"Any sign?" Cooper asked, glancing around. But as she said it, a man came into view. He was stocky, wearing a pale blue t-shirt with navy shorts, and was lumbered with a heavy, army-green rucksack. He wore brown walking boots and carried a hiking stick which pressed into the soft ground with each long, purposeful step.

"George?" Cooper called out as he neared.

Anderson lifted his eyes from the ground. His hair was short, his olive-toned skin carved with deep lines. "Yes?"

"I'm DCI Erica Cooper. These are my colleagues, DI Singh and DS Keaton. We're from Northumbria Police."

Anderson's eyes narrowed. "This is Lancashire."

"I'm aware, sir—"

"And I'm from the National Crime Agency. Marianne Grange. We'd like to speak with you."

Anderson continued walking. They followed.

"Has someone complained about the charity?" he asked defensively. "Every penny is accounted for. I don't take a wage from our fundraising, and you won't find any home spas being built for our directors."

"No," Cooper said. "George," her tone was cautious, "are you aware of the mass homicides that occurred in Gateshead, Scotland and Blackpool?"

"The ones that took out the grooming and trafficking gangs? Yeah. I'm aware." He spoke slowly, his voice laced with contempt.

Cooper chose her words carefully. She didn't want to refer to the people who died as victims. "While some of the dead suffered broken bones and dislocations, no weapons appear to have been used. Our pathologist believes the cause of death to be asphyxiation via blood chokes."

Anderson strode ahead, approaching the footbridge.

"Why are you telling me this?"

"Because it's our understanding that—"

"That I have such skills?" he snapped, striding ahead towards the footbridge. "Are you having this conversation with every skilled jujiteiro or judoka out there? Or just the ones whose kids have been..." His expression darkened. "Mick Hunter sent you, didn't he?"

"Please, George," said Cooper, feeling out of breath. "Can we stop and talk?"

"If you want to talk, then we walk."

Cooper exchanged a glance with Keaton, her mind racing. Anderson set a fast pace, and all but Keaton struggled to keep up. Grange, who'd stumbled a few times in her high-heeled office shoes, was falling behind. Singh walked with her, probably out of politeness rather than lack of fitness. A couple of local uniformed officers lagged further back, not interfering, just observing in case they were called upon.

"I asked Mick to sign an NDA when he started training me. I could sue him," Anderson said, his hiking stick thudding against the ground as they entered Lancaster city centre. Each bang of the stick like a symbolic knife through a heart. "Did it occur to you that Hunter might be covering up something closer to home?"

Redirection, Cooper thought.

"Actually," Grange panted from behind, catching her breath, "we've ruled Mick Hunter out of the investigation."

Lancaster centre was appealing, with many sand-coloured stone buildings and quaint churches. The garish, brightly coloured signage outside takeaways seemed out of place.

Anderson turned his head, glancing back at Grange as she practically skipped to keep up with him. "Mick Hunter isn't the only Hunter."

Cooper's thoughts immediately went to Kim, Hunter's waif-like wife. She was shorter and lighter than Cooper, and even with all the training in the world, she couldn't imagine her incapacitating anyone.

"Who suffered just as much as Mick and Kim?" asked Anderson. "Who was old enough to watch the news and read the papers? Who, despite being sheltered from it all, knew exactly what happened to MJ?"

That feeling of ice freezing her very core hit Cooper like an old friend. It was the good old adrenaline rush of having a name, or in this case, two names.

- Chapter 50 -

"Uriah and Catherine?" Cooper gasped, her heart racing. She paused to take it in, falling behind George Anderson as he strode purposefully through the streets of Lancaster on his way to the Forest of Bowland.

"Those poor kids witnessed it all," Anderson said. "Saw what it did to their parents."

Cooper knew firsthand the unbearable burden of grief, the way it twisted you up inside, leaving you raw and angry. She thought about Uri and Cat – tall, strong, and formidable like their father but carrying the weight of a tragic past they could never escape.

She ran to catch up with Anderson, her boots echoing on the old paving stones. "Did Hunter train his kids like he trained you?"

"Of course he did," Anderson replied, not breaking stride. "After MJ, he'd want to make sure they could handle themselves."

Keaton nodded. "Uri said his dad made sure they did their rounds every morning."

Cooper nodded, recalling his words at MJ's graveside. "Mick told me he trains everyone to a damn high standard."

Anderson finally paused at a junction, waiting for the lights to change so he could cross the road. "That he does. He might be a dick head, but the man's a wizard."

The thought of Uri and Cat, armed not with weapons but with skills and an unstoppable need to avenge their baby brother, made her extremities tingle. She imagined them learning to fight in a dimly lit gym, sweat dripping from their brows as they pushed their bodies to the brink, honing their craft for the inevitable day it would be called upon. Their father trained them to defend themselves; Uri and Cat trained for justice. Hardened daily by their father's relentless workouts, the pair were coached to become perfect little soldiers.

"We need to find them," Cooper said, turning to the others. "Send a team to Hunter's house."

The lights changed, and Anderson continued on his way, focused on his own mission. "Too late," he said. "They won't be there. My guess is Mick Hunter worked out it was Uri and Cat and sent you after me to buy his offspring some time."

He was probably right, Cooper thought, searching her pockets and finding a twenty-pound note. She handed it to Anderson. "For the charity."

He took the note gratefully and pressed his palms together in a sign of prayer.

While Anderson returned to his life of solitary pilgrimage, Cooper stopped at the crossroads, the shadow of Lancaster Cathedral looming over them. "Find out which catering college Uri attends, and call Sunderland Uni. Find out what Cat's studying and if she has lectures today."

"Already on it," Singh said, mobile pressed to his head.

Keaton turned her phone so Cooper could see the screen. "Uri's Instagram. His handle's rather ominous."

@Judge.Uri.and.Executioner.

"And check this out," Keaton continued, selecting a photo of Uri Hunter at a fancy dress party, dressed as Austin Powers with thick-framed glasses. "Remind you of anything?"

"Yes." Grange unlocked a tablet and opened a file. "The e-fit Willow made of the seventh man from Blackpool."

They stared at the black-and-white image, the similarities undeniable.

Singh ended the call. "Miss Catherine Hunter is enrolled on an electrical engineering course. She didn't show up for today's workshops."

Cooper swore. "They've already gone to ground."

"Electrical engineering?" Keaton echoed, realisation dawning on her face. "She must be the one who cut the power and disabled the alarms before the Team Valley and Lothian massacres."

"Any ideas where Cat and Uri might go? Relatives? Friends?" Cooper asked, her mind racing with possibilities. They turned, retracing their steps to where they'd left their cars.

"We can ask Hunter once he's in custody," Grange said.

"He's not going to tell us," said Keaton, "he'll just send us on another wild goose chase. Best we can do is get someone over to speak to their classmates, find out who their friends are, places they hang out, *et cetera*."

Cooper dialled HQ. "I'll action it."

Singh's bright eyes hardened. "If you want to find a stray cat, follow the mice. If we find their next target, we'll find the Hunters. We need someone on the dark web."

"Becky's doing her best," said Cooper.

"So are we," said Grange, doing better at keeping pace now they weren't trying to keep up with Anderson. "But it's like looking for a needle in a haystack. About eighty per cent of dark web traffic is related to child pornography. Europol managed to shut down a load of paedophile chatrooms last year, but they're essentially playing dark web whack-a-mole."

"You hit one, and another pops up," Cooper said, taking a quick side step left to avoid some dog mess.

Singh walked backwards. "If I may. Catherine and Uriah aren't targeting the sort of men who are after pictures or videos of children. They're killing the sort who want—"

"Actual real-life children," she finished. "You're right. Could that help narrow the search? What sites would they use to find events?"

Grange considered the question. "The darknet markets, I suppose."

"Like Silk Road?" Cooper asked. They'd reached the pedestrian bridge again and were heading to the north side of the Lune.

"Until the FBI shut it down. But there are plenty of others. Immoral versions of eBay or Craigslist where one can buy drugs, weapons, pornography, you name it."

"A ticket to a party?" Cooper asked, brows raised.

"I suppose so. Yes." Grange paused to look at the marshy footpath and then at her shoes. They were already ruined. She walked on. "People could bid and pay a deposit in Bitcoin, then pay the balance in cash at the venue."

Keaton visibly shuddered. "Is there really that much of a market for this sort of thing? I mean, they've already killed twenty-seven that we know of."

"Put it this way," started Grange, "the last network the German police managed to dismantle had over four hundred thousand members."

"Four hundred thousand?" echoed Cooper. That was just one site out of who knew how many. Even if she didn't have two children, she'd still feel sick to her stomach.

"Jesus H Christ," said Keaton, shaking her head and looking paler than usual.

When they reached their car, Singh held the driver's door open for Cooper.

"That's really not necessary," she told him.

"Manners maketh the man, DCI Cooper. I suggest we have a two-pronged approach. First, focus on Mick and Kim Hunter as well as any associates of Uriah and Catherine. They can't just vanish; the siblings must be out there somewhere. Second, have our friends in tech hone in on these darknet markets. If we can't find the Hunter children, we can find where they are headed."

Grange agreed and told Cooper she'd meet them at HQ tomorrow morning. She would buy herself a new pair of shoes and find a local hotel for the night.

Cooper got in the car, buckled up and promised Grange she'd have at least one Hunter in custody by the time she next saw her. She started the engine. The race was on.

- CHAPTER 51 -

SIX-THIRTY A.M. AND DCI Erica Cooper awoke with an unusual sense of enthusiasm. She couldn't wait to get to work, to press Mick Hunter on the location of his children, Uriah and Catherine. Though she had plenty of sympathy for the man and everything he had gone through, he'd given his adult children a head start, hindered their investigation and sent them to the other side of the country after an innocent man.

The morning light crept through the curtains, casting a warm glow across her duvet. Beside her, Atkinson stirred.

"Morning, beautiful."

"Morning, handsome."

They shared a shower, a fleeting moment of intimacy that occurred too infrequently between long work days and an infant son. Atkinson got out first to shave his face while Cooper stayed in to shave her legs. By the time she was out and dressed, Atkinson had brewed coffee and made toast. He was out the door before her too, planning to spend the day sweeping Uriah and Catherine Hunters' bedrooms for any of the victims' DNA. Cooper checked her emails while eating her toast until Danny's cries indicated he'd awoken. She changed him, fed him and cradled him gently, cherishing the moment before kissing his forehead and placing him back in the crib.

"Be good for Grandma, okay?" she whispered, tucking him in.

Julie arrived by half seven, excited to take her grandson to the aquarium while Tina was at school. She busied herself in the kitchen, making Tina breakfast and sending Cooper off to work with a sandwich wrapped in tin foil.

As she closed the door behind her, Cooper felt a feeling of unease wash over her. The world seemed darker now she knew the statistics Grange had shared with her. She couldn't comprehend the vastness of the problems Europol and the FBI faced. Wondering what kind of world Danny would grow up in, Cooper concluded it was a nasty one.

"Focus," she told herself, sliding into her BMW.

The drive to work was uneventful, but it provided Cooper with the time she needed to gather her thoughts and mentally prepare for the confrontation with Mick Hunter.

Upon arriving at HQ, she wasted no time. "Where's Hunter?" she asked a young officer – Lewis Haig – but before he could answer, she asked, "What the hell is that?"

A small bobblehead figure on his desk nodded perpetually, an unnerving grin plastered across its plastic face. Dressed in black trousers, a red and white striped t-shirt and a black mask over his eyes and nose, it could only be the man they'd dubbed the Masked Mackem. A few desks away, another officer sipped coffee from a matching mug, the same weird smile peering back at her.

"Lewis?"

"Masked Mackem madness, ma'am."

"Try saying that three times quickly," Cooper muttered, tapping the little figure on his bobblehead and sending it into a nodding frenzy.

"The papers have latched onto the story and the nickname. The Echo's offering a reward for whoever can unmask him."

Boyd and Whyte arrived through the doors to CID, and seeing the figure, Boyd said to Whyte, "Rumour has it, you're the Masked Mackem."

"Haddaway and shite," he said.

"That sounds like something the Masked Mackem would say," said Lewis.

"Is this based purely on me being the resident Mackem around here?"

"And no one's ever seen you in the same room," said Boyd. "It's like Clark Kent and Superman."

"Very funny," Cooper replied, rolling her eyes. "Back to my original question. Where's Mick Hunter?"

"He's in two," Boyd answered, pointing down the hall.

"Thank you." She made her way there, pulse quickening with each step.

Grange was waiting for her.

"Nice shoes," Cooper said.

"Shall we?"

Grange opened the door, and they took their seats opposite Hunter and his solicitor. The lawyer was small and squidgy with round glasses that seemed entirely too small for his face. He reminded Cooper of one of the Muppets. Scooter, perhaps.

"Mr. Hunter," Cooper said, staring straight into the man's eyes. It was hard to believe they were sharing a table in a bookstore coffee shop the last time they'd talked. Now, they shared a table in interview suite two. "We need to talk about Uriah and Catherine. They aren't at your home, and neither attended their courses yesterday."

But Mick remained silent, his face an unreadable mask. She knew this wouldn't be easy. Hunter had lost one child to murder; he didn't want to lose the other two to jail. She could see the pain in his eyes.

"Please, Mick," she pleaded. "Uri's car is gone, and every ANPR camera in the country is scanning for his plates. You know we'll find them eventually. Help us make this right."

For a moment, she thought she saw something flicker across his face – sorrow, maybe even guilt – but it was gone just as quickly. Cooper supposed that to Hunter, Uri and Cat were making things right. They were taking out Britain's worst scumbags. This was going to be a long, hard battle.

"My client will be exercising his right to remain silent," Scooter said.

"Fine," she sighed, taking a deep breath. "I'll talk, and you can listen. Forensic officers are combing over your home today. Through your electronics, diaries, calendars. They'll swab Uri and Cat's clothing and bedrooms looking for anything, no matter how microscopic, that shows they had contact with one or more of the victims."

She used the word *victim* on purpose to see if it caused a reaction in Hunter, but he sat motionless, his gaze fixed on the cold metal table before him.

Beside Cooper, Grange's face was stern, her auburn brows low. She propped her elbows on the table and said slowly, "Have you considered Uri and Cat may be in danger?"

He met her eye but said nothing.

"As I told my colleagues yesterday when you sent us to speak to George Anderson, the dark web is a vast, densely populated place. The sort of people we think your children have killed account for eighty per cent of the traffic on there. The FBI just closed a chat room with over a quarter of a million users. A quarter of a million people who, individually, might fear Uri and Cat and the urban legend-like status that now surrounds them, but collectively... Well, collectively, that's a lot of people to have a grudge against you. And that's just one chatroom."

Cooper liked Grange's idea. Hunter's instincts had always been about protecting his children. If they could convince him they'd be safer in custody, perhaps he'd talk.

"Then there's the pimps and traffickers," said Cooper.

"Yes," echoed Grange. "The people who make a lot of money selling tickets to these little paedo meetups."

"They must be losing a fair bit of income now," said Cooper. "It's not good for business having someone murder all your repeat customers."

Grange leant further towards him. Urging him to look at her. "We're going to brief the press later today, Mick. We're going to say how we wish to speak with Uri and Cat in connection to the massacres. We're going to ask the public for their assistance in finding them. Everyone in the country – including the people we just mentioned – will know their names and faces."

Still, Mick remained silent, barely even acknowledging their presence. His solicitor shifted uncomfortably in his seat but said nothing.

As the hours dragged on, frustration mounted within Cooper, her patience wearing thin. Needing a break, she stopped the interview, stepping out of the room and allowing herself some breathing space and time to regroup. She got herself a coffee and took it for a brief walk to Tennessee's bench. When she returned, not a lot had changed.

"Did you always know they were behind the killings, Mick? Did you know from the start?" she pressed, desperation creeping into her voice. "Or did you work it out recently? Did something I said or something in the news make you suspicious?"

"Or did they confess you to?" asked Grange. "Is this all a way of earning your approval?"

After twelve hours, the only words out of Mick Hunter's mouth were to ask for a toilet break.

There wasn't so much as a twitch when they told him that the press conference had gone ahead and that DI Singh had told the world Hunter's kids were suspected of murdering twenty-seven people.

Atkinson called to tell Cooper they found iPhone and Nokia chargers in Uri and Cat's bedrooms. They had monthly contracts for the iPhones, so he suspected the Nokias were burners used to communicate with each other.

"That's not evidence," Cooper said, disappointed.

"I also found an instruction leaflet for night vision goggles in Uriah's room."

"That's more like it." Owning the goggles wasn't a crime, and alone, they wouldn't be enough to charge the siblings, let alone convict them, but it was all part of a body of work they'd present to the CPS. "But I need more."

"I'll get you it," Atkinson said. "I now have hair samples with intact roots, which we can extract DNA from. Their toothbrushes too. Blackpool is the key. Team Valley and West Lothian were both pretty tidy crime scenes with no real blood and no fingerprints from what we can tell."

"They were careful," Cooper said, "but they changed their MO at Blackpool."

"And they made a considerable mess in the kitchen. I've seen the photographs. I'll liaise with the Lancashire SOCOs. If their DNA is going to be anywhere, it'll be there."

THE STEEL DOOR CLICKED shut, echoing through the empty corridor. Cooper watched as Mick Hunter walked away, his shoulders hunched and heavy with the weight of unspoken words. Thirty-six hours, and she hadn't broken him. She knew they had no choice but to release him.

She found most of the team gathered in the incident room with the same defeated expressions on their faces. They stared blankly at the murder wall, willing it to give up an extra clue. Martin was back, his foot encased in a heavy brace, a pair of crutches propped by the desk. He'd had a couple of therapy sessions and seemed oddly chipper to be back at work. Not that Cooper could talk; she'd always itched to get back to policing whenever she'd been forced to take time off.

As they looked around to greet Cooper, Singh gave her a searching look, then a smile that conveyed they'd get there if they gave it time. She admired his patience.

"I want one eye on Mick Hunter at all times. His wife too," Cooper instructed her team. "But I wouldn't get your hopes up. I don't think they're daft enough to contact their kids."

"You never know," said Singh. "Let's keep it positive."

"Yeah, you never know," said Keaton. "The kids might call home. If they do, we'll be listening."

As she paced the length of the incident room, Cooper's thoughts raced, searching for any angle they hadn't yet explored. It was a futile exercise; they'd been over every detail a thousand times already. Waiting for DNA results was like waiting for a watched pot to boil. And even if they got a match, it wouldn't help them find the Hunter siblings. There'd been a sighting in London – nothing solid – and ANPR was drawing a blank. They'd either switched vehicles or switched plates.

Her thoughts were wrenched back to the present by Elliot Whyte opening the door and tripping over his own feet.

Keaton snorted. "Well, if it isn't everyone's favourite superhero. This clumsy act's canny convincing. Good alter ego."

"Very funny," said Whyte, pushing his dark hair from his forehead. "That knacked." He twirled his ankle around a few times, wincing.

"At least your foot's still attached," said Martin with a grin.

"Aye, fair enough. Anyway, I come bearing news."

Keaton sat up. "And what say you, oh mighty Masked Mackem?"

"Give over." He turned to Cooper. "Our friends at Southwick Station have done us an absolute solid. They've completed a set of dawn raids and rounded up fifteen high-ranking members of the Roker Boys."

"Ha!" Cooper clapped her hands together. "That is good news. I could bloody kiss you."

Whyte took a small step back.

"But I won't," she clarified. "Don't go calling HR." Cooper grabbed her coat and ran a hand over her short hair. "We might not have the Hunters yet, but we have fifteen gangsters. Let's find out who killed Catalina and Mayor East."

- Chapter 52 -

Southwick, like all police stations, was designated a non-smoking area. That didn't stop it from reeking of stale cigarettes, sickly vapes and knock-off cologne. Cooper wrinkled her nose as she stepped inside, flanked by Singh.

"Smells like an ashtray in here," he muttered, voicing Cooper's thoughts.

Fifteen members of the notorious Roker Boys gang slouched on benches in the crowded booking room. Cooper eyed their gaudy tracksuits and heavy gold chains with palpable disdain. Dawn raids on their squalid flats and houses had unearthed a trove of illicit treasures: drugs, weapons, and piles of ill-gotten cash.

A heavy man in a white vest, a woollen hat, and shiny tracksuit bottoms was still wearing his slider-style slippers. Another suspect let loose a string of colourful curses as a uniformed officer confiscated jewel-encrusted knuckle dusters disguised as a harmless key chain. A third whined about missing his morning cup of tea. Cooper fought the urge to smack their smug faces. The destruction these thugs caused made her blood boil.

Amongst the crowd of reprobates, two individuals conspicuously stood out. Dressed more elegantly, they exuded an air of affluence and a slight amusement at the proceedings as if they knew they wouldn't be held for long.

"Toby Beck," Copper told Singh under her breath. "One of the four so-called top dogs."

Beck, in his sixties, with a polished demeanour, designer pyjamas and silky dressing gown, looked as though he'd stepped out of the Playboy Mansion.

Next to him, an attractive woman who could have been anything from late thirties to early fifties gave Cooper a slow look up and down. She wore a fur coat and high heels, her healthy raven hair styled into a French braid. Her teeth were as fake as her tan. The jury was out on her boobs.

"Kayla Dunn," Cooper informed Singh. "Another of the top dogs."

Singh sucked his cheeks in, concentration written all over his face.

"You're wondering how to make a *top-bitch* joke without offending me, aren't you?"

Singh smirked. "I was doing no such thing, Detective Chief Inspector."

"I wouldn't blame you. She's exactly that. And she has reason to hate us even more than your average mobster. Our very own Elliot Whyte sent her son, Harry, down for fifteen years."

Cooper folded her arms and scanned the room. She was slowly adjusting to the stench. "What do you think? Start with the top dogs and work our way down through the capos and soldiers?"

"I say we start at the bottom and work up. Far more fun to make the top dogs sit and stay, don't you think?"

She liked his style.

And so, ten minutes later, Singh found himself in a staring contest with a skinny bloke whose eyes were slightly different shades. Across the hall, Cooper met a shaven-headed gym monkey with gold teeth. His neck tattoo read, *Mama's boy.*

He looked up as Cooper entered and slammed her folder on the desk. He chuckled, ran a hand over his buzzcut, pointed at Cooper and said, "Nice haircut, pet."

It was going to be a long day.

"WHAT DO YOU DO for a living, Mr Nowak?" Singh asked Freddie Nowak, a pasty man with twitchy hands.

"Unemployed."

"I see." Singh opened a file. "Not many unemployed people drive Maseratis. Care to tell me where it is? The arresting officers reported no car at your address this morning."

"Where'd you get that pic?" Nowak huffed, pointing in the file at an image of himself driving the car in question through Seaburn.

"Please. You think you can drive a luxury car like this around Sunderland and people aren't going to take photographs? But that's what you wanted, isn't it? For people to stop and stare? People who value privacy don't drive cars like this." Singh waved the image in front of Nowak's face. "So where is it?"

"Sold it."

"Interesting. Had a sudden gambling debt to pay, did you?"

"No comment."

"Bet on the wrong boxer, did you?"

"No comment."

No, of course you won't comment, thought Singh. He'd had the same conversation three times already. As had DCI Cooper. It wasn't always a Maserati. Sometimes, it was a Bugatti, a Ferrari, or some other fuel guzzler ending in *I*.

"Where were you in the early hours of Sunday the 3rd of September?"

"Nee idea," Nowak said. "That was ages ago."

Singh tried not to sigh too loudly or show his impatience. "Allow me to refresh your memory. It was the night of the Ahmed–Jones fight. Where were you?"

On the other side of the corridor, Cooper interrogated Tommy "Two-Fingers" Smith, so-called not because he had two fingers but because he actually had eleven. Cooper could question his maths another time, but for now, she wanted the answer to one question: "Who killed Catalina?"

"Divint knaa."

"Come off it, Tommy."

Cooper propped her elbows on the metal table and toyed with a silver pen branded with the Northumbria Police insignia. With a rubber grip and a stylus tip, it was much nicer than the ones currently lying around the Wallsend station. She considered keeping it. That was the perk of police stationary; if it wasn't tied down, it was fair game.

"We know the Roker Boys are involved in match-fixing. We know you lost big time when Ahmed didn't stay down in the fifth. We know he hasn't been seen since."

Tommy swallowed. Had they thought no one had noticed? The general public might believe The Tyneside Terror was relaxing on holiday while he recovered from the big fight, but Cooper was inclined to believe Dylan Blackburn's theory.

"Where's his body?" she asked. "Come on, Tommy. Talk to me. Someone gave the order to kill Catalina, and someone carried it out?"

"It wasn't me."

"Oh, but it was," said Cooper. "You may or may not have been the one to slice her throat, but you were involved. You were all involved in this dirty little game." Anger built in the pit of her stomach, an acidic feeling of rage. "Catalina East, a new mum with an infant son, was beaten with a baseball bat and had her neck slit open. Would you like to see?"

"No." He was quick to answer.

"Have a look." Cooper slid the crime scene photographs across the table.

Tommy cowered. *Not as tough as he thought he was.*

"And she wasn't the only one," growled Cooper, sliding another photo into Tommy's line of sight. "You took her wife out just for the hell of it. Wrong place, wrong time? Wrong wife? Hope was a good woman and an excellent mayor. Now, I'm sure you have no qualms about what you did to Newcastle – about turning it overnight from a place of tolerance to a place of bigotry – but I do. I care what you did to my city." She was almost shaking with rage now, her face inches from Tommy's. "So mark my words, unless one of you starts talking, I will take every single last one of you on a joint enterprise charge. You will ALL be guilty of murdering Catalina East."

- Chapter 53 -

Cooper paced the corridor, the bottle of Lucozade in her left hand sloshing with each indignant step. Joint enterprise cases were a legal minefield, a contentious issue that blurred the lines of individual culpability. The difficulty of achieving a conviction for the fifteen waste-of-space criminals she'd had the displeasure of dealing with that day was immense, but it wasn't impossible.

Joint enterprise was a legal principle that allowed multiple individuals involved in a crime to be held accountable, regardless of their specific roles. It aimed to address the issue of group criminality and ensure that all participants could be brought to justice. Still, it was a doctrine that had become a source of deep-seated controversy and ethical debate.

The debate stemmed from what some considered unjust convictions. Someone egging their mate on while they stabbed someone could face the same legal consequences as the one wielding the weapon. Joint enterprise was a legal sledgehammer that could obliterate any semblance of proportionality in sentencing.

Frankly, Cooper didn't care.

Knocking on the door across the hall and entering, Cooper found Singh in conversation with Kayla Dunn.

"How are things, Detective?" she asked Singh.

"Ms Dunn would like to plead the fifth. I was just explaining that this is the United Kingdom, not the United States." Then to Kayla, "There is no fifth to plead on this side of the Atlantic, Ms Dunn, but you may remain silent."

Kayla's expression was one of outrage.

"Hello, Kayla," Cooper greeted, hoping to make the woman speak. "How are you?"

Kayla's response was more icy silence.

"Heard from Harry lately?"

The mention of her incarcerated son did the trick. Suddenly, it was hard to shut Kayla up. It lit a fire under her, and she shot a string of curses at Cooper, telling her to *keep her effing son's name out of her effing mouth*.

Singh quickly intervened, his calm, mellifluous voice cutting through the tension. "Ms Dunn, please, DCI Cooper was just making conversation."

"Like hell she was. Cocky cow, bringing my son into things. They framed him. My poor boy is innocent."

"We both know that isn't true, Kayla," Cooper said, taking her seat. "And we're not here to talk about Harry. As it happens, he's one of the few

Roker Boys we know wasn't involved in the murder of Catalina and Hope East. His alibi's good for the next fourteen years at least."

"YOU ABSOLUTE—"

"Who killed Catalina?" Cooper said, raising her voice over the torrent of swear words.

"How would I know?"

"Because you know everything," Singh said. "A woman rising to the top of an organisation such as yours? That's impressive, Ms Dunn. You're tough, I can see that. But toughness alone doesn't get one to the upper echelons of the hierarchy. You have to be wicked smart. I wonder how many of the men you command have made the mistake of judging you on your beauty and not your brains."

Kayla's lips formed a wry smile. "Are you flirting with me?" She turned to Cooper. "He's flirting with me. He can't do that, can he? You lot have rules about that kind of thing."

"I'm not flirting." Singh held his hands up innocently.

Though he wasn't flirting, Cooper recognised what he was doing. He'd used the same tactic on Chardonnay Long, complimenting her, calling her classy.

"You were. You dirty bastard. Trying to butter me up like that. Well, it won't work, sweetheart. You're not my type."

Singh changed tack. "Is that because I'm in the police or because my skin is brown?"

Kayla paused momentarily, her brows arched high in her forehead as she considered her response. Finally, she spoke with a directness that was both disarming and unsettling. "Both."

Cooper decided it was time for everyone to take a break. It was early evening, and they were tired from a long day of fruitless interviews. "I think we'll pause here," she said, the words a thin veil concealing her desire to avoid further confrontation.

As Cooper turned the recording devices off and they got to their feet, Kayla pouted her ruby lips and blew a kiss at Singh. She leant back in her chair, uncrossing her bare legs before recrossing them. It was a deliberate and provocative gesture designed to distract rather than charm.

In the corridor, Cooper exhaled a long, slow breath. "Wow. I always suspected she was all fur coat and no knickers."

"And you were right," Singh said, his eyes wide and slightly traumatised.

OUTSIDE, IT WAS SO wet and dreary that the break room at Southwick station seemed positively cheerful. They'd questioned the Roker Boys gang members for hours. It had been a relentless cycle of denials and half-truths, and they needed to clear their heads.

Cooper boiled the kettle and grabbed a sorry-looking sandwich from the vending machine. She opened a container labelled *coffee* and grimaced at the congealed mess of granules. The container labelled *tea* wasn't any more appealing. She was about to settle on hot water when Singh reached into an inside pocket and pulled out two square teabags.

"Turmeric, coconut and mango?" he said, bringing one to his nose and inhaling.

"Um, yes please," Cooper said. "What else have you got hiding in there?"

"Mints," he answered, brandishing an unopened packet of Polos.

"No thanks, don't want to spoil my dinner," she said sarcastically, holding up the ham and cheese sandwich.

The mention of dinner made her think of home. As much as she enjoyed her work, she felt jealous of Julie taking Danny to the aquarium. She pictured his awestruck face as he saw jellyfish for the first time, his little fingers touching the glass. She wondered how Tina's day had been and if Atkinson had had any news from the Hunter residence for her. They'd both been so busy lately that they'd hardly spent any quality time together. And to think, they should have not long returned from two weeks of sunshine and sombreros.

Singh brewed the tea and added a splash of cold water to each cup. Sitting on a low chair, Cooper closed her eyes, the frustration tangible.

"You seem troubled," Singh said.

"I am. This case is eating away at me. I keep thinking of the innocents: Hope, little Brandon, Whitney. I'm considering joint enterprise."

"Tricky," he said, tilting his head left and right. "But I do relish the idea of sending the lot of them down."

Cooper opened her notepad, her voice heavy with fatigue. "Beck admits to betting a large sum of money on Ahmed. Denies everything else and has given an alibi for the time the Easts were killed. I need to follow it up. See if it's legit. Tommy Two-Fingers wouldn't say a thing. Frankly, I thought he was too scared to. The bloke with the gold teeth, Bridges, says he lost money on the fight but denies being anywhere near Times Square. Says it's not his sort of scene, but the eyes he gave to the duty sergeant make me suspect otherwise. Big Les came the closest to admitting knowing about the match-fixing. I think we can get more out of him. He's not the brightest. I'm sure we'll be able to catch him in a lie or catch him changing his story."

She let out a long sigh. "How about you?"

"I felt like I was interviewing the seven dwarves at one point," Singh said. "Why do they always need a nickname? Instead of Grumpy, Sleepy and Doc, I had Crafty, Sweetie and Tats."

Cooper laughed. "Which one's Dopey?"

"Oh, they're all dopey."

"Is Kayla Dunn Snow White?"

"No, she's Sharon Stone." He opened his notepad and slid his index finger down a page covered in shorthand. "You mentioned Bridges. Would that be Perry Bridges?"

Cooper nodded.

"Crafty – that's Otto Craft – says Bridges was the one who told him to bet on Ahmed. He says he was the one who knew Catalina."

"Interesting."

"I thought so, too. After a string of fifty *no comments*, Freddie Nowak remembered where he was at the time of the murders. He was watching the fight in the Black Bull in Sunderland. That should be fairly easy to check. He had to sell his luxury sports car recently, which makes me think he's the gentleman Mr Blackburn was referring to. Like with Big Les, I think he'll crack if we press him further. As for Sweetie – that's Ian Sweetland – he said he knew Ahmed was a cheat and that Catalina had clients who would take a dive or miss a penalty when required, but he refused to say it was the Roker Boys who were the ones to turn them..."

Synapses in Cooper's brain fired up. She was transported to a green with bunny rabbits, a great bronze river god, a smart lobby area.

"...Again, he admitted to betting on the fight and was watching it in town, but no word on who demanded Catalina pay for Ahmed's insubordination."

"Sweetland," she repeated quietly, getting to her feet.

Singh went still, presumably the same connections being made in his brain. "Oh." He stood as well. "Sarah Sweetland, the receptionist at the Civic Centre? I commented that it was a lovely name."

"It is a lovely name. It's also an unusual one."

"That would be one hell of a coincidence. Wouldn't it?"

"I don't like coincidences, Daljit," said Cooper. She picked up her notepad and files. "Fetch Sweetie from the cells. I think I'd like a little word with him."

- CHAPTER 54 -

SINGH DRAGGED IAN SWEETLAND back into the interview room and pointed to a plastic chair. "Please, take a seat."

Sweetland sat opposite Cooper. He was heavy-set and dressed in a scruffy vest, beanie, baggy joggers, and hideous sliders. There was something oddly familiar about his face as his gaze met hers. His face was dark and rough, his features asymmetrical. His brown eyes were downturned and heavily lidded. He wore braces on his teeth.

Cooper leant forward, a clear bag in her hand. "Bag the beanie," she instructed.

"Why?"

"It's evidence."

Sweetland's curiosity seemed to be piqued. "How so?"

Cooper's response was to slide a photograph across the table. It was the still from a traffic camera that Martin managed to procure. It captured a man in a beanie hat in the heart of Newcastle City Centre on the fateful morning of Sunday, September third. He removed the hat, revealing a receding hairline, and dropped it in the bag.

"Is this you?" she asked, eyes locked on his.

Sweetland replied without a moment's hesitation. "No."

"Are you sure?"

"That could be anyone," he responded, attempting to deflect.

Cooper's gaze was unwavering. "But it's not just anyone. It's the man we believe killed Catalina and Mayor Hope East. So I ask you again, is this you?"

Sweetland's response stayed the same. "No. Doesn't look anything like me."

"I disagree," Cooper said, the ticking of a wall clock starting to irritate her. "Did you murder two women that night?"

"No, I did not. Thought it was that bloke who jumped in front of the train. That's what the papers said."

Cooper watched his body language. He didn't flinch.

Singh pulled his chair closer to the table. "Where were you that night?"

"I was in town. Watching the fight like everyone else," he replied.

"You told me you bet big on Ahmed because you knew he was supposed to take a dive in the fifth. How much did you lose?"

Sweetland looked around. "Thirty thousand," he admitted.

"Is that all their lives were worth?" Cooper asked. "Fifteen grand each?"

His voice grew insistent. "I didn't kill them. It was that councillor. You said so yourself at the press conference."

"We'll come to that later. Course, it's not just how much you bet," Cooper pushed further. "It's what you all bet. Collectively. How much did the capos lose? More than that, I'm guessing. And how about Beck and Dunn?"

Sweetland seemed evasive. "Nee idea."

"Mr Sweetland, it's not just this image that we have," Singh said, watching him closely. "We have a witness who saw you running from the scene. If we put you in a lineup, do you think he'd pick you out?"

"No."

"Why not?" Cooper probed.

"Because it wasn't me."

"So, you're saying," Singh said. "If we call this witness in and put you in a lineup, the witness will definitely not pick you?"

He hesitated again, his answer shifting. "Well, he might, mightn't he?"

Finally.

Singh pressed on, confronting the inconsistencies. "Why might he?"

"Well, this so-called witness might think I look a bit like the bloke who did it."

Cooper pushed the traffic cam still closer to him. "But you said that photo doesn't look anything like you? So, which is it? It either looks like you or it doesn't."

He faltered, and Cooper seized the moment. “Is this you?”

“No.”

“But it might look like you?” Cooper sighed, rested her back against the chair and eyed the clock. She got to her feet and took it from the wall, having to stand on her tiptoes. After removing the batteries, the infernal ticking came to an end.

Returning to her seat, she said. “You said you were in town in the early hours of Sunday, September third. By town, you mean Newcastle?”

“Yes.”

“Be more specific.”

He shrugged. “Just in pubs and bars, like.”

“Which pubs?”

“Dunno. Divint remember,” he mumbled. “I was drunk.”

He was lying. Cooper knew it. “Drunk enough to forget you murdered the Mayor of Newcastle?”

“No,” he snapped, moving to fidget with his hat and realising it wasn’t there. “I’d remember that, wouldn’t I?”

“You tell me. Because you’re saying, you were sober enough to remember that you didn’t kill anyone but that you were so drunk you can’t remember which pub you were in? Which is it? Drunk or sober?”

Again, he reached for the non-existent hat. Frustrated, he rubbed the back of his neck. “Neither. I was tipsy, a bit merry, like. Just can’t remember which pub I was in. That’s not a crime.”

“It’s also not an alibi. Who were you drinking with?”

Cooper could sense she was making headway. She was getting to Sweetland. The cocky edge had left his voice. He seemed more hesitant and confused. He couldn't sit still.

"Who were you drinking with?" Cooper demanded. "Maybe they remember."

He wavered. "Just a mate."

Again, she told him to "Be more specific."

"Erm... Freddie."

"Freddie Nowak? Are you sure?"

"Yes."

Singh chuckled as he interlaced his fingers. He turned to Cooper. "It's interesting Mr Sweetland says he was out drinking in Newcastle with Freddie Nowak, because Mr Nowak told me he was in Sunderland that night."

"So one of you is lying," said Cooper with a smirk. "I am going to put it to you, Sweetie, that you can't remember which pub you were in because either you were in the Pink Elephant and you don't want to admit it because you know that's where Hope and Catalina were watching the fight before a bloke in a beanie who looks a bit like you murdered them both. Or, you were waiting outside the Pink Elephant, and you don't want to admit that either because that would imply you were there to keep an eye on Catalina, right? To ensure her client, Abdul Ahmed, aka the Tyneside Terror, kept to the agreement?"

He swallowed, eyes flicking to the camera mounted in the corner of the room.

"We have all the CCTV footage from the Pink Elephant that night," Cooper said. "I didn't notice anything the first time I watched it because I didn't know who I was looking for. Are you telling me when I go back in and scour through that footage that I will absolutely definitely not see your face?"

He said nothing, working his jaw. Cooper guessed she'd have him within five minutes. If she'd left the clock on the wall, she'd have timed it.

"Well?" she pressed. "When I re-examine the CCTV footage of the Pink Elephant on the night Hope and Catalina East were almost decapitated, will I see your ugly mug?"

She waited patiently for the answer. It felt like an age.

"You might."

Getting closer.

"I might?"

"You might."

Cooper smiled. "That means I will. Why didn't you just say that? You could have saved us all a lot of time, Sweetie. So, I have you admitting to knowing Catalina threw matches for the mob. I have you admitting knowing Ahmed was meant to lose in the fifth. And I have you admitting you lost a lot of money when he didn't."

"We *might* have you on CCTV in the Pink Elephant," Singh continued, his fingers still laced over his belly. "And we have a witness who *might* pick you out of line up."

"We have a traffic still of a man who looks *a bit like you* fleeing the scene," said Cooper.

"Holding the murder weapon no less," added Singh. "It's not looking very good for you? Is it, Mr Sweetland?"

Sweetland said nothing, his eyes firmly fixed on the table.

"You're a gambling man," Cooper said. "So let me put this in terms you'll understand. There's a saying: The house always wins." She tapped her chest with her index finger. "And I'm the bloody house."

Picking up the evidence bag containing the woollen hat, Cooper asked, "Now, what are the odds we're going to find one or both of the Easts' blood on here?"

No answer. Cooper changed tack.

"Do you have children?"

He was caught by the question. "Erm, yeah. I do. Three."

"Girls? Boys?"

Sweetland's face saddened. "A daughter with my ex and two lads with my missus."

"They look up to you?"

He nodded, eyes still lowered.

"The Easts had a son," said Cooper, letting her comment hang for a moment. "So, I'll give you one last chance before I have forensics tear your house apart looking for evidence. Before I have them ransack your children's bedrooms, go through their toys, go through your wife's dressing table and underwear drawers. Did you kill Catalina East?"

She saw the moment he threw in the towel and conceded defeat – the way his posture slumped, his eyes closed, his lips parted slightly as if he were about to speak then thought better of it. Eventually, he said, "I didn't want to."

Hallelujah. She knew it. She bloody knew it.

"About bloody time," said Cooper. "I might get home today. And as Hope East was killed in the same attack, I presume you're confessing to that as well. Did you kill Hope East?"

Sweetland gave the tiniest nod, almost imperceptible. "I didn't want to."

Singh crossed his legs. "But you had to because someone gave that order. Who told you to kill her, Mr Sweetland?"

He shook his head rather violently. "No comment."

"Come on, Sweetie," Cooper pushed. "Cooperate. Things will be better for you if you do."

With a sob, Sweetland glanced at the camera again. "Not a chance."

"Give us a name."

"You know it was me. I admit it. I confess. But I'm not saying no more."

Cooper knew it would be incredibly hard to get Ian Sweetland to dob on any of the Roker Boys, especially the higher-ups. He was headed to jail, and he knew it. If he gave up a name, there'd be nowhere to hide; he'd be beaten, shanked, horribly burned or worse.

"Okay, we'll park that for now," Cooper said in a friendlier voice now she had the makings of a confession. She wished to turn her attention to something that had troubled her for a while now: Frank McKenna's apparent suicide.

- Chapter 55 -

The small interview suite was windowless, yet Cooper could still hear rain as it pitter-pattered against Southwick Police Station. The rhythmic tip-tap of falling water replaced the tick-tock of the wall clock. The top dogs of the Roker Boys were safe for now, but Cooper wouldn't stop. Even once Ian Sweetland was charged, sentenced and jailed, they'd still push for the truth. It was what Hope East deserved, and it was what Newcastle deserved. The whole city had inadvertently been scarred by the gang's manipulation of Catalina and her clients. She wanted to know how they did it. Threats or blackmail? Bribes? A combination of it all? More people would be sent down, she was sure, and they were still to locate Abdul Ahmed. But at least for now, she could tell the city – the world – that what happened on September the third wasn't fuelled by hate and bigotry or political ideology. It was greed, pure and simple greed.

A fluorescent light flickered overhead, casting a harsh glare on the cold interview suite. "All right, Sweetie," Cooper began, drumming her fingers on the table, "let's talk about Sarah."

He feigned ignorance, but his dilating pupils betrayed him. "Who?"

"Sarah Sweetland. Who is she to you? Sister? Cousin?"

"Never heard of her."

Cooper and Singh chuckled.

"Right," she said. "You know, I'm getting sick and tired of going round in circles like this. I ask you something. You deny it. I present evidence. You say it *might* be you, or you *might* be on CCTV. So, let's skip the bullshit where you tell me you might have heard of her or her name might sound familiar. I can find out. I can make phone calls, so save me the energy and the irritation and just tell me."

Sweetland clenched his jaw; Singh gave Cooper side-eye.

"Cousin," he said after a while. "Our mams are sisters."

"There, that wasn't so hard," Cooper said. "Are you close?"

"That's got nowt to do with you."

"Oh, but it does."

Singh turned to Cooper. "Perhaps I should bring Miss Sarah Sweetland here to confirm that? I could speak with Mr Sweetland's mother, too."

"Leave my mother out of this!" Sweetland snapped.

Cooper and Singh both gave him the same pointed look. They would leave his family alone if he answered their questions.

"Fine. Aye. We were close. Grew up together. So what?"

"I met Sarah," Cooper said, leaning in. Though this revelation didn't seem to shock Sweetland, it did grab his attention. He jerked in his seat, scratching his head. "I visited Newcastle Civic Centre on the fourth of September. We both did," she continued, gesturing to Singh.

"Yes," Singh said. "We wished to speak with Councillor Frank McKenna. We had reason to believe he had a falling out with the mayor. When he took his own life, it seemed to cement the theory."

"The mayor wasn't the only woman at the Civic Centre he'd had a falling out with, though." Cooper watched him closely, saw the flicker of anger in his eyes. "Several women, including your young cousin, had made complaints against McKenna. There were allegations ranging from over-familiarity and non-consensual touching to voyeurism and even sexual assault, possibly rape."

Singh took over. "When we arrived at the Civic Centre, Sarah was messaging someone. Was that someone you? And before you answer, let me please remind you that your phone was seized upon your arrest. It will be sent to our digital forensic experts. Even if you deleted your messages, we'll still find them."

Sweetland wiped his nose on the back of his hand and sighed. "Aye. She was texting me."

"What about?" Singh asked. "Again, we can check."

"She was upset about Mayor East, like. Said she was dead canny."

"How did that make you feel?"

"Guilty. Like I said, I didn't want to kill anyone. I was pissed off about the fight and the money, but I didn't think I'd be crossing that line that night."

"Still don't want to tell us who gave that order?" asked Cooper.

He turned away. "No. I'm cooperating, aren't I? Look, I'll answer all your questions but I won't tell you that. I'm not that stupid."

Sweetland looked visibly agitated, and Cooper knew a lost cause when she saw one. He was talking, and that was good enough for her. For now.

"So, when DI Singh and I arrived at the Civic Centre, we told your cousin we wanted to see Frank McKenna. She wasn't too keen on helping us. Was she, DI Singh?"

"No, DCI Cooper. We thought she was being uncooperative. But looking back, I think she simply didn't want to have to talk to Councillor McKenna or interact with him at all. In fact, when she returned from the chambers, she couldn't get away from him quick enough. She went straight back to her phone."

"What did she text you?" Cooper asked. When he didn't respond immediately, she continued, "Let me guess. *Hey, cuz—*"

"She didn't call me *cuz*."

"*Hey Sweetie—*"

"God, no. She called me Ian. Just Ian. And she was in a state. She was sad about the mayor, but I could tell something else was up. She told me the police had arrived to talk to one of the councillors, and he might be a suspect. She thought he might have been the one to kill the mayor. I was relieved hearing that 'cause it meant someone else was in the frame, didn't it? But then she tells me this councillor is a right creep and that she thought he'd drugged her one night, that the mayor had believed her even after HR didn't want to know, and the mayor was going to help, but now she was dead..."

The room felt colder as evening crept in. Cooper fastened the top button on her blouse. "You probably couldn't believe your luck. The nasty man who'd been harassing your cousin was suspected of the murders you committed?" A smile tugged at her lips. "It was probably too good to be true."

"And how did that make you feel?" Singh asked.

"I lost my shit. Like I said, we grew up together. She was more like a little sister than a cousin. So, yeah, I thought I could kill two birds with one stone, so to speak. Let him take the blame, like. And get revenge for Sarah."

"A week later, he was dead," said Singh.

"Took me a while to find out where he lived."

"McKenna's neighbour heard shouting that day," Cooper told him. "He thought McKenna was talking to himself, but it was you, wasn't it? How did you get in?"

"Easy. His back door was unlocked."

"And how'd you convince him to jump in front of a Metro train?" she demanded, her voice icy.

He scoffed. "I gave him no choice."

"Go on."

"When he came home, I hit him roond the head and tied him up. When he was *compos mentis* again, I told him who I was – I was the man who killed the mayor – and that I knew who he was. He was the dirty bastard who hurt our Sarah. Well, he started yelling all sorts, but I told him he was in no position to threaten me as I was the one with the knife."

"Which knife?" asked Cooper. "The one you used on the third?"

"Nah. That's in the Tyne. This was just one I found in McKenna's drawers."

"And where's that knife now?"

"I wiped the handle and put it back."

"Okay, what happened then?" asked Cooper. She'd seen the footage from the Metro station and knew no one had pushed McKenna.

"I told him I was going to castrate him right there in his kitchen – it was what he deserved – then I'd do to him what I'd done to the mayor. To be honest, I was hoping it wouldn't come to that. I knew I'd already crossed that line with Catalina and the mayor, but I didn't really want to do it again. I was hoping he'd take the other option."

"Which was to kill himself," Singh said.

"Yeah. I mean, if I killed him, then it would defeat the point of making him look guilty. I was prepared to threaten to harm his bairn as well – I wouldn't, of course – just a threat. So, I was very precise in my instructions. He had to do it by that evening, and it had to be in public, so there'd be no question that it was suicide. He knew I'd be following, watching."

Cooper remembered the vile message carved into McKenna's front door. Pen poised over notepad, she asked, "And who carved the message into the door?"

"He did."

This was what she thought. They'd only found McKenna's fingerprints on the screwdriver.

"Of his own free will?"

Sweetland gave a short, hollow laugh. "No. I made him."

It sounded like the rain was intensifying, a constant barrage of droplets drumming against the other side of the wall.

"Anything else to add?" Cooper asked, ready to charge him, put this whole sorry mess behind her and brave the wet drive home.

He grimaced. "Nah, not really. Just that Sarah had nowt to dee with it. I know you'll check my phone and that, but she didn't know what I did. She had no idea what I was going to do to him.

Cooper believed him. She pocketed the nice, silver stylus pen she'd had her eye on and asked, "You know what happens now?"

He nodded and held out his wrists in anticipation of being cuffed. Singh did the honours and read out the charges. "Ian Sweetland, I am charging you with the murder of Catalina East and the murder of Hope East, as well as the encouragement of suicide in relation to the death of Frank McKenna."

"Hope for Change. Vote Hope for Newcastle," Cooper said dryly as they led him from the room into the hallway and back towards reception. Sweetland's chances of getting bail were about as slim as Cooper's chances of making it home before Danny's bedtime. "I think Newcastle needs more than hope after what you and your associates did to it. Come to think of it, so will Sunderland once the public finds out it was a bunch of greedy Mackem gangsters who caused it all."

Singh's phone rang. He lagged behind to answer it while Cooper spoke to the booking sergeant. It was dark outside, the heavy curtain of rain crashing down on the car park. Inside, the harshness of the fluorescent lights was giving her a headache. She needed water, a painkiller and a hug from her children.

As Sweetland's charges and rights were explained to him, Singh said, "Pardon me, DCI Cooper." He held his phone, dark eyes burning. "That was Miss Hogg."

Cooper felt a sinking feeling in her stomach. "Is something up?"

"It's important," he replied, pushing the phone back in his inside pocket. "Let's sign the paperwork and get out of here."

- Chapter 56 -

Rain pelted against the roof of the car as Cooper strapped herself in and fired up the engine. Water trickled down the back of her head and under her collar.

"Talk to me, Becky."

Rebecca Hogg's voice crackled through the Bluetooth connection.

"The Hunters' next target – I think I've found it. At least, I hope I have."

Cooper could hear the strain in the digital forensic officer's voice. She could picture the bags under her eyes and the tremor in her hands. Becky had spent the last six days wading through the worst depths of what the darknet markets had to offer. They both knew what sorts of monsters lurked in the shadowy corners of the web. Exposure to these vile creatures and the disturbing things they posted would take a psychological toll on anyone. The horrors they saw in their world left an indelible mark on their soul.

Singh jumped in the passenger seat, and Cooper pulled away. The wind howled around them; fallen leaves and the occasional item of litter swirled around the edges of the road.

"Where is it?" Cooper pressed, feeling her pulse quicken. "We'll need to let Grange and the NCA know as soon as possible."

"I already have, Coop. Grange is on her way."

"What do you mean, on her way?" but Cooper already knew, already sensed it.

"Northumberland. A manor house not far from Hexham. It's an exclusive party for those sick enough to pay the price of admission. Food, booze, drugs... kids."

"Another all-inclusive." She felt ill at the mere thought of it and disgusted that it once again fell on her doorstep. Without thinking, she pushed the pedal harder, the engine growling beneath her. "Right, well, tell us all you've got, Becky, then we'll get a team together in the morning and make a plan. As much as I want to catch the Hunters, I want every last one of those perverts in jail, too. I want to find a way to watch the house discretely and arrest everyone as they arrive. If we catch Cat and Uriah in the act of cutting the power or forcing their way in, then it's a win-win. I'll need to arrange plenty of boots on the ground. I doubt guns will be necessary, but dogs will be a good shout."

"We'll want a battering ram," said Singh. "And tasers, too."

"But Coop—"

Cooper cut Becky off. "How much time do we have to get organised? When's the party?"

"That's just it." Becky's voice was urgent. "It's tonight. It's already started."

DS PAULA KEATON HUNG up the phone. She'd coordinated with Grange, updated Nixon and spoken with local officers in Haltwistle, Hexham and Bellingham. The exact location was somewhere between the three. An old country house off the beaten track between farms and woodland. Keaton looked it up on a holiday rental site. It was a three-storey, L-shaped stone building that slept sixteen and had a hot tub and sauna. If she didn't know what was going on there that evening, Keaton might have thought it very appealing, save for the twelve hundred pounds per night price tag.

The building looked to be surrounded by stone walls approximately five feet high. They were topped with wrought iron railings, taking the height up to around eight feet. Tall trees dotted the perimeter of the land, granting the occupants further privacy. Becky had spoken to the rental company and found the name used on the booking: John Smith. It was almost certainly a fake name, and the credit card used to pay was likely stolen.

"You ready?" she asked Whyte and Boyd as they pulled on stab vests.

They nodded grimly.

"You," she said, pointing at Martin, who was pushing himself to his feet. "Don't even think about it. Sit your tooshie back down. Cooper will kill me. Right after she kills you first. Stay here and help coordinate things."

Martin looked both disappointed for himself and worried for Boyd. She felt his pain. She knew what it was like to be benched – both in her sporting and professional life – but he'd get over it. Besides, they needed him to liaise with digital forensics and the various other bodies in play. She told him so, and the young man returned to his seat, ready to help however he could.

"Tick, tock," Keaton said, tapping her watch. "Cooper's meeting us there. Let's move it, people. Time to catch some crazy rich, coked-up kiddy-fiddlers."

A BOLT OF LIGHTNING flashed across the sky, illuminating the dark road ahead of Cooper and Singh as they raced northwest into rural Northumberland. They had the coordinates, and their satnav showed the house was at the end of a single-track road. That would play to their advantage.

"Only one way in means only one way out," said Singh.

Cooper cursed as they slowed for a red light. "As far as I'm concerned, the only way any of them are leaving is in our custody."

"Catherine and Uriah Hunter may have other ideas."

"Which is why," said Cooper, pressing the accelerator, "we need to stop hitting every red light on this bloody road."

She chewed on her bottom lip and asked Singh to call Grange. When it went to voicemail, she told him to keep trying. When it connected, Cooper tasted blood. She pressed the back of her hand to her mouth, examined it, and saw a patch of scarlet on her pale skin.

"Cooper?"

"You're on speaker with myself and DI Singh. Are we certain this is the target?"

"Yes." There was a pause. "But even if we weren't, I'd rather we raid the place regardless. Those vile..."

"I know what you mean."

Grange coughed before continuing. "Your digital forensic girl is quite something."

"Becky? Yeah, she's great," Cooper said, struggling to hear between the noise of the traffic and the rain beating off the car like hailstones.

"She found two usernames she thinks belong to the Hunter siblings: Justice and GA. GA stands for Guardian Angel. We believe that's Uriah Hunter. Justice is Catherine Hunter. Justice lurks in the forums and chats, doing the bare minimum amount of participation to not look suspicious and is quite adept at posing as a man. Justice and GA are in regular contact with each other. Becky hasn't been able to read their messages, but she knows how many have been sent and on what dates."

"Guardian Angel," Cooper repeated in a low tone, thinking of young MJ Hunter and all the events that had led them here. The massacres at Gateshead, West Lothian, and Blackpool haunted her – not just for the victims – the actual victims, but for the twisted minds that had orchestrated them. Two vigilantes that were hell-bent on delivering their own brand of Cat's username: justice.

"What's your ETA?" Grange asked.

Singh checked the satnav. "We're five minutes away."

"Same."

As Cooper made her penultimate turn, they spotted taillights ahead. "Is that you in the Audi?"

"Yes. I'm turning my lights off now for the final approach. I suggest you slow and do the same."

Cooper hung up and flicked the dipped headlight paddle, sending the country road into suffocating darkness.

After a minute or so of slow, careful driving, she brought her car to a stop behind Grange's. They'd parked a few hundred meters from the house to reduce the risk of being detected. She retrieved a VHF radio from the boot, turned it on, adjusted the squelch, and tuned it to the agreed channel. Singh opened an umbrella and held it over them both. They could hear other vehicles approaching on the same lane they'd just driven up. It wasn't until they were within twenty metres that she saw them; so was the absolute blackness of the rainy night. Keaton, Whyte and Boyd walked towards her, expressions grim, as several squad cars pulled up quietly. Beyond the stone walls and spiky railings, the holiday home looked warm and inviting, music playing from somewhere within.

"Let's have people stationed around the entire perimeter," Cooper whispered. "We don't want anyone legging it into the woods."

Grange agreed and sent some officers in each direction.

Keaton opened her tablet and showed Cooper satellite images of the property and photographs from the rental site. "Front door, back door, side door and doors leading to two conservatories. That's five main exits into the grounds if you don't count the ground-floor windows, which look big enough to climb through if they open up. Once into the grounds, there's only really the front and back gates. The front gates we have covered, and the back gate leads to a woodland walk that follows a small stream. If you ask me, we've got the bastards surrounded."

"I think you're right," Cooper said, watching officers leave for the back of the property, their boots heavy on the muddy ground. She scanned the walls and railings. "No one's jumping over those in a hurry."

"If they do, we'll be here to catch 'em."

Cooper's radio crackled. A quiet voice said, "Movement at the rear."

Cooper raised her fist. Everyone fell silent.

"Older IC4 man and younger IC3 female are getting into the hot tub."

"We're heading in soon," Cooper replied, wanting to get the young woman or girl out of there as soon as possible. "Keep eyes on. He might make a run for the back when we come through the front."

"Roger. But, no one's running out the back, ma'am. There's a heavy padlock and chain on it. Already checked, and it's locked."

That made things easier.

"Thanks. Just watch the walls for any jumpers. Update me if you see the Hunters."

"Roger."

Cooper shivered in the rain. She hadn't brought her outdoor coat, and though the umbrella kept the worst of it off her, her trousers were already soaked through. She turned to address the team who would be entering the house. "Be careful. We don't know if the Hunters are already here, but there's no sign of their vehicle. I need a group to patrol the surrounding areas and set up roadblocks to try and intercept them."

"I'll make it so," said Grange. "Leave it with me." She dialled a number and whispered into her phone.

"When we go in, I want every adult arrested and restrained," Cooper urged. "Preserve and photograph all evidence of drugs or grooming. Any children, reassure them as best you can. They may not speak English, may have had bad interactions with police in the past or may have been fed stories about how we'll arrest them for being illegal immigrants. We don't know what they've been through, so as softly-softly as you can."

"And any grey areas?" asked an officer, struggling to keep the rain off his face.

Cooper anticipated it might not be immediately apparent if some individuals were guilty adults, innocent adults or groomed children. Some children looked older than they were; some adults were masters at acting younger. Then there were men and women like Willow: adults who appeared to have a choice over their actions but whose lives were coerced and controlled by constant threats of violence.

"As long as every individual in that house leaves with us, then we're okay. I'd rather we treat someone as a victim and find out it's the opposite at the station than vice versa."

As they readied themselves and started walking towards the house, Cooper's radio crackled again.

"Just to confirm, ma'am, front gates are also locked with heavy chains."

That was odd, she thought, just as all the lights in the house went out.

- Chapter 57 -

"The Hunters! They're here." Cooper gasped, running the rest of the lane, her feet slipping in the mud, rain trickling down the back of her blouse.

"Give me your keys," Singh said as she ran. He took them, told Keaton to follow, and they returned the cars. Within moments, the beams from the police cars cut through the darkness, casting stark shadows across the sprawling lawn.

Cooper rattled the gates, the sound of metal on metal grating in her ears. "They've locked them all in." The partygoers were trapped inside, their fate resting in the hands of two dangerous vigilantes.

"Stand back!"

Cooper pivoted and moved out of the way as a member of the tactical team sprinted towards them, hacksaw in hand. Seconds later, the chain clattered to the floor.

"GO, GO, GO!" he yelled.

Cooper rushed through the gates, her heart pounding in her chest. The team surged forward, batons at the ready. They approached the house cautiously, moving in formation, their steps muffled by the rain and the damp ground. The darkness was oppressive, broken only by the glare of their flashlights and the car headlamps.

A man in a dressing gown and bare feet rushed around the side of the house, looking over his shoulder as if someone was chasing him. He practically ran into Cooper, who grabbed him by the arm, twisting his wrist to an uncomfortable angle. She pushed him towards Whyte, who cuffed him to the gate.

They continued into the ground, reaching the front door. Someone on the other side turned the handle repeatedly, shouting, "It's locked. Where are the keys?"

"Police! Stand back," someone yelled, and the man at the front of their formation burst the door down. Shouts and cries filled the darkened manor as partygoers stumbled and collided with one another in a frenzy to escape. The police team spread out, their flashlights carving through the darkness like blades.

Cooper moved quickly, following the team as they checked each room, looking for any sign of the Hunters. The team split in two: one heading upstairs, another covering the ground floor. When Cooper reached the bottom of the staircase, a hand grabbed her ankle. She almost fell, her torch illuminating a small face framed by raven-black hair. A girl crouched by a dresser. She was no more than eight or nine years old.

Cooper knelt down and spoke softly, trying to reassure her. "It's okay. We're here to help you."

The girl stared at her with big brown eyes, her lower lip trembling.

Cooper lifted her up and carried her to the living room, where Boyd comforted a boy in his early teens. He was crying, too scared to move. The room stank of marijuana and alcohol, and white powder dusted the coffee table.

"This is my friend Saffron," she told the child. "Saff, get them out of here. Straight in a squad car. Hospital first, then the station."

Separated from the team, Cooper pressed onwards up the stairs, careful of her footing. She could hear Keaton somewhere in the building wrestling someone into cuffs; she felt a surge of anger and disgust. She wanted to punch each and every one of them in the face for what they'd done. She wouldn't, of course. But if someone slipped in the dark and their face accidentally landed on Keaton or Whyte's fists, she'd find a way to explain it. Creeping forward, she opened the door to her right and saw a young woman, a girl really, cowering in the corner, tears streaming down her face.

"Please don't hurt me."

"I won't," Cooper assured her. She approached her slowly, trying to look as non-threatening as possible. "My name's Erica." She held out her hand. "I can help you."

But the girl didn't move. It was then Cooper saw the lump on the floor between them. She shone her torch on it, illuminating the dead body of a large, partly clothed male. Whether it was Cat or Uriah's handiwork, Cooper didn't know. Really, what did it matter? They worked as a team.

"He can't hurt you," she told the girl. She moved around the body and helped her to her feet. The pair of them shivering together, the girl from fear and Cooper from cold. "I've got you. Come on. Keep your eyes on me. Don't look down."

At the door, Cooper held the girl around her shoulders, speaking into her radio to request a female officer to the first floor. One arrived quickly, bringing a blanket with her. She then returned to the bedroom, pressing her fingers against the man's neck, feeling for a pulse. There was none. She paused, wondering who he was and what decisions had led to him being there that day. Were people like him born evil? Or did something in his upbringing or community make him that way? And if so, how? Her thoughts were so consuming she failed to notice the movement in the shadows until a powerful arm wrapped around her neck.

"Don't scream," whispered Uriah.

Cooper couldn't scream, even if she wanted to. She was gripped not only by his arm but by absolute, all-consuming terror. She kicked her feet, trying to remember her training. She kept missing his shins, so stamped at his feet, having no effect on his sturdy boots. She tried dropping her weight, but it was useless; he controlled her easily. She felt like a ragdoll in his grip, helpless and vulnerable.

"I don't want to hurt you," he said. "We're on the same side."

Cooper couldn't think straight. She clawed at his arm, her short nails making no difference to his gloved hands and the thick material of his sleeves. She might be agile and quick on her feet, but Cooper was light and frail, weakened from illness and the difficult birth of her son. She didn't stand a chance. And if there was one thing that Cooper couldn't stand, couldn't tolerate – it was anything around her neck. A year and a half ago now, she'd been held captive by a madman. Ever since, anything touching her neck would send her back to that cold, dark room. A tight necklace, a high collar, a scarf, it didn't matter. The thought of it was enough to drive her into a panic.

She writhed, trying to free herself, but his grip only tightened. Her body could feel his strength, the way his muscles bulged under her fingers, the feeling of his taught chest against her wet back. But her mind was elsewhere, back in that unlit, square room, naked with the metal slave collar locked around her neck and digging into her collarbones.

"You know I'm not the enemy."

His breath was hot against her ear, and in a moment of clarity, Cooper reached into her pocket, retrieved the shiny Northumbria Police pen and stabbed it into Uriah's thigh.

He growled in pain, trying to stifle his own voice by groaning into the back of her head. She stabbed him again, but his grip only tightened. He turned on the spot, moving with such torque her legs were lifted from the floor. Her arm slammed into the wooden bed frame, and she dropped the pen.

"Find me a way out of here," he whispered.

"Not a chance," she managed to pant between panicked breaths.

"There must be a way. A blind spot?"

Continuing to claw at his arm, tears streaming from her eyes, she managed. "The place is surrounded, Uriah. You're seriously outnumbered."

"I'm used to that."

The sound of footsteps and movement in the hallway caught both their attention. Cooper managed the first *H* of *Help* before he squeezed so hard she almost passed out.

"Shh. I told you I won't hurt you, but I will put you to sleep if you don't help get me out of here."

The footsteps faded away.

She tried to shake her head. "You're going to jail."

"Not yet, I'm not. I'm not finished. Once I've killed every last one of these bastards, then I'll happily go to jail. I'll do my time with a smile on my face. But Cat and I made a deal. We won't rest until every fucking paedophile in the fucking country knows what happens if they lay a finger on an innocent child. So, help me get out of here. Have all the police move to one side of the house. Cause a diversion."

Uriah's words chilled Cooper to the bone. She felt nauseous at the icy ruthlessness in his voice. Still clawing and writhing, she gasped, "I can't, you know I can't."

"We're not just doing this for MJ – for MJ's memory. We're doing the right thing for all children: to make the world a safer place. I looked you up; you have kids. You understand."

His muscles flexed with each impassioned word. Her neck was trapped in the crook of his right arm, his left hand pressing the back of her head. She couldn't turn her head to ease the pressure on her windpipe; even if she could, it would only increase the pressure on her carotid artery. Less and less oxygen was making it to her brain; she felt woozy, her peripheral vision flickering and fading to grey. He wasn't even trying.

"I will be the guardian angel this country needs. And to every sick, perverted child abuser, I will be the angel of death."

"Please," she begged. "Let me go."

"No," he said."You let me go. Tell me a way out."

She tugged at the material of his sleeve, finding a slither of exposed flesh into which she could dig her nails, but her hands felt numb and tingly; her legs were shaking.

"I'm sorry, Uriah. I can't help you," she said.

And as everything faded to black, she heard him whisper, "Then I'm sorry, but I can't help you."

He squeezed.

- Chapter 58 -

She thought she heard her name, distant, as if whispered in a dream. A flash of light followed, bright enough to be noticed through closed eyelids. Cooper felt her body twitch involuntarily, the way it sometimes did before she fell asleep. But the spasm didn't stop. It took a moment before she realised she wasn't the one convulsing; it was Uriah Hunter.

As Uriah bucked and contorted, his grip on her neck weakened. Cooper felt herself falling.

A pair of strong arms caught her just in time. Someone had discharged a stun gun at Uriah, the flashes of flickering electricity still sparking over his incapacitated body. Cooper, unnerved and traumatised, began to fight the arms holding her. Her hands slapped out in all directions, trying to pull imaginary objects from her neck.

"Where is it?" her voice trembled as she felt around her neck, fingers scratching for something that wasn't there.

"Cooper, calm down." Whyte's voice was gentle but firm, his hands on her shoulders grounding her. "There's nothing on your neck. It's over."

She didn't recognise him at first. When realisation hit, relief washed over her, and she sank into him, head on his chest.

"Thank God you're okay," he murmured. "When I saw he had you in a chokehold..."

She lifted her head, their eyes locking. Time seemed to rewind momentarily, and they were back at the beginning of their careers, two young officers struggling to find their footing in the chaotic world of policing. How time had flown. But the spell shattered as quickly as it had formed, and Cooper watched an officer, the one who fired the taser, cuff Uriah and read him his rights.

Whyte cleared his throat and helped Cooper to her feet. Her legs shook with fatigue and adrenaline. She kept hold of Whyte's hands for stability.

"We've got Cat," he told her, eyes on the floor, avoiding hers. "Six children on their way to Hexham General Hospital. Eighteen men cuffed and in the police van. Four DBs." He saw the half-naked body on the ground beside Cooper. "Five DBs."

"Taking their total to thirty-two," Cooper said, letting go of Whyte and wiping her clammy hands on her trousers, they were still sodden from the rain.

"That we know of." Whyte nodded toward the bedroom door, and they stepped out into the hallway. Two officers came running to help move Uriah downstairs.

Cooper brushed herself off, determined not to let anyone else see her so shaken. This was no time for vulnerability, and yet, she wiped her neck thrice more. She took a deep breath and raised her chin. "Come on."

They returned downstairs and through the back door into the holiday let's beautiful garden. The power was still disconnected, and the stormy sky provided no moonlight. Still, through torchlight and full-beam headlamps, Cooper watched officers swarm the grounds, leaving no stone unturned. There was a scent of chlorine from the hot tub and exhaust fumes as a van prepared to pull away.

"Cooper! Are you all right?" Keaton's concern was evident as they made their way across the lawn. "I couldn't find you. What happened?"

Putting a brave face on, she said, "Whyte caught Uriah Hunter."

Keaton slapped him on the back. "Nice one, mate. I'm not jealous in the slightest," she said sarcastically.

"You caught Cat."

"I know, but I'm pathologically competitive."

"And don't we know it."

Cooper appreciated the banter, even if it were short-lived. "Where's Singh?" she asked.

"At the hospital with Saff," Keaton told him. "One of the boys spoke Punjabi, so Singh's gone to translate until an official translator arrives."

Several cars rumbled up the track towards the house, tyres crunching on gravel and sliding in the mud. A car horn sounded before the noise of doors slamming. A man hoisted a video camera onto his shoulder, and another brandished a boom microphone. A third bombarded the nearest officer with questions. Journalists were like bed bugs, impossible to get rid of. Two women got out of the second car, and before they knew it, at least fifteen media members were angling for the best shot and the most salacious scoop.

"Who tipped them off?" Cooper asked, running names through her head: Becky? Martin? "Never mind, doesn't matter now."

She felt a twinge of irritation but knew she had to play nice. "Excuse me," she said, moving towards the crowd. "Can I have your attention, please?"

The reporters turned to Cooper, their cameras and microphones trained on her face. She was a far cry from the camera-friendly face of Northumbria Police, who had led the Frank McKenna press conference. Her clothes were wet, and her face no doubt pale and tear-stained.

"I can confirm that we have successfully apprehended Uriah and Catherine Hunter," she announced. "And we have arrested eighteen men for their connection to an online child abuse ring. I will update you all further tomorrow from Northumbria Police Headquarters. But for now, I need you to move your vehicles and clear the area.

This is a crime scene, and our forensic team will need access."

Just as the media circus began to disperse, a grip of officers emerged from the house with the Hunter siblings.

"There they are!" a journalist shouted.

Camera flashes lit the lawn like a strobe light; Cooper covered her eyes.

As the two avengers neared the gates and the awaiting police car, a smattering of applause broke out among the gathered press. "Good work," shouted one of them, and the applause snowballed into rapturous cheering and whistles.

"Can you believe this?" Keaton shook her head, disbelief etched into her features.

"I can actually," Cooper said. She toed the muddy ground with her shoe, caught somewhere between the bedroom she was just in and the breeze-block room with the metal slave collar chained to the wall. They were cold, dark places both literally and figuratively. As much as she wished the applause to drown out her thoughts, she couldn't shake it. She wanted to focus on the fact they'd arrested one of the Roker Boys, solving the Easts' murders, and now they had two of the most prolific killers in UK history under arrest. But she couldn't.

"Hey, Coop," Whyte nudged her gently. "You still with us?"

"Y— Yeah," she stammered. She glanced at him, then looked away, wondering if she'd imagined the intensity of the moment they'd shared earlier. She must have done. She was terrified, and he was there. That was all. It would have been the same with any of the team, she told herself. "It's just... hard to wrap my head around it all, you know?"

Whyte and Keaton nodded. Together, the three of them watched Uriah and Cat as they were guided past the press. Guardian Angel and Justice. The vigilante siblings walked tall, heads high and shoulders back. They looked straight into the cameras without a hint of shame. They were proud.

Despite their heinous crimes, they would become symbols of righteousness in a corrupt system that often failed its victims. They had risked everything, even their own lives and freedom, to find and kill paedophiles the police hadn't even had on their radar. They had taken matters into their own hands, but at what cost? Cooper's thoughts turned to Mick Hunter. A man whose life had effectively ended the moment he lost his youngest child. What was to become of him now? One in the ground; two in jail. He'd lost all three.

As the police car pulled away with the siblings in the back, the media dispersed, some following the car back to HQ, some headed straight for their respective studios and newsrooms. They'd rush to get the story out, and Cooper wouldn't be surprised if news were already breaking online. The three of them – Cooper, Whyte and Keaton – returned to their cars, passing the forensic team as they began their work. Cooper scanned their faces but didn't see anyone she recognised. No Atkinson.

"Back to HQ?" Keaton asked.

Cooper shook her head as she opened her driver's door. "Get home and get some rest," she said. "Grange and the NCA can take care of the Hunters. I'll go to HQ and give a statement supporting the lawful discharge of the taser. Then I'll get myself away as well. The rest of those... *animals* can wait until morning."

"You okay to drive?" Whyte asked, standing by his own vehicle.

"Yeah," she said. There was work to be done, papers to be signed and statements to collate, but Cooper had other priorities. She needed cuddles from her children and a kiss from her boyfriend. She needed a bloody great big drink. "I'll see you both tomorrow."

As Cooper collapsed into her seat and fastened her seat belt, she heard Whyte suggest he and Keaton go to the pub for a pint.

"Damn right," Keaton replied. "Let's pick up Martin and..."

Their conversation faded with the start of Keaton's engine. Tears rolled down Cooper's cheeks, and though it was a chilly night, she lowered the window to keep herself awake. She turned the car around, glancing at the house in the rearview mirror. It was a lovely building, and as a holiday home, it would have been the source of many fond memories for all the families who had stayed there over the years. No one who stepped foot in there that evening would feel the same.

All that death, she thought, following the two sergeants leading the way in the car in front. She turned on the radio, surprised to hear the same cheesy eighties soundtrack from their trip to Morecambe. But even Bananarama couldn't pull her tired mind from its conflicted thoughts between what was right in the eyes of the law and what was right in the eyes of the general public. She couldn't allow vigilantism in Northumbria, but deep down in her soul, she couldn't help but agree with Atkinson's earlier statement: The Hunters had done the world a favour.

- Chapter 59 -

The clinking of glasses and the warm glow of candlelight filled the dining room in Latimer Terrace on Friday evening. The Cooper–Atkinson clan gathered for their final meal together before three of them headed to Mexico for a holiday that had been delayed by a potential political assassination and hate crime, a culture war filled with protests, riots and looting, and a massacre that made heroes of the killers and villains of the dead. Across the table, Tina rolled her eyes at another one of Atkinson's terrible dad jokes while baby Danny gurgled happily in his crib. The atmosphere was light, but an underlying tension lingered.

It had been a busy few days since Ian Sweetland was arrested for the double murder in Times Square, and Uriah and Cat – the paedophile hunters – were paraded in front of an applauding media circus. They'd ID'd all the men at the party, including – with Margot Swanson's help – the ones who hadn't lived to tell the tale. Some of the men who survived were wishing they hadn't; they knew what shame awaited their families and what fate would greet them in jail. Of course, their lawyers would try to spin the old wrong-place-wrong-time line or the good ol' guilty by association, but the statements given by the brave children would sway any jury. Then, there was the evidence Cat Hunter had gathered. Though there was no doubting her guilt and the whole life sentence she would receive, she would prove a valuable and cooperative tool in prosecuting the men from the holiday let, and she relished the idea they might be sent to the same prison as her brother. The guards at Durham were going to have their hands full.

"Ooh, a night in Paris, then two weeks in Mexico. You lucky things," Julie said, raising her glass. "To sunnier shores."

Cooper smiled and met her toast with her glass of white. Still, her mind was elsewhere. It was with the dead man in the bedroom, who they'd identified as Peter Day, a fifty-year-old supermarket manager who volunteered at his local food bank. He had two daughters.

"I can't wait," said Atkinson. "Think of all the new experiences Danny will have. We can take him swimming. And imagine his little face when he sees an iguana for the first time. Erica?"

"Sorry. Sorry, I know I'm on another planet," she admitted with a sigh and a good glug of wine. "I'll switch off, I promise. Just... thinking about everything,"

She hadn't told him exactly what had happened in the bedroom. She told herself she was protecting him, not wanting him to worry. In the past, Atkinson had been overprotective of her, and it had driven her insane. The fact he'd been right in that instance was neither here nor there – she didn't need wrapping in cotton wool; she couldn't do her job if she were. She knew she wouldn't be able to keep the fact Uriah Hunter's arm had been around her neck secret for long. He had been in the process of using the same blood choke on her that he'd used on all his victims, and she had to put that in writing to justify the taser discharge. Atkinson would have found out sooner rather than later, so she confessed all – almost all – two days later. He was furious, hissing at Cooper while changing Danny's nappy, his anger not directed at Uriah but at Cooper for lying.

She'd stormed about, arguing that she hadn't lied; she just hadn't told him immediately. She'd tried to spare him the stress. He'd pointed a finger in her face and said it was the same difference. They were supposed to be a couple. They calmed down after twenty-four hours of not talking to one another and eventually made up, but the mood between them remained fragile. She could sense his disappointment in her, and though she knew he loved her, it was hard not to feel like she'd failed him in some way.

"Perhaps this break is coming at the right time," Atkinson said, reaching across the table to squeeze her hand. "Time to relax and spend time together, just the two of us – well, three of us – but it should be a nice opportunity to reconnect."

Tina pulled a face. "You two are gross." She flicked her glossy, artificially black hair over her shoulder and carved a slice of lasagne, steam billowing in the candlelight. "Let's eat before we all lose our appetites."

Tina portioned up the beef and pasta dish while Julie refilled their glasses and checked Danny's nappy. It was dry.

As Cooper took her first bite of lasagne, Julie said, "I'm so proud of you, my dear."

Cooper looked up, expecting to see Julie talking to Tina, but she was looking at her. "Who, me?" She almost choked.

"Yes, you. Honestly, you act like I'd never given you a compliment before."

Tina smirked.

"Twenty minutes ago, you had a go at me for leaving laundry in the machine, and ten minutes ago, you were horrified that dinner was store-bought and not homemade."

"I've had Mum's lasagne," said Tina. "Trust me, we're all better off with the M&S version."

Atkinson smirked.

"Stop it, you two," admonished Julie. "No, dear, I am proud of you. You put those two mass murderers away. I get their motivation, but taking the law into your own hands like that? No, we can't be having that. Not round here. And you solved that ghastly double murder in the town."

Tina nodded. "Got to say, Mum, everything seems more chill since the match-fixing became public knowledge." She took a bite of her food. "Mmm. This is good."

Her daughter was right. Some semblance of peace had returned to the northeast. There would always be outliers at either end of the political spectrum, those who hated anyone who looked or thought differently from how they did. And there'd always be the troublemakers who looked to exploit those differences. But for now, unity had largely returned to the toon. Nuance had returned to conversation, and the only thing purely black and white was the local football strip.

"Sad about Abdul Ahmed, though," Julie sighed. "I liked him. Do you think he'll turn up?"

"Alive? Doubtful," Cooper admitted, a shadow crossing her face. The one responsible remained elusive, but she knew time would reveal the truth.

Atkinson chimed in. "I almost feel bad stealing you away from the boys at HQ for two weeks."

Cooper swallowed and flushed, the food piping hot in her throat. "What do you mean?"

"I mean, how will the northeast cope without you for a fortnight?"

"Right," said Cooper, turning to Tina. "You will be careful, won't you? I know things have simmered down, but it won't take much for—"

Tina snorted, "Don't worry about us. If we get scared, we'll flee for Sunderland. The Masked Mackem's still out there."

Laughter filled the room, tension easing as they finished their meal, the conversation turning to Mayan monuments, jungles and jaguars. Cooper cleared their plates, and Atkinson arranged a taxi to the airport. It arrived on time, and he carried their suitcases to the waiting car. Cooper hugged her mother and daughter, picked up her snoozing infant and joined Atkinson in the street. The evening air was fresh and cool, the sky clear and full of stars.

As she settled into the backseat, Atkinson suggested, "Better turn our phones off, you know what happened last time."

She laughed and pulled hers from her pocket. "Damn right."

Three messages.

From Singh: *It was a pleasure working with you, DCI Cooper. Thank you for the warm welcome to the team.*

From Keaton: *Pint when you get back*?

And from Whyte: *Hope you have a great trip.*

The taxi pulled away. She was about to switch the phone off when it rang.

"Oh, you've got to be kidding me," groaned Atkinson. "What now?"

"Relax, it's Tina," she said, far from relaxed.

"T? What's up? I didn't leave my passport on the table, did I?"

Tina spoke in a blur or hurried words. When Cooper hung up, she couldn't help but smile from ear to ear.

"Well?" asked Atkinson. The taxi turned onto Front Street.

"Tina just got an email. Her goal the other week, the one that went viral, was seen by the right people, and long story short, she's been nominated for the northeast performance pathway."

"What does that mean?"

Cooper almost burst with pride. She had heard the happiness in her daughter's voice. Could practically see the smile on her plum-coloured lips. "It means next stop: England team. And after that, the Commonwealth Games."

They hugged on the backseat of the taxi, the driver beaming at them in his rearview mirror. "Congrats," he said.

Cooper snuggled her baby close, kissing his head. Atkinson held them both in a tender embrace, his warmth and her happiness for Tina thawing the sadness that had taken hold recently. She powered off her phone, vowing to keep it that way for two weeks. As she watched the screen fade to black, she thought of how the northeast was back on track, and from what she could tell, so was her family.

DCI Cooper will return.

- Message from the Author -

Greetings from North Shields, crime fiction fans and thank you for joining me on this latest adventure with The House Always Wins. If Cooper's journey resonated with you, I'd be over the moon if you could share your thoughts with a review on Amazon. Every word you write helps Cooper's stories reach new eyes.

This year has been a whirlwind, not just in the world of writing but in my personal life as well. Amidst trying to get this book ready, I also embarked on a new chapter of my own - getting married and enjoying the most unusual yet magical honeymoon, sailing around the UK. Balancing passage plans with murderous plots has been quite the experience!

I had a lot of fun raising the stakes with a potential political assassination and the highest death toll in a Cooper book yet. It was also a delight introducing DI Daljit Singh to the main cast. He might not drink or swear, but his character, like all in the Cooper universe, is far from perfect. I'm eager to see what dark secrets his future holds.

A few words of appreciation – a massive shout-out to Jane, my fellow ninja, and to my mum (not a ninja), for their invaluable feedback on the first draft. A big thank you to DI T and PC R for enduring my barrage of bizarre questions. And, of course, to you, my readers, whose unwavering support catapulted The House Always Wins to the number one spot in Amazon's LGBTQ+ hot new releases on pre-order. Your support means the world to me.

With warmest regards,

B x

- Be Sociable -

Newsletter: You can subscribe to the B Baskerville newsletter using the form on BetsyBaskerville.com. You'll mainly hear from B when she has something to share, such as a pre-order going live, a new book release or sale etc.

Facebook: B Baskerville - Author

Twitter: B__Baskerville

TikTok: B_Baskerville

Instagram: B_Baskerville_Author

- About the Author -

B was born and raised in Gosforth, Newcastle and is an alumnus of "Gossy High." Surprisingly, her academic journey led her to Sunderland University, where she studied sport and exercise development, a far cry from the creative writing path she would later tread.

Life took her to charming North Shields, a place that would become a source of inspiration for her writing. The local beaches and the bustling Fish Quay infused her work with a unique coastal flavour.

In a personal plot twist, in spring 2023, B and her husband embarked on an adventure by moving onto a boat, accompanied by their naughty Welsh terrier. Together, they sailed an impressive 1600 nautical miles, circumnavigating the UK's breathtaking coastline.

Away from the keyboard, B is a taekwon-do black belt and dedicated coach. While writing and fighting may appear markedly different, the discipline and perseverance required for both are the same and this sporting background gave her a unique ability to write realistic fight scenes.

When not wielding a pen or kicking something, B can be found walking her dog through North Shields, reading crime fiction and doing "boat jobs."

- Also By B Baskerville -

The DCI Cooper Series:
Cut The Deck
Rock, Paper, Scissors
Roll The Dice
Northern Roulette
Hide & Seek
Finders Keepers
The House Always Wins

Stand Alones:
The Only Weapon In The Room
Dead In The Water

Printed in Great Britain
by Amazon

38689463R00219